10·28

D1488199

THE MANTUA-MAKER'S BEAU

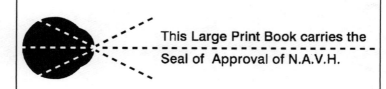

This Large Print Book carries the
Seal of Approval of N.A.V.H.

THE MANTUA-MAKER'S BEAU

ANNE HOLMAN

THORNDIKE PRESS

An imprint of Thomson Gale, a part of The Thomson Corporation

MAURY COUNTY PUBLIC LIBRARY
211 W. 8th Street
Columbia, TN 38401

Detroit • New York • San Francisco • New Haven, Conn. • Waterville, Maine • London

Copyright © 2006 by Sheila Finch.

Thorndike Press, an imprint of The Gale Group.

Thomson and Star Logo and Thorndike are trademarks and Gale is a registered trademark used herein under license.

ALL RIGHTS RESERVED

This novel is a work of fiction. Names, characters, places, and incidents are either the product of the author's imagination, or, if real, used fictitiously.

Thorndike Press® Large Print Clean Reads.

The text of this Large Print edition is unabridged.

Other aspects of the book may vary from the original edition.

Set in 16 pt. Plantin.

LIBRARY OF CONGRESS CATALOGING-IN-PUBLICATION DATA

Holman, Anne, 1934–
    The Mantua-maker's beau / by Anne Holman.
       p. cm. — (Thorndike Press large print clean reads)
    ISBN-13: 978-0-7862-9882-2 (lg. print : alk. paper)
    ISBN-10: 0-7862-9882-0 (lg. print : alk. paper)
    1. Women tailors — Fiction. 2. Bath (England) — Fiction. 3. Pennsylvania — Fiction. 4. Large type books. I. Title.
PR6108.O487M36 2007
823'.92—dc22
                                         2007026607

Published in 2007 by arrangement with Tekno Books.

Printed in the United States of America on permanent paper
10 9 8 7 6 5 4 3 2 1

THE MANTUA-MAKER'S BEAU

CHAPTER ONE

Bath, England, 1774

The continuous clanging of the Bath Abbey bells made Clementina Willoby exclaim crossly, "Why they have to make all that noise to announce Princess Amelia's arrival in Bath, I just can't imagine!"

Picking up her long skirts, she swished over to the workshop window to shut out the clamor. She also shut out the cool breeze of the sunny spring afternoon, making her wish she could be outside. Indeed, fresh air would have brought a rosy glow to her creamy complexion. And a pleasant stroll along the banks of the river Avon might have lifted her low spirits, which made her normally pleasant expression look strained.

Reluctantly she turned and walked back towards the long worktables where many seamstresses, who did not want to be accused of slacking, bent their heads over their sewing. Even the girls sweating from ironing with flatirons near the fire, and producing clouds of white steam, dared not protest the room was too stuffy. They were all aware Miss Willoby, their twenty-six-year-old supervisor, an expert dressmaker, had recently become more than a little short-tempered.

The workroom was strewn with cut pieces of materials: damask, brocaded silk, as well as mantua patterns of sleeves, half skirts, trains and side panels. And the tables were littered with off-cuts, bobbins of thread, scissors, needles and pins. But Clementina knew the clutter was all in order, and that quality ladies' garments were being made.

The small, three-storied, Bath-stone dressmaker's shop in Cheap Street, near the Abbey, with its bow-shaped front window and white shell-hooded front door, was thriving under Miss Willoby's management. Gowns, ribbons, laces, fans and suchlike fripperies were selling well, too. The high-toned city ladies, as well as visitors to the fashionable spa resort of Bath, were being attired there in the best of fashion.

The shop owner, Mrs. Elizabeth Hunter, would be pleased to see everything progressing well. She would have been, that is, if Mrs. Hunter hadn't died last week, leaving

Clementina in turmoil.

It was a tragedy Clementina was trying her best to ignore. She was pretending she could carry on the business as usual, as if the crisis would go away.

She gave a loud sigh before saying to the working girls, "No doubt it won't be long before Princess Amelia sends a courtier here demanding we make her several new gowns." Clementina sighed again as she pushed a wayward tendril of her auburn hair under her cap.

Bespectacled Matilda Brush, plying her needle quickly, with the expertise of an experienced, older dressmaker, ventured to say, "Princess Amelia has been a good customer, Miss Willoby. Although she frightens me to death when we take her garments for a fitting."

Clementina gave her industrious companion a wry smile, thinking of Princess Amelia, the almost-deaf and rather eccentric daughter of King George II.

"You shouldn't allow her to intimidate you. Her Royal Highness doesn't frighten me," she retorted. Which was true. Clementina did not lack courage, and she dealt with even the most awkward high-ranking customers with polite firmness.

But at that moment, Clementina felt

secretly afraid, worried she might lose her livelihood. This was because Mrs. Hunter had promised to leave her the shop and her business when she died, but Clementina had been devastated to hear from Mrs. Hunter's lawyer that she hadn't left her *anything* in her will.

Mrs. Hunter had left *everything,* including the shop, to her nephew, James Hunter, instead.

It was unusual for Clementina's heart to be pounding and to have her neck muscles feel tight. Her breathing was shallow as she fought to think what to do. She knew she couldn't avoid the problem any longer. She must try and deal with it. She needed to do something to save her living, as well as the jobs of all the seamstresses in the shop, who couldn't afford to be out of work either.

Of course, being a skilled mantua-maker, she could always find herself another job somewhere else. But she'd always worked for Mrs. Hunter. The dressmaking shop had been Clementina's home too. And after managing the business from dawn to dusk, which had been her life since childhood, she couldn't imagine being without it. Yet she feared she might if she didn't act quickly.

Deciding to go to the warehouse and

inspect the bales of luxurious flowered silks that had arrived from Spitalfields, she called, "Matilda, will you come with me? I'd like you to examine the new silks which have just been delivered."

Matilda put down the gown she was working on, glad of a rest from the exacting needlework she'd been doing. She yawned and stretched before following her supervisor into the warehouse.

While Clementina's mind tussled with what she was going to say to Miss Brush, the two women began to untie the packaging and unwrap the lengths of beautiful cloth.

They both gazed in admiration at the shiny white and cream silks decorated with asymmetrical cartouches of colored flowers: rosebuds, lilies, daisies, pansies and auricula, all with elaborately woven botanical details.

"I wonder which of these lovely designs the princess will want," chattered Matilda.

Clementina, lost in her own thoughts, said nothing.

"We'll need our wits about us to cut this cloth so that the design is correctly aligned," continued Matilda, engrossed in enjoying the fabrics and unaware of her supervisor's tenseness.

"Yes," agreed Clementina, coming out of her reverie and thinking she must be sure that she or Miss Brush cut the exquisite stuff, because only they possessed the skill to do it properly. Precious silks could easily be spoilt by careless cutting.

"I think this tobine pink on the diapered ground with the Flemish lace would suit the princess," Matilda suggested.

Struck by Matilda's ability to select the perfect trimmings for each garment, Clementina said, "You are right. Your sense of style is unfailingly good."

Matilda's face flushed with pleasure at the compliment.

Clementina knew Miss Brush deserved praise because not only was she skilled at sewing, she also possessed the gift of good color sense and of knowing which materials went with others.

But it had always been left to Clementina to talk to the fastidious, wealthy customers, who often had no taste or sense of style. She had to persuade them that the fashionable clothes that were admired by the *ton* in Bath, had to be tailored to suit their less-than-perfect-bodies. She also knew customers had to be comfortable wearing their gowns, so they would come back eagerly to the shop year after year to order more.

Clementina smiled at Matilda, saying, "It is necessary for you not only to choose what is best for the princess, but also to convince *her*. Just remember her royal bark is worse than her bite."

It had been drummed into Clementina since she was an undernourished child taken from the orphanage by Mrs. Hunter to be trained as a mantua-maker, that charming the customers was part of her job.

Mrs. Hunter had changed the little girl's name from Molly Pratt to Clementina Willoby, to give her class when she met the shop's customers. From Clementina's first day with her, Mrs. Hunter treated the poor child severely. There was no playtime for her. No time to meet friends. She was made to sit for hours in the workroom, sewing seams on scraps of material. Mastering the art of threading fine needles and using a thimble to make tiny stitches, the child had to practice until sewing became easy for her. Then she was shown how to make neat tucks and buttonholes. The arts of cutting cloth and pressing had to be practiced until she was skilful at it. But after several years, Clementina could sew gowns perfectly. As she grew older, she had Mrs. Hunter to thank for her dressmaking skill, and for being able to read and write and figure as well as any gentleman.

Clementina had also been taught to behave like a lady, too, as it would impress their well-bred patrons. She was shown how to engage in agreeable social intercourse with the customers, and to understand society's rules of etiquette. Clementina's clear voice, graceful carriage and polite attitude had become second nature to her.

As she grew to womanhood, Clementina became fond of, as well as grateful to, Mrs. Hunter. As the old dressmaker aged, she gradually let Clementina take over her business and began to pay her for doing it. Then she retired to her rooms above the shop.

When Clementina visited her before her sudden death, Mrs. Hunter had expressed the wish that Clementina should inherit the shop. So it had come as a nasty shock for Clementina when she found out Mrs. Hunter hadn't arranged the matter legally. This had left Clementina in a fix.

At that moment, anyone looking at the two mantua-makers in the warehouse, might have thought it was the middle-aged spinster, Miss Matilda Brush, who was in charge of the business, not the slightly built, younger Miss Clementina Willoby. But Clementina had every asset it took to run the shop successfully. Miss Brush was not

14

happy dealing with some customers, and although no fool, she was not able to manage the account books either.

However, Clementina had to make a decision. She'd thought about it long enough, staying awake at night wondering what she could do. Now she'd decided.

She stopped sliding her fingers over the luscious silks and looked intently at Matilda. "I must talk to you about an important matter," she said decisively.

Matilda blinked at her from behind her spectacles. "Yes, Miss Willoby?"

Clementina took a deep breath and said, "You are aware, I'm sure, that Mrs. Hunter intended to leave me this shop."

"I'm not surprised she did, Miss Willoby. You are her worthy successor. I congratulate you."

Clementina shook her head as she rubbed her hands together nervously. "Unfortunately, Miss Brush, she may have *intended* to give it to me. But I've found out she didn't."

"Oh, no!" Matilda's hands flew to cover her mouth in dismay.

Clementina pressed her lips together. Then she went on, "I've learned from Mrs. Hunter's lawyer that the whole of her estate has been given to her nephew, Mr. James

15

Hunter."

"Oh, dear me! I remember hearing James Hunter was such a wild boy," muttered Matilda. "His family found him untrustworthy."

Clementina knew that to be true. She'd been twelve years of age and was sewing in the parlor when a tall, fair-haired youth had visited Mrs. Hunter. To her he looked like a Greek god, strikingly good-looking and confident. He laughed a lot, too, she recollected.

Mrs. Hunter had taken him into her drawing room and Clementina could barely hear them talking. Then the door opened and they came into the parlor again. James was saying, "I thank you, Aunt, with all my heart."

Old Mrs. Hunter stood on tiptoe and kissed his cheek. "God go with you, James, dear boy."

"I'm not sure about that!" the lad chuckled.

Turning to leave, he noticed Clementina sitting as quiet as a mouse sewing in the corner of the room and gave her an engaging smile. Then he winked at her, making her pale face glow.

Clementina decided then and there he was the only man she would ever want to marry. Not that she knew anything about love and marriage. Her occupation gave her no opportunity to learn about that part of life. But she never forgot him.

She heard later that eighteen-year-old James Hunter had got himself into trouble with the law, which wasn't difficult if you were an undisciplined Oxford scholar. He'd been disowned by his father and had little choice but to emigrate to one of the colonies. He'd chosen the American colonies. Mrs. Hunter had provided some money for him to sail there and to set himself up in a small way. Being fond of him and having no children of her own as she was not married, although she had the courtesy title of Mrs. Elizabeth Hunter, she was sad to see the young man leave England.

Clementina explained to Matilda, "I need to find Mr. Hunter and ask him if I can have the shop, as it was his aunt's wish I should have it. I believe if I could get in touch with Mr. Hunter and prove to him how well we are coping with the shop, I might be able to persuade him to give it to me."

Matilda suggested, "Indeed he may give you permission to continue running the business, even if he will not part with it."

"Exactly so. I think, as he is now living in America, Mr. James Hunter wouldn't want a dressmaker's shop in Bath, would he?"

Matilda squeaked, "Oh Miss Willoby, is he in America? You can't go all the way to the American colonies! Why I've heard there are painted and feathered Red Indians there! Convicts are sent there too. And the French trappers attack the English."

Clementina had to laugh. Her mood lifted as she said, "Don't look so worried, Miss Brush, I will not come within miles of savage Indians, convicts, or hostile Frenchmen. Mr. James Hunter is in Philadelphia, which I'm told is a most orderly Quaker city."

"Oh dear me!" exclaimed Miss Brush, her eyes flashing from behind her glasses, big with alarm. "You're not seriously thinking of going there, are you?"

Clementina felt she had to confirm her intention. Deep inside her was a little voice telling her she had been repressed all her life and now she had the chance to break out. A few months abroad would give her the freedom to experience the wide world that she would never get if she remained cooped up in a little dress shop in Bath. She'd enough money for the fare because she'd saved her pay over the years. She'd never had the chance to spend her money.

"Yes," she replied firmly. "Indeed I have made up my mind to go to the American colonies and seek Mr. James Hunter. Even if I'm unsuccessful, at least I can say I tried."

"I admire you, Miss Willoby. Indeed I do. I'm not in the least adventuresome myself."

"No, you may not be. But I would like you, Miss Brush, to take my place and look after the shop until I get back."

Miss Brush blinked quickly at her. "Oh, my! Do you think I'll be able to, Miss Willoby? I can't talk easily to the clientele as you do, and I can't do the books and . . ."

"Don't worry. I'll teach you all I can before I go. I'm sure you'll do the job well enough until I return. And you'll just have to learn to put up with any awkward customers. And take no nonsense from those who don't want to pay. And as for Princess Amelia's whims — snap back at her if she barks at you!"

"Oh Miss Willoby. I'm all of a whirl at the thought of coping with all that new work."

Clementina said dryly, "*You* need not be. It is *I* who must face the unknown!"

A little later, when Miss Brush recovered sufficiently to return to the workroom, Clementina assured her they would both manage. She had also explained that, although she was a businesswoman and not a foolish girl just out of the schoolroom, she did not intend to travel abroad alone.

In fact, Mrs. Hunter's lawyer, Mr. Soames, had told Clementina about a respectable American couple, Mr. and Mrs. Redmarsh, who were sailing back to their home in Philadelphia next month and she might visit them and see if they were prepared to take her under their wing.

The long working day finally over, Clementina released her workforce and gave way to her feelings.

Alone in the shop, she walked around it as if in a dream. She'd never been allowed to dance and did not know how to. But with her arms outstretched she began to spin around the room on her toes, allowing her skirts to bell out. She'd never been permitted to raise her voice or to sing as a child, but now her heart was singing with the freedom she was about to have.

Grim childhood experiences at the orphanage, followed by Mrs. Hunter's strict and meticulous training in needlework, had left her little time to herself. Her life had been all work. It was as if she'd been cooped up like a wild animal in a cage for years. But now she was going to be free of the shop for a while. It was a heady feeling.

Really, it was remarkable that Clementina had reached her late twenties as good-natured as she was, as unbowed by the restraints that had been placed on her. She felt apprehensive, yet thrilled as any school-leaving miss ready to see the world.

As she'd been hidden away sewing all her life, no young man had had the chance to get to know her and ask for her hand in marriage. Clementina regretted the lack of love in her life especially. She considered herself now to be an old maid whom no man would want. Her peculiar training had made her a female oddity. She behaved like a young lady, but she hadn't a dowry. She certainly wouldn't be happy to marry a coarse workingman. She'd become far too genteel.

Puffed out from twirling around, she stopped to catch her breath. "Let the bells ring out as loud as they like," she said breathlessly, "the tightness in my head has disappeared. I'm bound for the American Colony of Pennsylvania, and I feel as free as a bird."

In her excitement she didn't even think of what Mr. James Hunter might be like now — if she found him.

She did, however, come to her senses and realize that she must go upstairs to her bed-chamber and prepare her best clothes so that she would make a good impression on the morrow, when she planned to visit Mr.

and Mrs. Redmarsh.

When morning came, Clementina felt strange to think she would not be spending all day in the sewing room, or having to serve customers. She was busy, however, as she had to accustom Miss Brush to the work she normally did, and to make sure all the girls knew what they were about, so she could leave the shop knowing all would be well in her absence.

"I do so hope, my dear Miss Willoby," said Miss Brush as she squeezed Clementina's hand before she left, "that you find those American Colonials agreeable."

The seamstresses, who were always quick to overhear gossip, and had found out what their manageress was about to do, chorused, "Good luck, Miss Willoby."

Clementina smiled back at them all. Whatever difficulties she faced, she felt sure they would be worth it, for their sake as well as her own.

Making sure everything would go on normally before she left took longer than Clementina had thought, and afraid she might be late for her appointment, she rushed upstairs to change. Slipping on her cream-and-brown Irish linen gown, which she had made herself and which fitted her slender figure to perfection, she hoped it made her appear a demure, well-dressed woman, although not a fashionable lady. She covered herself with her hooded cloak before she left the house, as the springtime wind was becoming a little sharp near three o'clock in the afternoon.

Clementina had only ever ventured out to attend church on Sunday with Mrs. Hunter and for their Sunday afternoon walk around the town. Clementina was then supposed to notice what the wealthy ladies were wearing so that she could make similar gowns for their clients.

To be going out for no other purpose than to please herself was indeed a new experience for Clementina, who tripped down the wide flagged walkways absorbing all she saw. She delighted to see the play of light on the spring's greening trees and the golden colors of the Bath-stone buildings with their elegant, classical style of architecture. There were cobbled streets where carriage and cart-wheels rumbled as horses were driven along. Horses were being ridden speedily up and down, so she had to take care as she crossed a street.

Toplofty ladies and gentlemen sauntered by, ignoring the plainly dressed Miss Willoby as if she didn't exist, just as they ignored the strident calls of the flower sellers and piemen. Neither did they appear to hear the vile curses of the sedan-chair bearers struggling with their heavy passengers.

But Clementina was enjoying being in the midst of the city bustle — until, after a while, she gave a shiver of apprehension. Was she being foolhardy, going off to a land she knew nothing about? Would she ever find Mr. Hunter? She'd heard America was a vast continent. Was she wise to use all her savings on this gamble? What if Miss Brush couldn't overcome her shyness with the customers and the rich ladies ceased to patronize the shop, and the business was ruined while she was absent? When she returned to England would she have to obtain a job as a lowly seamstress?

Many concerns such as these slipped into her mind and made her walk more slowly along Barton Street towards Queen Square, named after Queen Caroline, where terraced houses had been superbly designed into a unified palatial façade by the architect John Wood.

Yet when she got there, she stopped to gaze at the square, marveling at the sunlight on the tall obelisk standing in the quiet garden center, with its symmetrical beds of trees and pink and white flowering shrubs.

All she could hear was the twittering of the birds as they nested.

Enchanted by the scene, she forgot her worries.

Turning, she looked up, admiring the giant pilasters and columns of the Palladian-style building at the north side of the square. Her adventurous self returned.

She stepped forward purposefully because in one of those terraced houses lodged the people she had come to see: the American Colonials, Mr. and Mrs. Redmarsh.

CHAPTER TWO

"I wonder what has happened to that young woman," motherly and plump Mrs. Eleanor Redmarsh remarked to her husband, as she sat in the drawing room of one of the terraced houses in Bath's Queen Square. She was attired in an orange flounced and fur-belowed robe that did nothing for her figure. Tapping her foot impatiently, she went on, "Miss Willoby should certainly be here by now. It's well past the hour she said she would come."

As her husband didn't comment, she chattered on, "I've so enjoyed my visit to England and calling to see my English relatives and friends. And you, my dear, have been so kind to purchase this beautiful tea table for me. And this exquisite gilt-and-rose china tea set. My friends will be so envious when they see my beautiful things when we get home, won't they, my dear?"

Still receiving no reply, Mrs. Redmarsh

drew in air noisily. "Of course I'm not looking forward to the sea journey one bit." Then she added in an irritated voice, "If this young woman, who is supposed to be here now, is coming, and she is agreeable, it may help. Don't you agree, dear?"

"Harrumph!" Mr. Ralph Redmarsh replied. He was a large-sized colonial gentleman and charmingly amiable. But he was reading the *Bath Chronicle,* which he found more interesting than his wife's constant chitchat. It was in that paper several weeks ago he had placed an advertisement for a traveling companion for his wife. The long, tiresome sail across the Atlantic would seem far less so if his beloved Eleanor had a female companion to listen to her endless tittle-tattle, and he could be left in peace to read.

Mrs. Redmarsh frowned and, rising, left her new satinwood Pembroke tea table and walked over to the window to look out over the square. "Miss Willoby won't be of any use to me if she can't be punctual," she said. "I expect servants to be efficient. A scatterbrained girl is not what I want to keep me company."

Ralph Redmarsh gave an inaudible reply. As a wine importer, he was more concerned about the growing hostilities between his country and England than his wife's trivial conversation. The English Parliament was giving the American colonists a bloody nose by imposing taxes on them. Ralph, like most Americans, objected, calling them illegal and intolerable, as the Americans had no elected representatives in Parliament. Both sides were adamant they were in the right. There would be, he thought with deep regret, serious trouble ahead.

"Ralph. Ralph! Are you becoming deaf, husband?" His wife's voice jolted his concentration. "I said Miss Willoby is very late. I'm sure she's flighty. Ralph, I've decided, if she turns up, to tell her to find another family to travel to Philly with."

Mr. Redmarsh folded the newspaper with a sigh and rose to his great height. He strolled over to join his wife by the window, putting his large hand gently on her shoulder. "I don't think you should judge the young lady before you've met her, Eleanor. Her references, which included one from the Dean of Bath Abbey, are excellent."

"Oh, well! I'll see her then. If she comes. I've been wondering why this young English woman wants to go to Philly, anyway." Mrs. Redmarsh, as a Philadelphia hostess of note, liked to be informed about everything to do with social affairs in case her friends knew more than she did.

Mr. Redmarsh hoped sincerely the young woman was going to be suitable, but he knew that if Miss Willoby didn't come up to his wife's expectations, anything he might say in her defense would be useless.

Looking out the window, his keen eyes spotted a grey-cloaked young woman hurriedly approaching the house. "My dear," he said, "I think Miss Willoby has arrived."

"At last!" exclaimed Mrs. Redmarsh as she glided back to sit beside her tea table. Her hand moved instinctively towards the teapot handle, ready to pour out a dish of tea.

A few minutes later a servant showed Clementina up into the first-floor drawing room.

Clementina hid her gasp of admiration at the room's lavish proportions and fine furnishings, delicate craftwork she had never seen before. As her gaze wandered up towards the ceiling, she stood transfixed as she admired the decorative plasterwork.

Mrs. Redmarsh almost dismissed her on the spot, seeing the young woman was so uninteresting and seemed to have no conversation.

"Ah, Miss Willoby!" Mr. Redmarsh came forward to welcome her with a warmth that took Clementina by surprise. "Let me present you to my wife."

Unaccustomed to being treated as an equal by the gentry, Clementina's rosy lips parted but no words came, making her feel like a bashful miss.

But as she could see, there was something genuinely friendly in this big American gentleman's eyes, so Clementina overcame her shyness. She gave a little curtsy to him and then to the ample lady sitting behind him, who pointed to a gilt wood chair and said, "Sit down, Miss Willoby, and tell me about yourself."

Mrs. Redmarsh decided she approved of the young woman's demeanor, and her sober gown. She was just anxious to get a word out of her. "Will you take a dish of tea?"

"Yes, thank you, ma'am."

Old Mrs. Hunter's strict training had taught Clementina how to sit in a ladylike manner, although her stiff stays gave her no choice but to sit up straight, and drink tea in a refined fashion. Consequently, she felt quite at ease. She soon began to make polite conversation, as she normally did with the dress shop customers.

"What a charming tea set you have, Mrs. Redmarsh. It's quite the finest china I have ever seen." Clementina was accustomed to flattering ladies of quality.

"Oh, do you think so? I'm pleased to hear you say it."

"Indeed. And your tea table is so very fine too."

Mrs. Redmarsh beamed. "There, Ralph, what did I tell you? Miss Willoby can see the beauty of my purchases. Discerning ladies can always appreciate quality, and this tea table I bought to take home with me is true English craftsmanship. Not that we don't have our own fine craftsmen in America, Miss Willoby, because we do. But I like to have some English things around me to remind me of my ancestors."

"Indeed, you have good taste, ma'am," assured Clementina, a little tongue in cheek, as she could see the American lady had little dress sense, despite the money she must have spent for her ornate gown.

Mrs. Redmarsh was awash with pleasure at the compliment. This polite English miss was exactly who she wanted to accompany her on the long sea voyage. She felt sure they would have no difficulty finding plenty to talk about — as she would do most of the talking.

Ralph Redmarsh chuckled to himself as he sat in his wing chair. His Eleanor had taken an instant liking to the young lady, he could tell, and her approval absolved him from having anything else to do with the matter.

"In some ways you remind me of my daughter Nancy," Mrs. Redmarsh chatted on, her cornflower-blue eyes twinkling and her apple-red cheeks shining as she smiled at Clementina. "Nancy is a little younger than you. Just twenty-two in fact. I can see you are very alike, not in appearance, but in your . . ."

"Character, ma'am?" suggested Clementina.

"Exactly so. I'm sure when you meet her you will get on splendidly. Although, come to think on it, Nancy is a very lively girl, isn't she, Ralph?"

"Very," he replied with a fond smile.

Clementina was amazed to hear their twenty-two-year-old daughter referred to as a girl.

"But then so must you be very active, Miss Willoby. Prepared to cross the Atlantic. I do so hope you are a good sailor, because I am not." She lowered her voice. "I regret to say I get as sick as a dog."

Undeterred by the nursing task that lay ahead of her, Clementina just smiled. She had nursed old Mrs. Hunter before she died.

Mrs. Redmarsh sipped her tea and then nibbled at her sugar lump in a manner that made Clementina realize some things might be very different in America.

Clementina didn't show that Mrs. Redmarsh's remark about illness was hardly appropriate at teatime, or that chewing on a sugar lump would be considered bad manners in England. She said, "I'm afraid I can't say if I sail well, ma'am. I've never set foot away from Bath."

"My goodness!" Mrs. Redmarsh's eyes rounded. "What keeps you here?"

"My livelihood. I am a mantua-maker, ma'am."

Mrs. Redmarsh squealed and clapped her hands. "Ralph, did you hear that? Miss Willoby is a dressmaker. Isn't that splendid?"

Her husband for the life of him couldn't think why, but to indulge his wife he agreed.

Mrs. Redmarsh put her cup down and leant forward, saying quietly to Clementina, "Now, Miss Willoby, I consider your trade to be most fortunate. For me, that is. I have a blue silk that I like very much but I'm afraid it has become a little tight around the waist . . ."

"I'm sure I would be able to alter that for

you, ma'am," the practiced words slipping out easily from Clementina's mouth.

"Good. Now I wonder, if I gave you the money, would you purchase some dress lengths that could be made up during the voyage?" Mrs. Redmarsh's eyes were dancing with pleasurable anticipation at having a dressmaker thrown in with a companion.

Clementina nodded. She was demonstrating just the right degree of familiarity, and at the same time showing respect, as she did with her shop clients, which contributed to her high reputation as a dressmaker.

"And could you bring me some fashion plates?" Eleanor added hopefully.

"Of course, Mrs. Redmarsh, I'll be pleased to oblige."

Another squeak of pleasure came from Mrs. Redmarsh. "I have several gowns in mind for myself and for my daughter Nancy, too. I would say she's about your size."

"Miss Willoby," Mr. Redmarsh's deep voice sounded from across the room, "do not allow my wife to inveigle you into doing more work than you wish to do."

Mrs. Redmarsh swung round to face him, saying, "Ralph, pray do not interrupt. Miss Willoby is a strong-willed young woman. I can see that. I'm sure she'll not take on more sewing than she wishes to do."

Clementina smiled. She felt more relaxed, realizing they were talking as if they had already selected her for the position. And she liked them both. She said to the American lady, "May I suggest that you visit my shop in Cheap Street before you sail, ma'am, and select the stuffs you want? We have just received a consignment of beautiful silks from Spitalfields."

"A new selection of silks! My, I can hardly wait to see them! In Philly the ladies are most fashion-conscious you know, and many of the Quaker ladies are becoming far less puritanical in their dress. The ladies love to see the latest fashions from Europe."

"Then I shall make some fashion dolls for your friends," Clementina said enthusiastically. The fourteen-inch-high wooden dolls were dressed in exact replicas of the latest Parisian modes. Sandaled and bewigged, the little figures were made with every small detail, including the hooped underpinnings. Clementina had loved to make these dolls since she was a child and sewed each miniature garment lovingly. A few of her customers, including Princess Amelia, liked to see them before selecting their gown designs.

Mr. Redmarsh stood and walked over to the ladies. "I hope you will remember, Eleanor, that there are restrictions on the importation of many articles and materials from England. We have been told to manufacture our own goods."

Mrs. Redmarsh was taken aback for a moment or two. "Yes . . ." she said slowly, but then went on, "but *no*. I shall get what I want. I don't intend to let our country's representatives, who are all men, dictate that we ladies should not dress well because of their quarrels with the government of England." She looked at Clementina again. "And don't forget to bring plenty of pins."

"Pins?"

Mrs. Redmarsh nodded. "Yes, Miss Willoby, we are short of pins in America."

Before his wife could say more, Mr. Redmarsh, who realized the conversation about clothes could last another hour — and he was anxious to start a game of whist — ventured to bring the ladies *tête-à-tête* to a close. "Miss Willoby." He raised his voice. "I think we can say that we would like you to accompany us to Philadelphia. Is that not right, Eleanor?"

"Yes, oh yes indeed, and Miss Willoby, I —"

"There's no time to say anything else right now, my dear," Mr. Redmarsh interrupted firmly. "I expect you'll be meeting Miss Willoby again several times before we set off, and further arrangements can be discussed then."

Clementina stood up and wished the delightful American couple a polite good-bye, thinking that, as she had to go to America, going with them was going to be as pleasant a sail as she could hope for.

After Clementina left the room, Mrs. Redmarsh scolded her husband. "You should have escorted Miss Willoby back home."

Ralph rubbed his chin. "My dear, Miss Willoby came by herself, didn't she? So she should be able to find her own way back. Anyway, she strikes me as the kind of woman who is quite capable of taking care of herself. Now, how about a game of whist?"

Mrs. Redmarsh was still thinking out loud about her new companion when they rang for a servant to clear away the tea things and set out the card table. "That girl has taste, admiring my lovely tea set. And she has style too. It shows in her simple but beautifully made gown. I'm sure she'll be able to advise me about what to wear. My goodness, Ralph, I'll be the envy of every lady back home! Yes, indeed, I like her. We'll have so much to discuss. But, dash it, I clean forgot to ask her why she wants to go to Philly!"

Clementina took her favorable meeting with the Redmarsh couple as a good omen, indicating that she was right to go ahead with her plans to depart for the American Colony of Pennsylvania.

The next few weeks were hectic ones for her, as there was so much for her to do.

Miss Brush brought along her fifteen-year-old niece, Mary, for Clementina's approval, to fill her place as seamstress, and Clementina was happy to find the girl was as good at sewing as Miss Brush said she was.

Clementina had more difficulty training Miss Brush in the rudiments of bookkeeping, though. Matilda blinked uncomprehendingly at Clementina through her glasses. But, by the end of the month, Matilda suddenly got the hang of it, and Clementina breathed with relief thinking at least some records would be kept, and she could sort out any muddle when she got back from America.

The shop business was discussed and every eventuality considered, until Clementina was happy she was leaving everything to run smoothly while she was away.

Princess Amelia ordered two new mantuas and a riding costume, and several other customers requested gowns, which filled the order books nicely.

When Mrs. Redmarsh arrived at the shop, she was enthusiastic about everything she set her eyes on in the place. Clementina made a great fuss over her, which, of course, she enjoyed, too.

"How I wish there was a shop like this in Philly!" the American lady exclaimed.

Mr. Redmarsh had wisely set a ceiling on his wife's dress allowance, but she had fun selecting dress lengths and accessories with the generous amount he'd allowed.

Clementina tactfully guided her choice and stacked her up with boxes of pins before she left.

"How I am looking forward to you making up my gowns," the beaming Mrs. Redmarsh declared. "Now you just let me know, Miss Willoby, if there is anything I can help you with."

Clementina was delighted to find herself accepted so readily and to have the opportunity to ask a few questions about the adventurous trip. For example, she wondered what the weather would be like and if she would need to bring an umbrella. Such information, which was not essential, was of great comfort to Clementina. She was thrilled to find herself on such friendly terms with the colonial lady and hoped all the colonials would be as easy to deal with.

However, James Hunter was her real objective, and naturally she began to wonder about him a great deal. When she went to pay a final visit to Mrs. Hunter's lawyer she asked about him.

Mr. Soames was a pompous man. He cleared his throat, then he looked down his nose at her. "Miss Willoby, I've not heard from Mr. James Hunter since I wrote to tell him that his aunt had died and he was the sole beneficiary of her estate," declared the lawyer.

"Do you know where he is, sir?"

Mr. Soames looked at her suspiciously, making Clementina feel uncomfortable.

The lawyer knew the plainly dressed woman seated before him had been rescued as a child from the orphanage by Mrs. Hunter. She was, in his opinion, an opportunist who was after part of the old lady's estate. He only had Miss Willoby's word for it that Elizabeth Hunter had intended to leave the shop to her.

"I do not. He did not acknowledge my letter. He may have died," he added with a ghost of a smile.

"Oh, dear me!" exclaimed Clementina. That was something she hadn't thought of.

But then she thought, *why should I let this lawyer put me off doing what old Mrs. Hunter wanted?* The shop was hers rightfully, if not legally. She must fight for it. She shifted in her chair. "Mr. Soames, do you know what James Hunter is like?"

The lawyer gave a guffaw. "Well, if I tell you he was sent down from Oxford University as a student for stealing a great deal of money from a professor, it may perhaps tell you something about him," he told her sarcastically.

"Indeed?" Her eyebrow rose. "His aunt thought well of him."

"Of course, his crime wasn't proven. But if it had been, he'd as likely to have been hanged or sent for hard labor to Australia. As it was, his father disowned him and he fled to the American Colony of Pennsylvania. So, Miss Willoby, if you are foolish enough to go there to beg him to give you the shop you say his aunt wished to give you, bear in mind the place is probably full of criminals like him."

Clementina allowed her mind to dwell for a moment on Mr. and Mrs. Redmarsh. She smiled. "I don't think," she said positively, "I shall come to any harm there, even if I can't find Mr. Hunter or, if I do find him, if he is unwilling to make me the owner of the

41

shop. I firmly believe that it would be Mrs. Hunter's wish that I should seek him and at least ask him. I have saved my wages over the years and have a little money of my own."

Mr. Soames had to admire her. He could tell that warning her of the perils of the sea voyage would not deter her. He also knew that, living in the cultivated city of Bath, she had no idea how primitive the colonies were.

He got up from his chair, and going to a tall chest, opened it and took out a letter from a drawer. Returning to his seat, he fingered the letter, saying, "I have written a letter for you to take to a Philadelphian lawyer, Mr. Kenrick, explaining the matter of the estate. If Mr. Hunter is located, perhaps he would ask Mr. Kenrick to confirm he is able to inherit his aunt's estate, and" — his steely eyes pierced Clementina's — "what he wishes to do about his shop here, in Bath. And I'll write one to Mr. Hunter too — in case you find him, like the needle in the haystack."

Clementina refused to be offended by his sarcasm, and accepted the letters before wishing the lawyer a polite goodbye.

He hadn't upset her. People were not always pleasant, and she considered the lawyer was only doing his job efficiently.

She was, however, dismayed to learn James Hunter was, or could be, a thief. Was it true he was a rogue?

The days flew by and soon Clementina's long voyage was due to begin. On her last evening at the shop, tears came to her eyes as she bade farewell to her workers.

Matilda Brush, who had been helping her pack away Mrs. Hunter's gowns and belongings, as the house would be empty upstairs for perhaps months, until the shop's fate was known, said, "Don't you think it's time you packed your trunk now, Miss Willoby?"

"Oh, I haven't very much to take," replied Clementina. "It won't take me long to pack what I own."

Which was true. Clementina now had only a few more belongings than when she'd come from the orphanage.

But there was one thing she'd discovered Mrs. Hunter owned that she wanted. She'd found it as she looked through her old employer's wardrobe and drawers, putting tissue paper over the contents to keep them free of dust.

It was a drawing of a youth. James Hunter. The artist, Thomas Gainsborough, had stayed in Bath for several years. Mrs. Hunter had obviously persuaded the painter to draw James before he left England, so that his aunt would have something to remember him by. Gainsborough was an excellent draughtsman. The portrait was not only a beautiful picture; it was exactly as Clementina remembered James. There was a hint of his engaging smile captured by the artist in this small work of art.

Clementina lay awake that night, tossing, not only with the thought that she would not be sleeping in her own bed again for weeks, but because she wanted to have the Gainsborough drawing of James.

Did she dare take it? She'd never stolen anything in her life. But, she argued with herself, wouldn't Mrs. Hunter have told her she could have it if she'd asked for it? What use would it be to anyone else? His family had disowned him, so the drawing might get thrown away if the house was eventually cleared for sale.

Clementina finally pushed her blanket aside, put her bare feet on the floorboards, then flitted in the dim light towards Mrs. Hunter's bedchamber. She opened the drawers to search for the picture, and, finding it, she took it out. She couldn't see the drawing in the dark, but she hugged it to her bosom for a moment. Then she returned to her room and slipped it in her small hand case.

She felt her heart pounding as she thought of her criminal act. Not only was she leaving England, she was leaving stained with sin.

Her life had already changed. She had become a thief. Like James Hunter?

She shrugged, gave a sigh, and snuggling under her bedclothes was soon asleep.

CHAPTER THREE

Bristol's harbor vibrated with the hum of nautical life and its lively sea trade, capturing Clementina's complete attention as she gazed about her. The shipping and the bustling Broad Quay so fascinated her she was almost knocked off her feet by a heavily laden donkey pushing by her.

"Whoa!" yelled the driver. "Sorry, ma'am. Them donkeys never look where they's agoing."

Clementina smiled at him. She didn't mind being shoved by any man or beast, because she was enjoying being free to see the world. But she decided to walk through the noisy crowd of carriers and harbor workers to a row of chandler's shops where she could observe everything going on without getting in anyone's way. Standing with her back to the shops, she feasted her eyes upon the towering masts of the sailing ships moored along the quay. She could smell the tang of the sea water as it lapped at the side of the great bows and could hear the cawing cries of the swooping seagulls as gusts of wind swept by and tugged at her skirts. Everything was exhilarating for her, although she had to keep her hand on her bonnet to prevent it from blowing away.

Seamen with baggy trousers rolled up to their knees were climbing about high in the rigging. Dock porters were rolling barrels to be filled at a standpipe, ready to be hoisted on board, and overseers were checking the cargoes coming on and off the great ships. Skilled shipwrights in leather aprons were busy chipping wood as they made repairs, while gentlemen in three-cornered hats stood on the cobbles in huddles, discussing their next voyage. Clementina's heart beat fast when she thought she also would soon be off and sailing on the sea.

"Ah, there you are, Miss Willoby. I've been looking for you everywhere. My maid's been looking for you too." Mrs. Redmarsh's voice sounded a little out of breath from dodging people on the quay while searching for her companion.

Clementina woke from her reverie and went to join a flustered Mrs. Redmarsh. "I'm sorry you lost me, ma'am. It's so intriguing here. Those tall ships are truly magnificent."

"Yes indeed — if you like that sort of thing," Mrs. Redmarsh replied somewhat dryly. What concerned her was that the packing case containing her precious table and tea set was stored away securely on board the ship on which they were about to sail.

Mrs. Redmarsh took Clementina's arm and said, "Come with me. We have time to take a coffee before we leave. Mr. Redmarsh is over there talking to the master of the *Heron,* Mr. Millard. I can't say I like the look of that man."

Clementina looked over to where Mrs. Redmarsh pointed and her first glimpse of the captain was not favorable either. Mr. Millard was short, crimson-faced and belligerent-looking. "Nor I," agreed Clementina.

"He was very curt with me when I asked him about the safety of my luggage. He merely snapped that it would be stowed on a sound ship owned by a reliable Philadelphian trader."

"I expect he has a great many concerns at the moment," said Clementina soothingly.

"That is as it may be, Miss Willoby, but I doubt if we will get much conversation out of him during the weeks on board. Now come along and we'll find the coffee house, and get out of this wind."

Clementina would have preferred to remain on the quay, where she found interest in everything she saw. Being enclosed in a coffee shop was not her idea of passing the time profitably when there was so much to observe. But she wanted to humor the lady who, despite her ability to wag her tongue all day long, was a kindly woman and had readily befriended Clementina.

Since they had departed from Bath by private coach two days earlier, and Clementina had sat half-listening to Mrs. Redmarsh's tittle-tattle and making the odd reply while the hours went by, she'd stared avidly out the coach window. The undulating countryside, dewy fresh and green with spring growth, was a treat for Clementina's eyes, and she didn't want to miss even a little of it. She felt nature was a bit like herself. Having been shut away all the winter, it was now coming out into the wide world.

Fortunately, Mrs. Redmarsh didn't seem to notice Clementina's lack of total attention, and her husband was able to read or doze as happily as the potholed road allowed, knowing he did not have to reply to his wife's constant prattle.

They'd spent the night at The Dolphin Inn in Bristol. Their stay wasn't long enough for Clementina to see more than a fraction of the new Georgian rebuilding of the thriving commercial city of Bristol. Mr. Redmarsh had informed her that trade with the American colonies was big business. In exchange for lumber, wheat, cotton and tobacco sent over from the colonies, Bristol traded in manufactured goods such as cloth, axes and clay pipes.

He commented, "Although now the colonists are refusing to buy some English goods." Then he mumbled. "I smell trouble brewing between us before long. The sooner we get home, the better."

The subject of the purpose of Clementina's visit to the American Colony of Pennsylvania was also discussed. Clementina could understand why the British government wanted the colonials to pay for their army, while the colonials resented being taxed. But she resisted becoming embroiled in the argument, and told Mr. Redmarsh she only wanted to find James Hunter and persuade him to give her the shop.

"It is not only my job that is affected, Mr. Redmarsh," explained Clementina. "There are six other sewing girls who might lose their employment. So I must find him."

"Just because I've not heard of Mr. James Hunter," Mr. Redmarsh told Clementina, "does not mean he is not in Philadelphia. It is a large city. He may be living outside the center. It's an expanding place. Immigrants are arriving all the time and many make their way into the hinterland."

Mrs. Redmarsh chipped in, "My husband knows a good many people in Philadelphia because his wine business gives him access into the social life of the best families. The wealthy Quakers: the Logans, the Miflins, the Norrises, the Pembertons, the Powles, and of course, our friends the Whartons. Then there are the Presbyterians: the Allens and the Shippens we know quite well. And the Anglicans: the Willings, the Hopkinsons —"

"Eleanor," interrupted Mr. Redmarsh, "I'm sure all those names mean nothing to Miss Willoby."

"She'll soon get to know them," retorted his wife.

Clementina knew her station in life would not permit her to mix with the gentry, so she smiled. She'd not been surprised to hear the man she was looking for was not amongst the better sort.

She had the feeling he was probably one

of the daredevil breed of men who'd gone forging into the American wilderness. A man who could fell a tree, or swim a fast-running river, ride like a trooper — and even kiss a girl with passion!

My goodness! Whatever had made her think of anything so intimate as a kiss? Why she'd let her imagination run away with her she didn't know. Love, and anything to do with it, was not on her mission list. Her mission was to find the missing owner of the shop, get his permission to have it, and to sail back immediately — particularly as the colonials were becoming unsettled. She didn't want to be caught up in a conflict.

When the time came for them to go aboard the American ship *Heron,* Clementina felt a frisson of excitement. As her party walked up the gangplank the crew was shouting in seaman's language to each other as they scurried about in bare feet making the final preparations for the lengthy sea crossing. The wind was gusting, encouraging them to set sail.

Their cabins were very small, but even a wooden cot and room for their trunks in the tiny area gave them valued privacy on-board which was more than the servants and steerage passengers were to have for the next four or five weeks. There was a larger dining-cum-general-purpose cabin for the cabin-class passengers' use. Unaccustomed to luxuries, Clementina found nothing wanting and settled in eagerly, anticipating their departure at the height of the tide.

It was only when she met the sullen, heavily jowled master of the 140-ton, three-masted ship face to face that she sensed all might not be ideal for everyone aboard the American vessel.

"The captain may be a thoroughly disagreeable fellow," Mr. Redmarsh explained to the ladies confidentially, "but I don't want us to remain another week or so in Bristol waiting to find an alternative passage. First-class cabins are hard to obtain at the best of times, and I understand from talking to the crew that the rift between England and America has widened and taken a sharp turn for the worse recently."

"How so?" demanded Mrs. Redmarsh.

"I dislike having to tell you this, Eleanor my dear, but the matter concerns tea."

The ladies looked at each other in amazement. "What has tea to do with the matter?" questioned his wife.

"I understand Boston Port is going to be closed by order of King George as a punishment because the citizens of the Massachusetts Colony refuse to pay tea tax." He gave a chuckle. "Some of 'em dressed up as Indians and boarded some English tea ship in Boston harbor and threw three hundred and forty-two chests of tea overboard!"

"What a waste of tea! But it shouldn't concern us," said his wife.

"Oh but it does, my dear. You'll have to know about it sooner or later. You won't be able to serve tea any longer, as Americans have decided not to drink it anymore. They will drink coffee instead."

Slowly the truth dawned on his wife that her beautiful new tea set would not be needed. She gave a squeal of anguish.

Seeing Mrs. Redmarsh so clearly upset, Clementina hurriedly put her arm around her. "Ma'am, I'm sure your china teacups will be admired filled with coffee instead of tea. And your beautiful table can be renamed a coffee table, with no trouble at all."

Mrs. Redmarsh's glazed eyes looked at Clementina in gratitude. "Yes, yes, I suppose they can be used for coffee just as well, Miss Willoby. Thank you, my dear."

However, Clementina realized the shock of hearing how angry opposition to British rule was becoming in the American colonies had distressed the colonial lady. Having

English relatives, Mrs. Redmarsh didn't like hearing about the growing bad feelings between the two countries she loved. Nor, of course, did Clementina, who once again hoped she would get there and back before any skirmishes broke out.

The experience of leaving Bristol harbor was both thrilling and stomach-churning for Clementina. As the *Heron* slipped away from its anchorage and sailed smoothly through the Avon River's high, winding banks towards the estuary, she felt sadly that a part of her was being left behind, and yet she was thrilled to be off. And keen to realize she was on the way — she hoped — to finding James Hunter and sorting out her future.

They had sailed past the cutters, hoys and other smaller boats and reached the deeper waters when they came across the impressive sight of a majestic seventy-four-gun Royal Navy ship-of-the-line.

Nothing, she thought, would be able to conquer that monster. The rebellious colonists had better watch out!

As the day passed into night and the ship's lights were lit, all sailing craft and land had been left behind. They were now completely surrounded by Atlantic rollers.

■ ■ ■ ■

In the first few days of sailing, the ship made good progress across the Atlantic.

Mrs. Redmarsh was happy to begin discussing clothes and working on improving her wardrobe. Clementina was happy to advise and sew for her.

The weather was sometimes sunny and sometimes showery, but the sea was calm. Clementina enjoyed being on deck and seeing the wide expanse of sea and sky. She quickly found her sea legs and was able to cope with the swaying motion of the ship. She comforted Mrs. Redmarsh, who hadn't.

At dusk she liked to see the wonderful orange and crimson colors across the sky that tinged the moving clouds. The peacefulness, however, was sometimes broken by what she thought sounded like cries from afar. Was it the sirens of the deep? Or some aquatic animals calling to each other?

It wasn't until a week had passed that some blustery weather hit them. A fierce northwester, caused the ship to pitch and toss. Poor Mrs. Redmarsh suffered horribly from seasickness as the wooden ship heaved and groaned as it rolled relentlessly.

Clementina stayed constantly at Mrs.

Redmarsh's side, trying to comfort the distressed lady. The crew was not at all helpful, but she realized they did have their work to do onboard the vessel. The master seemed to be missing most of the time, leaving them to get on with it as best they could.

Mrs. Redmarsh's face had turned pale green, and her conversation dried up. "You are so good to me, Miss Willoby," she said in a strained voice. "My abigail is sick too. Without your help I don't know how I'd manage."

"Rest assured, ma'am, I am accustomed to tending the sick. My late employer, Mrs. Hunter, was infirm for some months before she died, and I attended her."

Clementina had not thought before that her nursing was of any consequence. Her motherly instinct had taken over and she'd done what had to be done to make Mrs. Hunter as comfortable as possible. That she'd to run the shop at the same time hadn't seemed significant to her then. She just got on with it, although she was often very tired. Now those skills she had acquired came in useful in nursing Mrs. Redmarsh.

One evening, as the pounding sea buffeted the ship and the sails were taut, Clementina went out on deck to get some fresh air into her lungs. She saw Mr. Redmarsh fighting his way towards her against the wind. She wondered, as she stood shrouded in her cloak and clinging onto some guy ropes to steady herself, if she was needed below.

"Miss Willoby," he said as he came up to her and shouted over the humming of the rigging, "I'm concerned for your safety up here in this storm. I think you should go below."

Struck by his concern for her, Clementina smiled up at him. She used her fingers to comb back long strands of her hair the wind had flattened against her face. Raising her voice she replied, "I will not stay long here, sir. I don't intend to walk about on deck. I enjoy the fresh air and the salty spray after being confined below most of the day."

"It's most good of you to nurse my wife."

She looked up at his worried expression and replied, shouting back over the wind, "I'm sorry she has been so ill, sir. But I'm sure she will overcome her seasickness in time."

He shook his head slowly, saying, "I wish Eleanor could get some sleep, but those children in the steerage are making such a commotion."

Clementina had been vaguely aware of the noise coming from the deck below. Noise that she thought had been from the sea.

Now she realized that the sounds were children playing noisy games to amuse themselves. The children of the poor were not made to behave as quietly as the delicately nurtured offspring of the quality, whose boys were regimented in harsh boys' schools and whose girls were made to behave docilely.

They couldn't converse easily, as the thrumming of the rigging and the sea made talking difficult. Mr. Redmarsh bade her goodnight and moved off. Watching his shoulders hunched in misery as he staggered away from her along the heaving deck made her long to ease his wife's discomfort.

When she saw the figure of the narrow-as-an-arrow boatswain an idea occurred to her, although his hooded eyes made her wary of him.

"Good evening, Mr. Hugill," she shouted, making her way towards him.

"Good evening, ma'am. You should be below in this weather. A slight woman like you could be tipped overboard by a big wave."

Clementina gave a shudder. She intended to go to her cabin, but wanted to speak to him first. "I wondered if you might ask the children below to make less noise? Mrs. Redmarsh has been so ill and needs rest."

59

The look on Mr. Hugill's face was not pleasant. "Ho, ho! You can hear the brats below, can ye? I'll soon make 'em as quiet as lambs or they'll feel my cat-o'-nine-tails!"

Immediately Clementina regretted having mentioned the rowdy children. His offer to go and threaten them with a whip was excessive. Children needed to let off steam at times.

But as she opened her mouth to protest, the swarthy boatswain moved away from her with the nimbleness of a trained seaman used to wet, slippery decks.

She struggled to follow him as the noise of the wind lashing the sails drowned her cries to stop him. She saw him disappear down some steps and followed him as quickly as she could. Then she spotted him lowering himself down a hatch. Although the ship's movement made progress difficult, she reached the hatch and lowered herself down the ladder backwards to the deck below, where she heard the boatswain bellowing an order to one of the crew: "No rations tomorrow, tell 'em, unless they belt up!"

Horrified to hear the harshness in his voice Clementina renewed her effort to call the boatswain. "Mr. Hugill, I need to speak to you. Please wait . . ." she pleaded, but her voice had become a croak.

Hugill vanished. She'd no alternative but to rush after the seaman as quickly as her long skirts permitted. Only the light the seaman carried enabled her to see in the darkness. Unfamiliar with this section of the ship, she found she had to lower her head to avoid the beams above.

The man ahead suddenly stopped, and bending down, lifted a large hatchway ring, which he yanked open. Clementina heard children's voices. The man bellowed Mr. Hugill's instruction into the hole in an ugly threatening voice.

For a while, the cries of the children below became quieter. But despite their parents' efforts to pacify them, they began crying again.

Clementina listened in dismay. These weren't the strident sounds of children playing noisy games. Oh, no. Clementina recognized from her childhood in the orphanage that these were the pitiful cries of children in distress!

Horror made her cover her face with her hands. She hadn't known there were children and infants down in that gloomy hold. Instinctively she drew nearer. She couldn't check her natural desire to see for herself the deprivations suffered by those people at the very bottom of the ship.

It was like a jail: an airless tomb below sea level. No wonder the poor children were upset and crying as the ship was being tossed and buffeted.

Forgetting any danger she might get herself into, Clementina ignored the utter surprise and foul language of the seaman as she clambered down the steps into the hold. The stench that greeted her took her breath away. It took her several seconds to adjust to the darkness. Then she beheld the crowd of pinched faces and the mournful eyes of the men, women and children who stared at her.

She panicked, and almost climbed straight back out of the hole. But a woman's plaintive cry, "Help us, ma'am!" prevented her from bolting.

Her presence brought a hush to the cries and moans of the steerage passengers. Suddenly Clementina felt a small hand take hers, and looking down, she saw a grimy, thin-faced child, whose eyes looked beseechingly at her. "I want a drink," the child said.

"We need fresh water," chorused others.

"Food, ma'am, we must have more food."

"Please, for my little one!" an anguished mother, clutching her baby, cried out.

The heart-rending cries and sobs made

Clementina angry. She knew what it was like to be thirsty. Hunger, too, she'd suffered as a wee child. These people were not rogues who had been sent to prison for wrongdoing. They were worthy folk, families, people wanting a passage across the Atlantic to a better life. Indentured servants, they were called, because they couldn't afford the cost of the passage and had to work for anyone who would take them when they arrived in America, to pay off their travel-ticket debt.

Poor they might be, but Clementina knew they shouldn't be suffering like this.

"I promise I'll try to do what I can to help you." She found herself grinding her teeth as she spoke the words. She decided then and there that she would confront the lazy master of the ship and demand that these unfortunate passengers be treated humanely. She didn't want to involve the Redmarshes, as they had Mrs. Redmarsh's acute seasickness to contend with.

Resolutely, Clementina clambered out of the hold and ordered the seaman to take her to see the master of the ship.

He protested. "Ma'am, I . . . I can't disturb the capt'n."

"Oh, yes, you will. Take me to see him at once!" she ordered, her eyes blazing in the lantern light.

Clementina Willoby's slight shoulders were back and her chin was high. Her years of experience as a shop manager gave her the appearance of someone used to authority. But inside she boiled with rage.

Whoever was responsible for the ill treatment of those pitiable steerage passengers, she would find him and put the matter right. The ship's owner was wicked. He should be ashamed of himself, allowing such suffering. Whatever kind of man would permit his ship to carry a cargo of human suffering?

The seaman pulled his forelock when he recognized her determination. He might get flogged for taking her to the master's cabin, but then, he didn't relish the consequences of disobeying this small harridan of a woman who might be after his scalp if he did not.

CHAPTER FOUR

By the time Clementina arrived outside the captain's door, the uncontrolled fire of her anger had abated. Her ability to think rationally returned. She was aware her hands were clenched, so she stretched out her fingers. Her bosom heaved. With her heart hammering, she took a number of deep breaths before she knocked on the door.

There was no reply. She knocked again, louder.

"Enter!" came Mr. Millard's gruff voice from inside the cabin.

Taking another deep breath, Clementina opened the door and went in.

What she saw shocked her. The cabin was unkempt. The master was lying prone on his cot. He was unshaved and his bleary eyes looked up at her in amazement.

Seeing Clementina, he rose unsteadily, holding his head as if it hurt him.

"Ma'am?" He tried to sound efficient, but Clementina could smell the rum on his breath.

It took all her courage not to turn and leave. But her duty was clear. If she did not protest and get something done to improve the conditions in the hold, some people would die before they arrived in Philadelphia.

"I've come to inform you," she said, adopting the imperious tone Princess Amelia used, "that your passengers in the hold urgently need fresh water. And more food."

It took him some time to understand what she'd said. Then he slurred, "Ma'am, it is the bos'n, Mr. Hugill's, job to make sure the crew feed those people."

"Indeed? So why has he not been doing it? The people incarcerated down there — which include little children — are crying out for water. Is the ship short of drinking water?"

The master swept his hand over his florid face and jowls as if he were trying to think of an answer.

Clementina could see he was drunk. He was incapable of thinking properly. But drunk or not, Mr. Millard was still captain of the ship, and Clementina knew the crew still had a duty to obey him. So she realized he needed enticing to tell his bos'n to improve the conditions of those suffering passengers.

With as much charm as she could muster, Clementina said, "Mr. Millard, I can see you are unwell. May I ask you to order Mr. Hugill to have fresh water and food provided in the hold immediately? And to save you the bother of having to think of the matter again, you can put me in charge, if you will, to make sure the crew doesn't forget again."

It obviously hurt the master to nod his head as she heard him groan. He seemed to step backwards as if he wanted to collapse onto his cot.

"Call Mr. Hugill, right now," she ordered, before he fell unconscious. "Give your bos'n the order that I shall oversee the needs of those steerage passengers in future."

She went to the door and opened it, calling as loudly as she could, "Mr. Hugill! Mr. Hugill, the master wants to speak with you."

She prayed, watching the captain's contorted face, that he wouldn't fall asleep before Mr. Hugill arrived. "Sir," she came up close to his swaying body and hissed in his ear, "stay awake, sir! You don't want those children to starve, and have to bury them at sea, do you?"

He jolted upright. "No!" he said, "I don't wish them harm."

Before this captain had let drink get hold of him, he was probably a decent man, Clementina thought. "Then tell Mr. Hugill I will look after them," she said firmly. "The crew shall do as I say about this matter."

Years of managing the dress shop allowed Clementina to assume an air of command that impressed even Mr. Hugill when he appeared. He listened to the master ordering him to tell the crew they must obey Miss Willoby, and get victuals down to the hold without delay.

But the look Mr. Hugill gave Clementina was intimidating. It was also lascivious, and although knowing nothing of men's lust, it made her flesh creep. It was fortunate for her, however, that a crewman who disobeyed his captain's order was flogged, and Hugill didn't want to risk that. "Aye, aye, sir," he said reluctantly.

Clementina had great difficulty maintaining her commanding stance, as her knees felt in danger of giving way. But she kept her eyes steadfastly fixed on the loathsome seaman until he pulled his forelock and backed out of the cabin.

She had won the battle, but felt exhausted. Sheer willpower made her follow him and make sure the captain's order was obeyed.

Hugill grumbled to her as she watched two members of the crew lower some water and biscuit below. "Ma'am, those passengers down in the hold are indentured. That is, they are going to be sold for seven years' labor as bonded servants to whatever gentlemen in Philadelphia will buy 'em. They are taken in lieu of a cargo. Those 'redemptioners' are ridin' free, so to speak. So they get half rations. See?"

Clementina took a deep breath in before she said, "No, Mr. Hugill, I do not see it that way at all. It's not right for passengers to be stuffed in a ship's hold for weeks, and that little children should be crying for water!"

"It's business, ma'am."

"Business? It is not the kind of business I know, and I'm a businesswoman." She wondered again who owned the *Heron* and was responsible for "redemptioners" traveling in those dreadful conditions. "I can't approve of that method of making money." She took another lengthy breath in, and said determinedly, "Therefore, Mr. Hugill, I'll make sure that not only will the crew feed these people properly, but they will also get an airing from that dungeon every day when the weather improves. See to it, if you please."

She was thoroughly worn out when she eventually crept to her cot. She lay shivering as the ship tossed her. Eventually she slept, knowing the people under the waterline had been comforted.

Overnight the storm abated.

Next morning she questioned Mr. Redmarsh about the master's drunkenness.

"I fear he becomes intoxicated at times," she said primly.

"Yessiree." Mr. Redmarsh obviously knew. He was sharp, and seemed to have developed an understanding with his wife's companion. They could discuss a problem like rational business people. "Now," he told her, "don't you go worrying about it. Mr. Hugill, the bos'n, although a surly man, is a capable sailor. I've watched him at work."

A look of relief spread over Clementina's face.

"Don't mention the master's condition to Eleanor, will you?"

She smiled. "I won't. But in her present unwell state, I don't know if she'd care."

Mr. Redmarsh gave a laugh. Then he became serious. "If I didn't have you to take care of her, Miss Willoby, I assure you I would not be as amused. I appreciate you being here and looking after my wife."

Clementina smiled, knowing she appreciated traveling with Mr. and Mrs. Redmarsh as much as they seemed to approve of her.

Eleanor Redmarsh recovered as the weather improved. So did her abigail, who was therefore able to resume her duties and tend to her mistress and listen to some of her chirpy chatter. This gave Clementina time to continue sewing the lady's new sack-back gown with the material she'd brought from the shop in Bath. When she'd finished it, Eleanor was delighted, clapping her hands with joy.

"Why, you are so very clever with a needle, my dear Clementina. This blue silk taffeta with the little fleck in it is so elegant. This gown is quite perfect for me. My friends will be so envious!"

And indeed it was a much better fit and style than any other gown she owned, thanks to Clementina's expertise. The little Bath mantua-maker was pleased to be thanked profusely for her work and to see the colonial lady well and happy again.

Clementina didn't tell her she went every day to check on the rations being given to the people in the hold, but Mr. Redmarsh had observed and approved of her mission of mercy. Perhaps it was because Hugill knew Mr. Redmarsh was keeping a fatherly eye on Clementina that her request was granted to allow the poor passengers up on deck at a certain time during the day to exercise and wash their clothes while their children could play in the sunshine.

As the sun shone most days, the hardships of the long voyage eventually came to an end. Excitement ran through the ship as the coast of the New World appeared on the horizon. It was a particularly momentous time for Clementina.

As the *Heron* sailed up the Delaware River in the sunshine towards Philadelphia, Clementina's eyes were fascinated by all she saw. The sunlit meadowlands, farms and forests looked not unlike England, only everything seemed much bigger to her eyes.

"I'd no idea the colony would be so . . . beautiful!" She almost shrieked her admiration to Mr. Redmarsh who was standing near her on deck.

She heard him chuckle. "That's right, it is, Clementina." His good humor had returned now that his wife was fully recovered, and he was calling her by her first name just as Mrs. Redmarsh did.

As they progressed upriver, she marveled to be sailing past so many other ships and river craft skimming over the water, ferrying cargoes of iron, bricks and lumber. Mr. Redmarsh informed her such commodities as paper, glass, cloth and potash were also carried up and down the many navigable rivers and creeks of the Delaware.

"Our economy is thriving," Ralph Redmarsh said with pride in his voice.

Soon the ship was gliding by many busy shipyards. "I'm surprised to see so many craft being built here," she commented, thinking she'd imagined America to be a backward country, but it appeared very prosperous.

Swiftly the *Heron* reached the two-mile stretch of the Philadelphian wharfs with their great clapboard warehouses.

"Over there is Stumper's Wharf, and the shipbuilders' yard, Davey and Carson," exclaimed Ralph Redmarsh, sounding glad to be home and able to recognize familiar landmarks.

It was home for the Redmarshes but not for Clementina. She had to find somewhere to lodge. "Do you know of a respectable boarding house where I can stay?" she asked Mrs. Redmarsh as they got ready to disembark.

"Oh, but you will be staying with us!" cried Eleanor. "Ralph, dear, we want Clementina to stay with us as our guest, don't we?"

Ralph Redmarsh, busy checking his luggage, called back, "Yessiree."

Clementina went pink. She was overwhelmed at being invited as a guest.

"We have so many bedchambers being unused. You will be welcome. And our daughter Nancy will love you, I know she will."

Clementina didn't argue about their generosity. She knew they were wealthy and owned a large house. She'd learned during the voyage that Eleanor Redmarsh had given birth to six children. Sadly, five had died in infancy. Only Nancy had survived, and that was why she was their pride and joy.

Not worried any longer about where she was to stay, and content in front of the fire, in the warmth of the sun, she went out on deck to see the ship berth at the wharf.

They had finally arrived and the sailors called to each other as they ran about securing the vessel. Then the task of unloading the ship began.

Clementina watched them. And as her eyes wandered she was suddenly struck rigid.

She gasped as she saw the name of the

wharf written in large letters on a board. The name was *James Hunter!* It was Hunter's wharf.

It couldn't be the James Hunter she was looking for, could it? The man she had to beg for her little shop in Bath from? She frowned. He was not the same pleasant-looking young man so accurately depicted by Thomas Gainsborough, was he? There was, in the picture, a slight devil-may-care attitude in his engaging smile — but no hint of cruelty. Surely Mrs. Hunter's nephew wouldn't be making money from shipping poor families over the Atlantic in the hold instead of a regular cargo?

Although the weather was hot, Clementina gave a shudder, as though a cold draught had whistled by. Had she come all this way to meet a cruel tyrant?

It made her feel she wanted to stay on board and return immediately to England. But then the steel inside her made her want to find out if he was the owner of the ship, and if he was, to tell him exactly what she thought of him! The more she thought of Captain Millard and James Hunter pocketing sovereigns made from a human cargo, the more it made Clementina fume.

She could hear Eleanor Redmarsh calling her, so shelving her feelings, she rushed to

assist her. The Redmarshes were far too occupied making sure their trunks and chests
were taken carefully off the ship and piled
on wagons to be sent to their house, to
notice they had landed at James Hunter's
wharf.

"Home at last!" declared Eleanor delightedly.

She was looking at a large, rose-colored
brick, classical style residence set well back
from the road, amidst trees. As the carriage
swung towards the imposing paneled front
door, the face of a dark-haired young
woman could be seen for a instant looking
out of one of the downstairs sash windows.

In less than a minute the same attractive
young person had thrown open the front
door, and holding her skirt up so she didn't
trip on it, she tore down the flight of steps
and straight towards the newly arrived carriage, crying, "Mama, Papa!" until, panting,
she ran up to where her parents dismounted
from the carriage.

"Dearest Mama," she said, hugging and
kissing Eleanor delightedly as she jumped
about, "I'm so pleased to see you back safe
and sound. And Papa, it is truly lovely to
have you back home."

"Bless me, Nancy, how splendid you

look!" Her father regarded his daughter fondly and kissed her.

Clementina looked on and thought that the bright-eyed, exuberant young lady in her flower-sprigged cotton gown was indeed a Philadelphian society belle, and felt instinctively she would like her.

Embraces and exchanges of family endearments over, Eleanor turned to Clementina. "Now, Nancy, you must meet my English companion who has journeyed with us from Bath. She was so kind to me when I was very ill with seasickness. She's going to be staying with us for a while, and I'm sure you two will get on just fine."

Clementina found herself being examined closely by Nancy and was pleased to see the young lady's dimpled smile. Nancy gave a little curtsy and said politely, "I am indeed glad to make your acquaintance, Clementina."

Amazed as the American young lady curtsied to her, Clementina gave a little gasp.

"Why, you needn't look so proper, Clementina! I'm sure we're going to have loads of fun together," trilled Nancy. Eyes sparkling, she turned to her parents, saying, "One exciting event is that we have been invited to the Governor's Ball. Isn't that wonderful? And Mama, I can hardly wait to tell you. Since you've been away I have made the acquaintance of the most admirable young gentleman." She clasped her hands and raised her eyes skywards. "I just know you will love Henry, when you meet him at the ball. And you will too, Clementina. He's so handsome, so amusing, and so affectionate. Henry's my new beau!"

Her parents exchanged smiles while Clementina was stunned. Surely this young lady wasn't thinking of her going to a ball?

"Nancy," Clementina said, as they began to walk indoors and the servants came, smiling, to see the master and mistress return from their long voyage overseas and to cart in their luggage, "I'm not a lady. Not a fashionable young lady like yourself. I'm a mantua-maker. I do not go to balls."

Nancy looked at her sharply, "What difference does it make what you do?" Her eyes twinkled. "Once you've taken off that rather drab traveling gown you're wearing and put on a pretty summer one, you will look as attractive as any of the ladies at the ball."

Clementina smiled ruefully. She didn't own any ball dresses. How could she make Nancy understand she was in trade? She was a businesswoman and a companion —

a servant, really — not one of the gentry.

But Mrs. Redmarsh had chimed in and was informing her daughter that Clementina was an excellent dressmaker. "She has brought over some fashion dolls so you can see what they are wearing in Paris and London!"

"Oooh!" Nancy's mouth opened into a wide smile that showed her white teeth, then she jumped up and down with excitement. "I can't wait to see them. In the next few days we shall be making our new ball gowns. Clementina, will you make one for me?"

Clementina nodded and chuckled to see the lack of restraint evident in the American young lady's behavior. It made her feel she didn't have to be too stiff and formal either. And she was delighted to think she'd be able to sew for the family, in return for the hospitality they were so generously offering her in their lovely home.

When it came to unpacking, Eleanor wanted to show off her purchases, the fine coffee set and table first. But it was the silks, satins, gauzes, ribbons and fine lace that Clementina had in her luggage that made Nancy squeal with delight.

"That rose-red damask would suit you, Mama. And Clementina would look very charming in the embroidered cream silk, while I just love that yellow taffeta."

Clementina was thrilled by the notion that she could wear one of the fine creations she'd made for years for other ladies. But ball gowns were not for the likes of her.

"I can't dance," she confessed to Nancy, as the American seemed set on the idea that she should go to the ball.

Nancy looked surprised. "Well," she said after thinking about it, "you could always learn. I could teach you quite enough dances for you to get by."

Clementina gave a short laugh. "At my age I don't suppose any gentleman would want to dance with me!"

Nancy put down the piece of lace she was holding and put her hands on her hips. She regarded Clementina with a frown. "Fiddle-sticks!" she exclaimed. "Now Clementina, you must cease thinking of excuses why you cannot attend the Governor's Ball. Here in Philadelphia we have our own ways of doing things. We might not be as grand as the Quality in England, but we have our etiquette — and we have fun. You are still a young woman. True, you are older than many of the unmarried girls, but some mature men, Henry tells me, don't care for the younger girls who giggle and tattle excessively. They prefer poised young women like yourself."

Clementina's mind whirled. Would she dare dress up like a lady and dance with the Quality, just for once in her life? Yes, she would! When she got back to Bath and was working again in the sewing room, she would be able to smile, thinking how she once pretended she was a lady and danced at the Governor's Ball.

The loathsome task of finding Mr. James Hunter and begging him for ownership of the shop, as well as telling him how odious she thought he was to be shipping indentured servants in a ship's hold, could wait a while.

She had every intention of making herself as beautifully dressed as the other ladies, and enjoying her first ball. Why, she might even find the prince of her dreams!

CHAPTER FIVE

During the evening of the Governor's Ball, the daylight remained until late, and the weather was pleasantly balmy. The city ladies' silk and satin gowns shimmered under the outside lanterns in the garden and inside under the candlelit chandeliers in the ballroom.

Eleanor Redmarsh, tightly stayed, looked matronly and elegant in her rose-red gown trimmed with delicate lace. Dark-haired Nancy was a picture of youthful exuberance in her yellow taffeta, and Clementina, her auburn hair fashionably dressed by the Redmarshes' hairdresser, wore a cream and gold silk gown with touches of tiny crimson flower buds.

"Ladies, you are decked out as exquisitely as butterflies," declared Ralph Redmarsh gallantly, bowing to them.

Clementina, however, felt as if the butterflies were dancing around her insides.

She could not quite believe that she, a foundling child from the orphanage in Bath, was being accepted into the highest level of Philadelphian society.

The Redmarsh carriage bowled up to the Governor's residence, past the ornate wrought-iron gates, which were opened by liveried footmen for the visitors' carriages to enter the grounds. Along the tree-lined drive towards the magnificent Philadelphia fieldstone and brick mansion, Clementina heard Nancy whisper to her, "Do smile, Clementina. Ladies look prettier when they smile."

Made nervous by the role of a lady she was to play, Clementina could only force herself to raise a little smile.

Nancy didn't need to be told to smile as she was glowing with happiness, knowing she would soon be dancing with her beau, Henry Fisher. After they arrived at the ball, they were presented to Governor Penn of Pennsylvania and his gracious lady.

Clementina then met strapping young Henry, and deemed him a perfect partner for Nancy.

The first minuet was danced sedately to the string orchestra in the white and gold ballroom, whilst the chaperons sat looking at the dancers and gossiping behind their fluttering fans.

Clementina was overawed and thankful she'd not been asked to dance. After a while she began tentatively to enjoy watching the spectacle, tapping her slippered foot in time to the music, until she became aware that she was being scrutinized. An exceedingly bold gentleman had her in his sights. He had obviously not been taught one of the rules of polite behavior: one should not stare.

After a while, she began to feel uncomfortable being studied in this insolent fashion. Consequently, she turned away from him to hide her reddening cheeks.

But as the dance ended, out of curiosity she glanced at him again and was immediately annoyed with herself when he turned to meet her gaze. It infuriated her he'd singled her out to be ogled at, as if he'd recognized her to be out of place. As if he knew she was of indifferent breeding and did not really belong at the ball with American people of quality.

How cross she was with herself to see the glitter of satisfaction in his protruding eyes and the smirk on his thick lips when he saw her look at him.

Confound the bold man!

Clementina felt like getting up and telling

him off. She was quite capable of doing that. Many a tradesman in England — the delivery carter, the milkman or the butcher boy — needed to be scolded at times.

She was saved by Ralph Redmarsh, who came up to her. Bowing he asked, "Clementina, may I have the honor of this dance?"

The gavotte took all her concentration. "I regret a few dancing lessons from Nancy hasn't allowed me to master the intricacies of the gavotte," she apologized as her faltering steps embarrassed her.

"My dear, your feet may be occasionally wayward, but I appreciate dancing with such an attractive lady as yourself," said Ralph graciously, who did indeed appreciate her light-footedness and sense of rhythm.

Somewhat pacified that she was not dancing as badly as she feared, she relaxed.

As the dance progressed, Clementina enquired, "Tell me, sir, do you by any chance know the gentleman in the burgundy suit standing over there by the door? He keeps looking at me."

As Ralph looked over to where her tormentor stood, she added, "Pray do not look now," but she realized as she said it, that it was too late.

"No, I don't know the man. However, he

seems to have his eyes riveted on you."

Clementina found her knees unstable. "Why do you think he stares at me?"

Ralph chuckled. "Men like to watch pretty females."

"But I am not more than tolerable-looking. And there are many prettier girls in the room."

"He obviously doesn't think so. He's probably plucking up enough courage to ask you to dance. Although he doesn't look to me as if he is the kind of man you would choose to dance with."

Clementina agreed.

"What ails you, Clementina? Why, I believe you are too warm." Ralph had stopped dancing and was looking at her with concern. "As this dance is ending, shall I take you out into the garden? Maybe dancing is a little too much for you when you are not used to it."

"Thank you," Clementina murmured, taking his arm and strolling out the double doors into the refreshing breeze in the garden air.

"How beautifully tended this garden is," she remarked, trying to forget the gentleman in the burgundy suit. How sweetly the box fragrance soothed Clementina as she walked on the gravel around the herb garden. Rosemary, lavender, mint, purple sage and golden marjoram were laid out to great advantage. Balm-crickets chirped noisily, and they could just hear the strains of the ballroom music in the background.

"Shall I fetch you a lemonade?" asked Ralph.

A refreshing drink did sound good to Clementina. "Mmm, thank you," she said, and he marched off to get one.

Finding an alcove nearby with roses trained to grow around, she sat and felt composed again.

Until she heard the crunch of leather shoes on the gravel. She felt like a hunted animal as she saw the man attired in the burgundy silk suit approaching.

"Ma'am," he said, giving an elaborate bow, "I observed your eyes sought mine in the ballroom. Am I to understand you favor me?"

Clementina stiffened. She said, "No, sir, you are wrong. It was you who chose to stare at me."

He ignored her icy manner and seated himself very close to her so that she could smell his breath, which reeked of garlic. She moved farther along the seat, but his arm shot out and his clammy hand grasped her slight body, drawing it back towards him again.

Scared and shocked, Clementina gave an indignant cry.

Being so close to a man was a new experience for her. Being attacked was alarming. She had no idea how to get rid of him.

He picked up her hand, and although she tried to snatch it away, he held onto it fast. She froze with displeasure as his thick, wet lips pressed into her palm. His unwanted kisses moved up to her arm and over her shoulder to her exposed breast.

"Stop, sir. I beg you!"

But her protest only seemed to encourage his advances.

Horrified, Clementina gave another cry. "Go away!" she begged, acutely frightened. Her maidenly modesty had been cruelly invaded, and it was a situation she had no idea how to deal with.

Suddenly she was aware of large hands that yanked him off her. A powerful gentleman had come to her rescue!

Through tearful eyes she watched as her molester was dealt a mighty blow, sending him sprawling on the gravel. He had fear in his eyes as he got off the ground. Taking a last look at the man who had floored him, he hurried off, dabbing his bloodied face with his lace handkerchief.

The rugged young gentleman now sat beside her and asked with concern, "Have you been hurt, ma'am?"

It was only her dignity that had been invaded. Her composure was lost. She swallowed, to try and moisten her dry mouth, wanting to regain her voice. But only a sob escaped her. She could not explain that she was upset by the encounter because she'd never had any intimate dealings with a man before.

Yet, wiping her eyes with her fingers, she sensed this powerful man sitting patiently by her side understood her distress. Through wet eyes, she noted that although his physique looked superior to most gentlemen at the ball, she sensed he would not harm her. Indeed, she liked the look of him. She appreciated his large but rough hand that patted hers to comfort her.

"I do not know how to thank you," she gulped at last.

"Men like him are the very devil! But an attractive lady like you should not be left alone." His voice was deep and robust like himself.

Clementina could not hide another sob. The experience had truly shaken her to the core. Everyone was calling her attractive, but she was convinced it was only her costume that made them say they admired her. After all, she was only an ordinary businesswoman, whom normally nobody would notice or remark on, until tonight. She longed to take off the fashionable gown she was wearing and let her hair down, put on her cap and be plain Miss Willoby again.

"Mr. Redmarsh is fetching me a drink," she said, hoping the young man would remain with her until the gentleman returned.

"Harrumph!" Ralph was there with a glass of lemonade in his hand.

Getting up immediately, her savior bowed. Clementina was thankful he didn't mention the embarrassing incident between herself and the lecherous man in the burgundy suit.

Ralph, seeing the confusion that had struck Clementina at being caught seated with a strange gentleman, was as gallant as ever. He handed the glass to Clementina so that she could take a much-needed sip, then he bowed at the young man, saying, "I am, sir, Ralph Redmarsh. Allow me to present this lady who is newly arrived from England: Miss Clementina Willoby."

"And I am James Hunter, at your service, sir." The fellow then turned to bow to Clementina. "Ma'am."

The name James Hunter rattled Clementina. She gave an audible gasp, her hand shook, and she spilt some of the lemonade on the front of her gown.

Mr. Hunter quickly took the glass from her hand, in case she spilt more.

She found it impossible to say anything coherent. "Oh! Mr. Hunter. I . . . that is, if you are Mr. Hunter. I mean, are you Elizabeth Hunter's nephew? James, from England? Who owns a dress shop?"

Mr. Hunter frowned at the stuttering young lady.

Observing Clementina's loss of coherence, Ralph immediately eased matters by saying with a chuckle, "Mr. Hunter, this is indeed fortunate. Miss Willoby has come all the way from Bath, in England, to find you."

It was the young man's turn to look astonished. And Clementina was able to study him closely.

He'd changed considerably since she'd met him as a boy, of course. He'd adopted an American accent. He also looked dashing and was obviously successful. Her trained garment-maker eyes detected the superb cut and quality of his dark blue velvet suit and the expensive lace at his wrists. His brown hair was tousled, and she thought his broad shoulders would be equally impressive attired in a workingman's linen shirt and breeches. But it was his features she studied particularly. The same features that Thomas Gainsborough had so expertly depicted many years ago. Of course as he'd grown to manhood, he didn't look like the soft-faced youth who'd left England. But he was just as handsome. Indeed, he was even more attractive. Her cheeks became rosy as she recollected her daydreams about him.

"Harrumph!" Ralph interrupted not only Clementina's concentration on James, but the stalwart young gentleman's attention to her.

James was the first to find his voice. "Perhaps, ma'am, you will tell me why it is you braved the Atlantic to find me?"

Struggling to find the right words Clementina stammered, "I, er, I have two things I wish to say to you, sir."

"Indeed?" James looked surprised.

Ralph gave a polite cough. "Excuse me. I have no wish to meddle in your affairs, Miss Willoby. So I will leave you both to discuss your business."

Then, before Clementina could think to say that she did not wish to be left alone with the man she had to accuse of scandalous shipping practices, Ralph strolled away.

Clementina felt she could not call him back. But she didn't feel frightened to be left alone with Mr. Hunter, although he looked even more powerful than the man he had thrashed.

The couple looked into each other's eyes, and Clementina found his eyes very beguiling for a moment or two before Mr. Hunter enquired, "Well then, why not start with the first thing you have to say to me, Miss Willoby?"

She swallowed, and he handed back her glass of lemonade so she could have a drink and try to put her thoughts in order. Should she ask for the shop first, or berate him about the indentured servants?

Sitting bolt upright, her delicate nostrils flared as she took a long breath in. Deciding to get the worst part over first, she breathed out, saying, "Do you own the ship *Heron,* sir? And run a shipping line to England?"

"I do."

Haunted by her memories of the terrible conditions she'd witnessed of the poor families in the hold of his ship, she snapped, "Then you should be ashamed, sir!"

Taken aback, Mr. Hunter's mouth formed a straight line. A dangerous man glared back at her. "I beg your pardon, ma'am?" he said in a thunderous tone.

She took a wavering breath in and said as boldly as she could, "I traveled from England in your ship, the *Heron,* sir. I was appalled that you were shipping indentured servants — men, women and children — without adequate provisions, in the hold of your ship!"

He bellowed, "Untrue!"

Clementina was frightened at that moment. He certainly seemed taller, stronger and more angry than any man she'd encountered before. He continued to talk loudly: "I ship manufactured goods from Bristol. Things that can't be made here in America."

Determined not to be shouted down, she said quietly but clearly, "Surely you know there are restrictions in force now on the import of manufactured goods from England?"

She noticed a twitch on his handsome face. A crack appeared in his armor. Encouraged, she pressed on, "I presume your captain wanted to fill the empty hold so he could gain something from selling indentured servants. I did not imagine those poor people. I saw them living in terrible conditions, Mr. Hunter. *On your ship, sir.* And I think it is disgraceful to make poor people suffer so much. Men, women and children were stuffed below and shamefully neglected. You may ask Mr. Redmarsh if you wish to confirm my observations. He saw them too."

For a split second the young gentleman seemed caught off guard, vulnerable. He frowned and ran his fingers through his hair, making it look more untidy, as he muttered, "There must be some mistake." Then he shot at her, "Was Mr. Millard the master in charge of my ship?"

She felt like replying *you should know,* but instead she said, "Oh yes — when he wasn't drunk."

"He was intoxicated?"

"Even I could observe that!"

"Well, I . . . don't know. . . ."

She had floored him, but only for a moment. He cleared his throat and she saw his wide chest expand as he took in a deep breath. "If that is so, I assure you the matter will be promptly dealt with."

She should have left it at that, but Clementina, erroneously thinking she'd felled her man, continued to lay on condemnation in her cutting, managerial voice. "Language cannot describe the horror and indignation I feel about your conduct. I could hardly believe that Mrs. Hunter's nephew would do such a barbaric thing as ship indentured servants in such horrid conditions. You do it for money, I suppose. Is that how you've become rich, Mr. Hunter? Mrs. Hunter would be ashamed of you if she knew."

He breathed fire. "What do you know of my Aunt Elizabeth?"

"I've been employed by Mrs. Hunter since I was a little girl." Then she added softly, "May she rest in peace."

His eyebrows shot up. "*What* did you say?"

"I said — or I meant — I was very sorry she died."

This was clearly news to James Hunter, who let out a moan of lament.

Clementina's eyes blinked fast. She hadn't realized he didn't know about his aunt's death and was mortified she'd mentioned it to him so casually.

He clasped his hands behind his back and walked along the path away from her, as if he needed the time to mourn alone. Clementina sat and watched, sorry he was taking it so hard. Perhaps, she thought, Mrs. Hunter had been the only relative he had left behind in England who'd cared about him. And he'd loved the old aunt who'd helped him to start a new life in America.

He returned, his suntanned face afire, and barked at her, "When did she die?"

As sympathetically as possible, Clementina told him of his aunt's last days, of her sudden illness and death, assuring him that everything that could have been done was done for her by the doctor, but that several lettings of blood saw no improvement in her condition. She went on to explain how Mrs. Hunter was tended day and night by her. And that when the end came it was without any apparent suffering.

He listened thoughtfully and did not interrupt. "You must be the little orphan girl she adopted," he said suddenly. "I remember now. My aunt often mentioned you in her letters."

"Yes, Mr. Hunter. And I developed a great affection for her. She taught me her trade very well. And . . ." She drew in breath, then rushed to say what she'd come all the way from England to say to him. "She told me that when she died I could have her business and the shop." She gave a sigh as she looked down and plucked the lace on the sleeve of her gown. "But her lawyer told me she did not put it in writing. Legally, everything she had is to go to you."

He stared at her as he rubbed his chin. "It is curious I've not heard a word about this before." He took some steps away, stared into the distance and spoke as if to himself.

"And yet I suppose I've been occupied for a year or more in the backwoods, building a sawmill near Lancaster." He swung round and shot at her, "I guess some things have been going on behind my back." Then, again talking to himself, he muttered, "Maybe, when my aunt was planning her will, she wrote to me, but I've not received any letters for months."

Clementina had the feeling he was telling the truth. Seemingly, he hadn't received any mail from England recently, and he was wondering why.

Bringing him back to what concerned her, she said, "I'm anxious to keep my shop."

He eyed her keenly. "Did I understand you to say the shop was left to *you,* or to *me?*"

He was sharp. Clementina crimsoned as she squirmed. "I beg your pardon, sir. You have inherited your aunt's estate, and the shop. I have been in charge of the dress-making business recently. I work in it with other seamstresses, and we are all worried about losing our livelihoods. I have come to request that you allow us to work in the shop, even if you do not wish to give it to me." Clementina looked up at him challengingly and said clearly, "Although your aunt told me she wanted me to have it."

He thought for a moment or two before he spoke. "Miss Willoby," he said, "my aunt's death has come as a shock to me. I'll have to find out about this. I can't give you my answer straight away."

He watched the disappointment on her face as she said, "I understand, sir."

"As far as the other business you accuse me of is concerned," he went on, "I've been working, building a new sawmill in Lancaster for the past year. But I shall get down to my wharf and see Mr. Spear, my shipping agent, as soon as I can. I assure you, I will find out if there are any irregularities going on, and rectify the situation."

He seemed sincere, and Clementina breathed more easily.

Whatever else he or she might have said was lost, as Nancy's cheerful voice sounded as she tripped along the path towards them on the arm of her beau, Henry Fisher. "So there you are, Clementina! And this must be Mr. James Hunter. Papa told me you had found him."

James bowed politely. Henry returned the bow. Nancy gave James a curtsy and they all smiled at each other.

As it was an important social occasion, and since James seemed to be able to put aside his personal concerns, Clementina knew she must do so too and smiled.

"The light is fading. I've come to bring you in to dance. You must dance at a ball, you know." Unaware of the tension between Clementina and James, Nancy chattered on happily, just like her mama. "They are about to form for the cotillion." Nancy gave James a flirtatious wink from behind her fan. "I can see why Clementina wants to keep handsome Mr. Hunter to herself."

Clementina blushed. She was attracted to James Hunter, but hearing Nancy saying she was, although she was only funning, embarrassed her. There was far more between them than attraction. There was business. But Nancy could only think Clementina had been seeing a man she liked in private.

Clementina was partly relieved that James had seemed disturbed when she'd told him about the indentured servants. That made her think he had been unaware of them being transported in his ship. She prayed that he would stop the cruel practice. Also, he hadn't said he would not be giving her the shop.

Feeling she'd done all she could that evening to obtain the ownership of the shop and to secure her future livelihood and those of her fellow workers, she allowed herself to relax.

As if in a trance, she let Mr. Hunter escort her back to the dance floor.

The music transported her into the joyous world of dance. James's strength supported her steps, guiding her smoothly and effortlessly with the throng of dancers. And for once in her life, as hundreds of candles made her eyes shine as she looked admiringly at him, her English reserve vanished as her romantic dreams of him came true.

CHAPTER SIX

When Clementina awoke the next morning, her first thoughts were of James Hunter. His strong physique and well-formed, sunburned features, as well as his dazzlingly grey-blue eyes, were now engraved on her mind.

She lay in her bedchamber, luxuriating on a high-post bedstead covered by a patchwork quilt. She stretched slowly, like a waking cat, happy in the knowledge she didn't have to get up and go to work in the sewing room. Still sleepy, she let her mind wander.

There was something fascinating and exciting about a man who had chosen to live in the wilderness, close to nature and free from the restrictions of the orderly city of Philadelphia. Wealthy, thanks to his shipping business, James could return to civilization whenever he wanted. His well-developed physique and healthy skin, as well as his merry laughter, showed he enjoyed a rough out-of-doors life and the challenge of building his sawmill.

Clementina sighed at the thought of being in James's strong arms . . .

She suddenly sat up, bewildered by the powerful urge in her body that yearned for him.

Amazed to find her puritanical and decorous dressmaker façade crumbling, she realized that she had become a sensual woman. She wanted a man. She laughed softly to herself.

What kind of a person was she? Being an orphan, she'd no idea of what her parents were like. Maybe her father had been lusty, and her mother flirtatious . . .

Last night she felt she had passed the test, making her first foray into genteel society among the august company of Philadelphian people of quality. But the experience had been made memorable because of James Hunter — and the discovery of her suppressed feminine desires.

Then, remembering their conversation and the ownership of the little shop in Bath that lay between them, her smile disappeared. She'd better not abandon the strict, prudish principles she'd been brought up with or forget her frugal life as a seamstress, laboring long hours stitching, as she would probably have to return to it, with or without ownership of the shop.

But then, she thought with spirit, she would enjoy her freedom while she could.

She rose, and after a wash, began putting on her clothes. As she fastened her stays and slipped on a plain lilac cotton dress and apron, her eyes lingered for a moment on her beautiful silk ball gown. She stroked the lush silk lovingly. Perhaps she would never get the chance to wear it again but, like she would a wedding gown, she would always treasure it.

The aroma of coffee floating up from downstairs dispelled further wayward thoughts. Clementina hurried down the wide staircase and entered the breakfast parlor where the Redmarsh family was sitting around a long wooden table on Pennsylvanian Windsor chairs, having a dish of battered eggs and puffy bread rolls for their first meal of the day.

Good-morning greetings were exchanged and Clementina took her place with the family. Martha, the servant girl, poured her coffee and offered her something to eat. Mrs. Redmarsh, although suffering slightly from the vapors after the previous evening's exertions, was chatting away merrily about the ball with her daughter. But having covered most of the essential highlights, such as the other ladies' dresses, and who was dancing with whom, and gossip they had heard while they were there, Eleanor was ready to question Clementina about her thoughts about the glittering social event of the year.

"Now Clementina," said Eleanor, "did you sleep well? Yes, I believe you did, as your eyes have a brightness about them. We want to hear —"

Nancy chipped in, "I think her beau, Mr. James Hunter, is responsible for her bright eyes, Mama."

Shocked to hear the suggestion that there was any amorous connection between herself and Mr. Hunter, Clementina spluttered and quickly put down her cup of coffee. "No, no. Mr. Hunter is not my beau. He is —"

"A most presentable young man," finished Eleanor, "and I was dying to talk to him — but you hogged him all the evening, Clementina. What does he do?"

Clementina gulped. She didn't really want to discuss the man of her dreams. So she adopted her shop-girl reserve. "I don't really know, ma'am. That is, he told me he owns a ship and a sawmill." Clementina gave a sad sigh. "And my — I mean his — late aunt's dressmaking shop in England."

Eleanor clasped her hands together. "Aha! A man with considerable assets. I thought so. You must understand that here in the American colonies we use little actual money, or bank it, as they do in England. We put our money into land, property, and enterprises. And frequently we exchange goods rather than buying them. So your Mr. Hunter has done exceedingly well for himself in the years he has been here. Now what did you find out about him being a possible suitor?"

Clementina bristled. "His eligibility for marriage? That I do not know."

Eleanor glared at her. "Oh, I found out he's not married. That much I did find out from an acquaintance last night. Every girl should know who is available to wed. And I could see he was polite, and he struck me as being a most honorable gentleman."

Clementina dabbed her mouth with her napkin. Mrs. Redmarsh didn't know about his roguishness. She hadn't seen the indentured servants on his ship, and she didn't know that he'd been considered a wild youth who had been disowned by his father and sent away from university for thieving.

"I cannot say if he is honorable, ma'am. I can only hope he is, because as you know I want him to give me the dressmaking business Mrs. Hunter promised me."

Eleanor Redmarsh hid a sigh. It was clear to her that the little dressmaker was not going to reveal her secret thoughts about the gentleman she danced with last night. It might be English reserve that prevented Clementina from wanting to chat about it, which was a pity, as Eleanor had already decided James would make Clementina an excellent husband. But young people had to find these things out for themselves. So it was better to let the subject rest.

She nodded at Clementina, and smiled. "Ah, yes, dressmaking. Now that is another matter that is of interest. My friends were most impressed with the gowns you made, they said —"

"Mr. Hunter danced well," Nancy commented, turning to Clementina, "and I was very proud of my pupil last night. Watching you two together, I would say . . ." She raised her voice. "He is most definitely interested in you."

Annoyance made Clementina's face flush crimson.

"Pray do not interrupt your mama, Nancy!" scolded Eleanor. "Now as I was saying about the gowns Clementina made for us. My friends were full of praise, and asked me to ask you if —"

"Harrumph!" This time it was her husband who interrupted her by rising hastily from the table. Pushing his chair back, he explained, "My dear Eleanor, you will please excuse me. Having heard you go over in the minutest details the happenings of last night's ball, I will leave you to prattle on about the ladies' apparel. I shall retire into the peace of my study with Benjamin Franklin's *Pennsylvania Gazette,* which chronicles events that interest me far more."

Eleanor gave the girls a rueful smile as he left the room, remarking that her husband always had his head in the clouds and didn't know anything about society, as he never listened to what she had to say. Then she poured herself another cup of coffee, and launched into a flattering account of what the ladies had said about the gowns Clementina had made. She ended by telling Clementina that if she had it in mind to do any more sewing, her friends would love her to make them some gowns — and they would pay her well.

Delighted to be given such praise, Clementina assured her hostess that she would be willing to oblige them. "I'm happy to do some sewing for your friends, ma'am. For as long as I am here."

Eleanor's face beamed and she clapped in delight.

"I think you have enough customers already in Philadelphia to set up shop here," declared Nancy. "That is, if your beau is unwilling to give you the one in Bath."

Clementina frowned. If Nancy were one of her shop girls, she would have given her a dressing down. But she had to tolerate Nancy's teasing about James being her beau, although she wished it would cease. But just as she was thinking how she might put a stop to it, Nancy suddenly shot up from her chair and ran to the window, calling excitedly, "Speak of the devil, if it isn't Mr. James Hunter, come riding up for a visit. And you don't need to tell me who he's come to see — Clementina, of course!"

Clementina was not amused, as she tried to control her pounding heart. This was going to be far worse than a session with the Princess Amelia. She lifted her chin, pushed back her shoulders, and said frostily, "I expect he might well have come to discuss business with me. Which reminds me, I have a letter upstairs from Mrs. Hunter's lawyer to give him."

Eleanor rose from the table, saying, "He's making his morning call very early! I must fly upstairs and change out of my wrapper.

Now you girls preen yourselves. Have him shown into the drawing room, but if he wants to discuss business with Clementina, then I suppose the back parlor might give them more privacy. And tell Martha to make a fresh pot of coffee for him, Nancy dear."

Eleanor having left them, Nancy came over to Clementina and said, "Let me fix your hair prettily around your cap." She took a lock of Clementina's hair and curled it around her finger and laid it over her slender neck. "There, that looks most fetching."

"Now, let *me* adjust *your* gown," Clementina said, to prevent Nancy noticing her cheeks were heated. She went behind Nancy and pulled the folds of her skirt straight.

"Heavens, Clementina, I'm of no concern to James Hunter. You are his belle."

Angrily Clementina retorted, "No, no, Nancy, I am not. And I would be obliged if you would forget that whim of yours once and for all."

A giggle from Nancy told Clementina that Nancy wasn't going to oblige her. Clementina would have to endure the teasing. She just prayed Mr. Hunter would not hear of it.

The sound of the doorbell sent Martha

rushing into the hall to open the front door, and soon James Hunter's deep, seductive voice was joined by Ralph's, who'd come out of his study to greet him.

It wasn't long before Martha came into the breakfast room announcing, "The gentleman what's just come, wants to speak to Miss Willoby. He's been taken to the back parlor, ma'am."

"There, what did I tell you!" Nancy poked Clementina playfully. "You hoped he would call all along. I know you did. And now you can go through to the parlor and enjoy a nice long visit with him. I just hope Henry Fisher comes to see me soon."

Clementina swiftly left the room to hide her discomfort. She took several gulps of air to stop her heart from fluttering before trotting upstairs to collect Mr. Soames's letter for Mr. Hunter. Then she took another few slow, deep breaths before entering the parlor.

James Hunter's appearance was very different this morning than it had been the evening before. He was still handsome and confident-looking, but gone were his fine clothes. Instead, he was turned out in a serviceable riding coat and coarse cloth breeches that fitted his muscular figure to perfection. His leather boots were somewhat muddy.

And his face looked serious. It was a businessman who had come to see her, not the carefree dancer of last night.

He bowed to Clementina and she curtsied.

"I find you well this morning?" he asked with a hint of his delightful smile.

"I am, thank you," she replied. "And you?" she asked, sitting down primly on the settle.

He clasped his hands behind his back and replied just as formally that he was well.

"Then, sir, pray be seated."

He sat down on the chair opposite the settle as if he were fascinated by the formal manner of the woman he had come to see. Recollecting her carefree behavior last night, his lips curved. "I have come to apologize," he said, looking straight into her eyes and making her blink nervously. Another slight twitch moved his lips before he continued, "I saw my shipping agent this morning. You were quite right about the indentured servants." He looked away and gave a cough. "Captain Millard has been dismissed. It will not happen again, I assure you."

She had no doubt it would not. James Hunter would intimidate even the likes of

Mr. Hugill when his blood was up. "I'm thankful to hear it," she said primly, and was pleased no more suffering would take place in the hold of his ship.

"Now about the other business . . ."

"Oh, I have this letter for you, sir." She got up and handed him Mr. Soames's letter, then sat down again while he broke the seal. He took out the letter and read it.

Clementina hoped the letter did not put her in a bad light. She was aware that Mr. Soames was not entirely sympathetic to her claim.

Folding the missive slowly, he rolled it and tapped one palm with it as he said with a grimace, "He refers to a letter from my aunt that I did not receive. It is obvious some of my mail from England has not reached me. I would stay and investigate the matter, only I have to return to Lancaster today. The sawmill construction is at a crucial stage. It is almost ready for production. I must be there to oversee the men. I will return to Philadelphia as soon as I am able to, and look into this matter."

Clementina said tentatively, "And what about your shop in Bath, Mr. Hunter?"

"Ah yes. Now tell me, Miss Willoby, are Mr. and Mrs. Redmarsh being hospitable? Are you happy staying with them?"

Confused, Clementina nodded. "Yes, indeed, they have been most kind. But I must get back to Bath. I only put Miss Brush in charge of the business temporarily."

"Quite so. Is Miss Brush competent?"

"Why yes. She's an excellent seamstress. She knows all the skills of dressmaking."

James rose. "So there is no rush for you to return to England."

Clementina's face fell. "But, sir, I can't stay here indefinitely."

It was all she could do to control her dismay. She'd come all this way to see him. And he was playing with her like a fish on a hook. What had she done wrong? What would Miss Brush and the seamstresses say to her now? How could she convince him to part with Mrs. Hunter's shop?

Seeing her fighting to know what to say to him, he smiled at her. He came over to sit next to her on the settle, putting her head in a worse spin. His closeness made her body stiffen.

"I know nothing of sewing gowns, Miss Willoby, but I can't think that anything drastic will happen in the shop for the next few months if you are away. Can you?"

Clementina's head shot round to face him. "Oh, indeed, things can go wrong very rapidly."

Hadn't he been neglecting his shipping business? And look what had happened to his shipping business! But in this tense moment, with him so near, she thought it better not to refer to that.

She said, "The expensive materials we use can easily be spoiled if they are not cut and sewn up properly. And we can displease our toplofty clients very easily too. Some, like Princess Amelia, are very difficult to handle at times. And poor Miss Brush is inclined to be afraid of the royal lady."

James gave a chuckle. "I shouldn't imagine you frighten easily."

"No!" she lied, because she was very scared at that moment as his arm slipped around her shoulders. His face came closer and his lips were poised above hers. She felt her bosom rise and fall with the rapid beat of her heart. Yet she didn't have the strength of mind to push him away.

Seductively, he pronounced the words: "I am certain, Miss Willoby, that there will be no difficulty about you acquiring the shop" — his voice lowered and he breathed heavily — "in due course."

Whether she kissed him or he kissed her, she wasn't sure, but their embrace was short-lived as a rap on the door drew them apart. Martha entered, bearing a tray of coffee.

The diversion enabled Clementina to regain her composure. Handing him a cup of coffee with trembling fingers, she accidentally touched his skin, which sent a spasm of warmth through her.

Sitting upright, alone on the settle again, she wondered as she watched him drink his coffee if he knew she was falling in love with him. And that thought completely removed from her mind the reason she had come all the way from Bath to see him.

James hadn't come to visit with the intention of courting Clementina. What had prompted him to kiss her he didn't rightly know — unless it was the desire to upset her prim, old-maid's behavior. Which wasn't very gallant of him, considering the hold he had over her.

He'd come swiftly to sit by her, drawn like a bee to nectar. She'd been startled, yet he was sure she was unafraid as she let him place his lips over hers.

As they kissed — although lightly — he became aware that she was a woman with feminine ardor and that she was trying to hide it from him.

What he hadn't taken into account was

how the brief, passionate experience affected him. This was a new aspect of Miss Willoby he hadn't expected. He discovered she was a desirable woman, and she stirred him deeply.

Suddenly he realized he was a man who needed a woman — and Clementina was that woman. Disturbed by the recognition of his lust, James decided he must have time to think about his strong attraction to her. Bachelors were frowned upon in the American colonies. Men were taught it was their duty to marry and beget children, but he'd never considered matrimony seriously before. Now the specter of marriage rose up before him, and he decided he'd better leave before he did something else rash — like propose to her!

"Hum," he said, looking at her rosy cheeks and lips and admiring the way she'd so quickly controlled herself, as if butter would not melt in her mouth. "I'm afraid I didn't behave as well as I should have done," he muttered.

"Don't let that concern you," she answered prudishly, as if the kiss hadn't happened. But she looked at him, reluctant to take her eyes away from his.

"Now, about the shop. I trust you will be patient and wait until I have the time to sort out my affairs properly. I must hurry away right now." He gave her one of his magnificent smiles and said jokingly, "Just remember, good things come to those who wait."

She gave him an uncertain smile.

He said, "As I explained before, I must get back to the sawmill today. But I promise you I will not forget about the shop." And going to the door, he was thinking that what he really meant was that he would never forget her.

Clementina was fixed in his mind. She was a most tantalizing female. More than any he'd known and bedded previously. He would court her seriously on his return.

"Thank you." He barely heard her weak reply. He left her sitting in a trance.

Clementina refused to cry, although she felt like it after he'd gone. She'd thought all she wanted in life was the little shop in Bath. Now she realized she wanted James more than anything else in the world. Nay, she needed him! And there was no chance of her getting him.

He didn't need her any more than a dose of salts! James Hunter was an up-and-coming colonial gentleman. Wealth, position and looks: he had them all.

She had nothing. Not even the shop in Bath — although he'd made a vague promise to let her have it.

Later, Nancy was all ears to hear about what had occurred between Clementina and her beau. "I saw him leave. I could swear his eyes looked dreamy. And you have the look of someone in love!" she said delightedly.

Clementina was just thankful James Hunter was well out of earshot, riding his fine black horse back to Lancaster.

CHAPTER SEVEN

The next few days passed slowly for Clementina. She was in a curious state after James kissed her in the parlor. The kiss had been unlike any other sensation she had experienced. Excitement bubbled inside her, and yet she had a sense of unreality, too.

She couldn't share her strange feelings with anyone, any more than she'd ever been able to confide in her Bath shop girls. But it comforted her to know that Mrs. Redmarsh and her daughter seemed to have her best interests at heart. They treated her like a friend, despite constantly provoking her about her "beau," as they called James Hunter.

Disturbed about her situation, which had become more complicated since she still did not know if she would ever own the shop in Bath and she was obliged to stay in Philadelphia longer to find out, she had the added concern that she couldn't shake James out of her mind. And knowing James was not married added to her torment. Could he ever be, as Nancy said he was, her suitor?

When she left England, she'd considered herself a female who would never marry. Now, although older than most unmarried women, she wondered if she was, perhaps, a little attractive, as the Americans kept saying she was. And wearing light, pretty summer gowns she'd made for herself, she looked quite different from the way she'd looked in the less flattering working clothes she'd worn in England. Even her golden ginger hair was no longer pushed tightly away under a head-covering cap, but curled around her oval-shaped face. She also wore a pretty cap or, sometimes, a feathered hat perched on top of her head.

Her heart did a little dance of hope that perhaps she was not, after all, a frigid old maid as she'd feared when the man in the burgundy suit had made the advances she'd abhorred. A maiden's prayer of getting married and having children was not impossible. Would that prayer ever be answered for her? And was James Hunter her man?

Or was it all wishful thinking?

But she also worried about the kind of man she thought James was. Could he be the sort of daredevil and reckless man she shouldn't be associating with — even if she was attracted to him?

She didn't know the circumstances about the money he was supposed to have stolen at university. It pricked her conscience that she, too, had stolen something: Mrs. Hunter's drawing of James by Thomas Gainsborough. James did admit he was guilty of not keeping a close eye on his shipping business so that, unknown to him, his drunken captain had conveyed people across the Atlantic in terrible conditions. That showed he could be remorseful, even if he had faults.

But, could she trust James's promises? How long would it be before he returned to Philadelphia and saw his lawyer about giving her the shop? Or had he thought about it and changed his mind?

James hadn't bothered to send her a message, and it was now the end of July. Did that mean that her daydream — thinking that he had some amorous regard for her — was merely in her imagination? Had he forgotten her already? Did his kiss in the parlor mean nothing to him? Virile men like him would take many a girl to kiss and cuddle. What was momentous for her might mean nothing to him. He might well have even forgotten he'd kissed her!

She often wondered how Miss Brush was managing in the shop. Would she get back and find the business gone to pieces? Should she now return to England and hope James would write to his lawyer, who would then contact her about his decision regarding the shop in Bath?

One fine summer day, she and Nancy were strolling back from the shops along the attractive tree-lined streets of Philadelphia with their neat terrace rows of houses.

Fierce sunlight was filtering through the leafy water beeches and Clementina, unused to America's stifling heat, was glad of the shade.

Nancy remarked, "I think you've become a little sad of late, Clementina. What ails you?"

Clementina gave her companion a quick smile. "Oh, you must know. I've not yet heard from Mr. Hunter about the shop."

"I guessed it was your beau, James, that was tying up your thoughts."

Clementina decided it was about time she stopped Nancy's speculation. "It's not as you think, Nancy," she retorted crossly. "Mr. Hunter can't be interested in me when I've heard nothing from him for so many weeks, now can he?"

Not giving Nancy a chance to make an excuse for him, she continued, "No, he has settled back to his work in the backwoods and forgotten all about me. So I'm in a quandary about whether to return to England and let Mr. Hunter's lawyer correspond with Mrs. Hunter's lawyer in England concerning his decision whether he will allow me to have — or run — the shop."

"Oh you can't go back yet, Clementina!" shrieked Nancy. "I'm getting married soon, and I want you to make my wedding dress! And Mama will want a gown of your making, too."

Clementina smiled at the happy girl. Nancy had become officially betrothed to Henry Fisher recently, and in her happiness she'd not noticed Clementina's unhappiness until today.

"Of course, I will make your gowns," Clementina assured her, "before I leave."

"Thank you, dear Clementina. You are such a wonderful dressmaker. I just can't imagine how we will ever do without you. And I don't mean that I just appreciate your sewing skills. We all like you. I've become very fond of you."

Flattered to hear Nancy's words of affection, Clementina was so taken aback she couldn't think what to reply.

They were walking by small houses whose balconies had benches for the owners to sit on next to the brick-paved sidewalks. The houses looked so friendly — so different — from the beautifully elegant, but aloof, Bath architecture. Clementina liked Philadelphia, and was fast becoming accustomed to American scenery and ways.

"Let me advise you . . ." Nancy said, then stopped to smile and wish good day to an old gentleman sitting on his balcony with a puff of smoke rising from his long clay pipe. Clementina received a nod too; Americans she found most friendly.

"Yes," Nancy continued, walking on, fanning her face with a new fan she'd just bought, "it is indeed a very hot day." She walked on a few steps. "I was distracted. Now what was I talking about?"

Clementina could see Nancy was becoming just as much a gabble goose as her mother and smiled. "I think you said you were going to advise me?"

"Ah yes. So I was. Now, I think you should stay with us much longer. For there are many exciting events coming up. There's a Ladies' Tea and Dainties next week, and dancing at the Assembly House the following month. And we need your help at the Sewing Bee; no one sews faster than you, Clementina. There are so many poor people from the frontier districts who were made homeless during the French and Indian War needing garments."

Clementina assured her she would be glad to help.

"Then there are the rural parties coming up. The Turtle Frolic. And several picnics that start in the afternoon and end at moonlight that are always fun. And you haven't visited our mineral springs yet. But most of all —" Nancy's voice faltered. "I shall miss you if you go. You are like an elder sister I never had."

Clementina was much touched to be encouraged to stay in such a genuinely warm manner. She dreaded the day when she would have to say goodbye to the Redmarsh family, who had been so generous to her. She wasn't really looking forward to leaving the loving Redmarsh home and going back to an empty flat over the shop and becoming plain Miss Willoby again. Just another shop girl.

Regretfully, her decision day drew nearer as another month of pleasant social engagements passed and the wedding gowns were almost finished. Still Clementina had heard nothing from James, and she decided he must have cast her from his mind. Sadly, she must return to England.

She made an appointment to see the lawyer, Mr. Kenrick, who told her where Mr. Hunter's sawmill was situated in Lancaster. Mr. Kenrick, who'd read the Bath lawyer's letter, offered to contact Mr. Hunter's lawyer. She was told she would be informed as soon as Mr. Hunter had decided what to do about her claim to the shop.

Telling the Redmarsh family of her decision to leave would not be easy, so she decided not to mention it to the ladies until she knew for sure that she was going.

When Mr. Redmarsh made his next visit to the harbor to see about his latest consignment of Madeira, Clementina asked to accompany him. She intended to slip off to the shipping office and see if she could book a passage to England.

The Philadelphian shipping offices were as busy as beehives on the morning when Clementina was taken there in a gig driven by Mr. Redmarsh. She saw the comings and goings of sailing ships making their way up and down the Delaware from ports in North America and abroad. Not only England, but ships from the West Indies, Holland, Africa and the Spanish Main, were in evidence.

"All this trade," she commented to Mr. Redmarsh, "makes me realize that the Americans are no longer like children needing their mother country for support."

"That is true, Clementina. We are capable of making decisions for ourselves now, and resent interference from the British. And what is more, a convention was held earlier this month in the House of Burgesses at Williamsburg, where it was agreed to send seven delegates to a Continental Congress in Philadelphia. Being an intelligent young lady, I am sure you will understand that the colonists are meeting to challenge British rule."

"Will it lead to trouble?"

"It need not. But I fear it will," replied Mr. Redmarsh as he flicked the whip and steered the horse around a convoy of Conestoga wagons on the quayside. "Some of the British are very stiff-necked. And some of our colonists are hotheaded."

Clementina could think of a hotheaded colonist immediately: James Hunter.

Mr. Redmarsh gave a loud sigh. "Many British colonists fear for the worst and are already leaving and going north to Canada."

She looked at him enquiringly. "And what

will you do, Mr. Redmarsh?"

"I intend to stick it out. This is my country and I'm staying here. My wine imports come from Portugal, not England."

Clementina's teeth bit into her lower lip as she pondered the possible difficulties ahead for the colonists. Of course, being English, she was loyal to the crown. But she understood how the colonists felt about being ruled by a country on the other side of the Atlantic.

Mr. Redmarsh had been confidentially told by Clementina of her plan to return to England and made no comment on it. Especially in front of his wife and daughter. He'd always had straight dealings with Clementina, finding her a sensible and capable young woman whom he liked. Besides, he had no hold over what she did, although he seemed dismayed to learn she was planning to leave his family.

"I will tie up my horse here," he said, drawing his gig up where carriages could be parked. "I'll wait for you if I get back first. And if you do, you can sit and wait for me in the gig."

Clementina, clutching her reticule with money she'd saved from dressmaking for her fare, walked towards the shipping office. She stopped and looked the tall building up and down, trying to make a final decision as to whether she really wanted to leave this land where she felt, even after a few months, strangely tied. Especially to James Hunter, her love, who, she realized with a pang, she would probably never see again.

Then, with a heavy heart, having made up her mind it was for the best, she pressed on through the entrance and up the stairs to where a notice informed her passages to England could be booked.

All shipping entailed much bookkeeping. Ships went from Philadelphia harbor to all over the world. In numerous small offices along the quay, shipping clerks were scratching entries into their ledgers with goose-quill pens, as marketable items and amounts of credit were carefully recorded.

In one counting office, Mr. Nathaniel Spear, shipping agent for Mr. James Hunter, was talking in sibilant tones to the master of Mr. Hunter's ship, *Heron.* Mr. Millard was supposed to have been dismissed, but Spear had retained him for his own convenience, knowing Mr. Hunter wouldn't learn about it until too late as he was engaged with Indian raids on his sawmill in the back-woods and was unlikely to appear in Philadelphia for some time.

Spear, a short-necked, stocky man with

eyes that were close together but moved about as quickly as a bird's, hissed his s's and tended to spit through his blackened front teeth, which obliged Millard to choose a seat well away from the agent's desk. This made Spear talk loudly so that he could be heard. "You only have the latest batch of indentured servant to sell and collect the monies before the business is over for you."

Miserable Millard mopped his sweaty face with his less-than-clean handkerchief. Even with the doors and windows open, the shipping office was unbearably hot on this sultry summer morning.

"Aye," Millard said unhappily as he leant forward in his chair and rubbed his bloodshot eyes.

Spear's smug smile, which had fooled James Hunter and was now intending to cheat Millard too, spread over his square face.

Once Mr. Millard had been a first-class seaman, a capable captain. Drink had been the captain's downfall. Rum had put him at the mercy of Spear, who was a dishonest, jumped-up shipping clerk.

Millard was no fool when not intoxicated; he knew Spear was intending to cheat him, but if he refused to do what Spear told him, he would find himself destitute. Hugill and

Spear would sail off and leave him with nothing. Hugill, he knew, was quite capable of sailing the *Heron* to the Caribbean without him on board. The most he could hope for was to pocket some of the money from the last sale of the indentured servants and disappear before James Hunter returned and found out he'd been robbed of his ship.

His better nature had made him loathe having to go to the courts in England to acquire indentures, promising to convey prisoners to the American colonies at no cost to the crown. Hugill couldn't do the job because, being an ex-convict, he lacked an air of authority that was needed to impress a Bristol judge.

For that reason Spear had retained Millard.

Millard crammed the prisoners, together with poor families requiring a free passage to America, into the *Heron*'s hold. The unfortunate people were cooped up for as long as six weeks, depending on the wind and weather, so that he could sell as many as possible at fifteen pounds a head to satisfy Spear's greed.

Then, as now, he had the detestable task of having to parade them in their rags on the wharf in Philadelphia, offering them for sale. Some Philadelphians were so against the trade, he had to arrange for the buyers to see them out of sight in a shed. Seven years of their just and fair labor he was offering the buyers, and then they were to be freed. Released from bonded service with fifty acres of land, two suits of clothes, a hat and a gun — and a sack of corn. Some made it, and some died, trying to survive the harsh American winter climate.

Millard found it an abhorrent business. Some of the sniveling children, the older and sick men and women, were the devil to get rid of. He was often obliged to sell them for work they were not strong enough to do. Families were sometimes split up, and as for some of the young women — he didn't like to think of their fate!

It was, Millard thought miserably, all right for Spear, sitting in his smelly little shipping office. He was not obliged to hear the captives' cries of distress for weeks on end onboard ship. He didn't have to dole out the skimpy rations as he and his crew did. He was not there to officiate at the burials at sea most of his transatlantic crossings entailed, which were often children weakened by the long sea voyage in the hold unsuitable for passengers.

Millard regretted the day he'd met Nathaniel Spear and silently damned him to hell.

Millard knew Mr. James Hunter was an honest ship owner. But he was also a trusting young fool! It was disastrous that he'd left the shipping side of his business in the hands of Spear and moved away into the interior for his timber enterprise.

Even when Mr. Hunter had come on a quick visit a couple of months ago because he'd heard about the ship's "redemptioners," Spear had given him one of his deep abeyances and feigned shock.

"I will send the master packing," Spear had informed James Hunter, who foolishly believed him.

"If you can't fill the ship with a decent cargo then you must not send the ship to England." James Hunter's temper was up.

"No, sir." Spear's eyes looked humbly down, but his lips smirked.

The agent's grin vanished, though, when Mr. Hunter thundered, "I'd rather sell my ship than allow it to be used to transport indentured servants."

Spear was alarmed. The ship had brought him in a good, if fraudulent, income, and the thought of losing it did not please him. He had to cunningly pull the wool over the young owner's eyes to enable him to keep the ship, so he promised to get rid of Millard.

But as soon as the young man had ridden off, what had he done? He'd called Millard and sent him off to England to collect another load of redemptioners!

The agent was evil, and so was the ship's bos'n, Hugill. Millard wished them both to hell.

He regretted, with all the decency he had left in him, that he'd not informed James Hunter years ago about his embezzling little shipping agent, Spear. Spear had begun with petty pilfering and steadily grown worse and worse, until now he was after Mr. Hunter's ship — and would most likely succeed in stealing it from behind that young idiot's back!

Millard stood to leave, hardly able to look at the crowing pirate, as Spear joked, "Mr. James Hunter will get a nasty surprise when he finds his ship has flown, eh, Millard?"

All Millard wanted was to get out of Spear's office and creep into the nearest tavern. He looked helplessly along the unpolished floorboards and traveled up to the doorway, where he caught sight of frilled feminine skirts. In a flash, he raised his eyes to behold the neatly dressed young lady. He blinked twice. Wasn't that the same young woman whom he had onboard the *Heron* during the voyage from Bristol to Philadelphia not above three months ago? Now somewhere deep in his brain he remembered hearing from the wine merchant, Mr. Redmarsh, who'd also sailed on that trip, that the young lady was going to seek for a Mr. James Hunter about some matter concerning a shop in Bath.

"Spear, look!" Millard said, pointing at Clementina's startled face.

"What is it, man?" Spear demanded rudely, because the young lady had vanished, like a phantom, out of sight.

In consternation, Millard wondered how much of their conversation she might have overheard. His guilty conscience made him incoherent.

Spear was obliged to produce a bottle of rum from his office cupboard to make the captain relate the whole story.

"That young woman was Miss Clementina Willoby. She traveled on the ship with Mrs. Redmarsh — as her companion, I remember. Mr. Redmarsh mentioned she knows James Hunter. If she overhead what you said, she might inform him of your plan."

Spear was beside himself. He crashed around the office, slamming the door and shutters on the window and bolting them.

His clever plan to steal Mr. Hunter's ship would be wrecked if that eavesdropping English wench got word to Mr. Hunter.

"Find Miss Willoby . . . and kill her," he told the captain callously. "I'll arrange for us to sail away with the ship long before Mr. Hunter can get back here."

"Kill her?" gasped Millard. Even in his half-intoxicated state, he could not consent to murder.

"Yes, kill her, or *your body* will be floating in the Delaware."

Frightened, and being the weak man he was, Millard agreed that he would dispose of Miss Willoby. Now he was involved with Spear up to his neck, and it would be a hanging matter if he were caught. The sweat oozed from the captain's forehead.

A short time later, when Millard slunk away from the shipping agent's office, he took hold of himself. No, he could not — *he would not* — kill Miss Willoby. He would order his bos'n, Hugill, and mate, Big Jack Toms, to find her, kidnap her, and restrain her somewhere so that she couldn't warn James Hunter. Later, he would release her.

Captain Millard decided he would have no more to do with the criminal activities of Spear and Hugill. He would vanish. He couldn't prevent them from stealing Mr.

Hunter's ship, but he would not sail the *Heron* to an island in the sun where James Hunter's ship could be sold to pirates.

With the money he'd pocket from selling the last lot of indentured servants, Millard hoped he could look forward to a modest retirement in another colony, where the people would not think of him as other than some harmless old sea captain who enjoyed his tipple of rum.

CHAPTER EIGHT

Without intending to listen to a private conversation, Clementina had stopped by the shipping office door, lettered with Mr. Spear's name, when she heard some men inside talking about James Hunter.

Mesmerized, she strained to hear more, without thinking she was eavesdropping.

She stayed long enough to be horrified about what she heard. There had been another group of indentured servants sent over from England despite James's assurance that there would not be. And she was sure she recognized Mr. Millard, whom she understood had been discharged. Then she almost cried out — the hairs on the back of her neck pricked — when she heard Spear bragging that he planned to steal Mr. Hunter's ship!

James had told her he suspected some underhanded work was going on. Obviously his short visit to see Mr. Spear when he was in Philadelphia hadn't cured anything. Or had James lied to her? Had he a cruel streak that allowed him to continue shipping the poor "redemptionists"? Or had his absorbing interest in his sawmill and his absence left his shipping business unsupervised and open to abuse from these villains who were about to steal his ship?

With these alarming thoughts rushing through her brain, Clementina fled. Her feet took her swiftly down the wooden office stairs, and holding her bonnet so that it did not fall off in her haste, she ran to the gig where she was thankful to find Mr. Redmarsh waiting for her.

"Oh, Mr. Redmarsh, a dreadful thing is about to happen!" she cried as she jumped up into the carriage. "Please leave here at once. I must get to Lancaster as soon as possible."

"Dear me, young lady, what has upset you?" But without waiting for her to tell him the details, Mr. Redmarsh got down and untied the horse, then stepped up again to sit beside her. He looked questioningly at her flustered face.

"I've discovered some men are planning to steal Mr. Hunter's ship," she gasped.

"The *Heron?*"

"That is what I overheard outside his shipping agent's office."

"Are you sure?"

Clementina, thinking she'd always been able to discuss things in a rational way with Ralph Redmarsh, turned to look pleadingly up into his eyes. "Yes, I'm sure. I heard those men say they intend to sail his ship to the Caribbean and then to sell it. Mr. Hunter should be warned without delay."

Ralph flicked the reins and the horse trotted along the quayside and out onto the road. His instinct told him Clementina was very disturbed. She'd obviously discovered some dastardly plot to harm James Hunter. She was not, in his opinion, the type of woman to embroider the truth.

"Did you see the men?" he asked as they bowled along in the carriage.

"Well, I couldn't be sure, but I thought I heard and glimpsed Mr. Millard, the master of the *Heron.* The other man could be Mr. Hunter's shipping agent, Mr. Spear."

"Ah. Very likely."

Clementina, grateful Mr. Redmarsh was taking her seriously, thought out loud. "I must get a message to James Hunter immediately. He must be told." She was struggling to think how she could do that when she burst out, "He has been so stupid to trust that shipping agent. I only had to hear that man's voice to know he was not trust-worthy!"

"Humph! Some people have not much ability to judge the worth of others. But are you sure Mr. Hunter is not aware of this treachery?"

"That I cannot say." Then she added, "But I told him about the ill treatment of the passengers in the hold, and although he told me the trade would be stopped, it obviously hasn't been, because I overheard the agent say another group had been transported! They are about to be sold down at the quay."

Ralph's comment was not fit for a lady's ears.

Clementina was too upset to take offence. She went on, "I'm convinced all this has happened because James has been far too lax. Stupid, foolish man! Now see what has resulted from his negligence!"

Mr. Redmarsh no doubt agreed but said nothing for a while. Only the horse's trotting hooves on the cobbles could be heard as they made their way to the Redmarsh residence.

"Are you sure those men you overheard didn't see you?" Mr. Redmarsh asked suddenly.

"I cannot be sure of that. But I don't think so."

"Let us hope you are right."

That was a concern Clementina hadn't thought about. But she was sure they couldn't have seen her. Or could they? She quickly pushed that worry out of her mind.

As the house came in view, Clementina suddenly announced, "I will have to go and tell Mr. Hunter myself. It may be too late, of course. Those men might have absconded with the ship by the time he can get back to the quay to stop them."

Mr. Redmarsh flicked his whip to encourage the horse to go faster. "You can't go. I'll send Hawkes, my Indian manservant. He can be trusted."

"Why can't I go, sir?"

"Because the wilderness is no place for young ladies."

Clementina protested, "But I'm *not* a lady, as well you know. I'm used to rough ways. I think it's essential for me to speak to Mr. Hunter. Besides, I have to see him about another matter too. I've been waiting for ages to hear from him about the shop in Bath." She looked sideways at Mr. Redmarsh. "I came all the way from England to find out if he would give me the shop. And he still hasn't given me his answer. So a few extra miles up the great Philadelphian Wagon Road to get it will be no hardship for me."

"Now listen to me, Clementina. While I agree that you must let Mr. Hunter know straight away what you overheard, I think you should abandon any idea you have to go there yourself. A young woman, brought up in civilized society, can't imagine the wilderness. It is vast. There are hostile Indians and wild beasts, and the men living there are not gentlemen. Lancaster is a frontier town, an expanding town, I grant you, but a far cry from the elegance you found in Bath and here in Philadelphia. It's not a fashionable place to visit."

"But, sir, I'm not going there for a social visit." Clementina was not going to be put off by his warning. In fact, it made her want to see America's interior. She could just imagine Matilda Brush's face when she told her that she'd seen Red Indians and bears roaming in the wild! As for men who were not gentlemen, she'd seen enough so-called gentlemen in Bath who were far from well-mannered.

James was half a gentleman, as she was half a lady. She wouldn't be surprised to find him working like a laborer. He had left England under a cloud. Yet he could behave like a gentleman when he chose, as she knew how to behave like a lady. Coming from an orphanage, she knew her mother might have been a harlot — or she might be a duke's bastard child.

Then, of course, she had a compelling urge to see James again before she left for England.

She couldn't explain all this to Mr. Redmarsh. Consequently, she just said stubbornly, jutting out her chin, "Despite all you tell me about Lancaster, I intend to go."

Looking at the determination on her face, Mr. Redmarsh sighed. He had no authority to prevent her from going anywhere she pleased. She was not his wife, his daughter, or his servant that he could forbid her to go. And he had the strong feeling she would survive no matter what she did.

"Very well, Clementina. I will help you as best I can."

"Thank you, sir."

"There is a stagecoach from the metropolis to Lancaster tomorrow morning. I am sending a consignment of wine to customers I have there. I can arrange for you to take the stage, with Hawkes as your bodyguard. I intended him to deliver the wine, as I would not trust a case of Madeira to travel on the stage west without being broken into."

Excitement and apprehension boiled up together inside Clementina.

"Hawkes is astute. He is an Indian who comes from the Appalachian Mountains. He will protect you."

Clementina hoped she would not need protecting, but she was grateful to know she would have a knight traveling with her.

"Mr. Rogers of Lancaster is a man you can trust, too. He will be able to direct you to the sawmill. I will send him a letter of introduction."

Clementina felt a little less keyed up.

"There is one thing I ask. Please don't tell my wife or daughter what you intend to do. Say, if you will, that you would like to travel to Lancaster purely for pleasure."

Clementina smiled.

As the gig rolled into the Redmarsh stables and a groom hurried out to hold the horse's bridle so the passengers could dismount, Mr. Redmarsh remarked, "I'm aware you will need a female companion, too. There is one overnight stop at a post tavern. I will see what I can arrange."

Taking his leave of her, he said confidentially, "Clementina, much as I abhor your decision to make this journey into the wilderness to find Mr. Hunter, I believe you have good reason to do so. As a merchant myself, I would appreciate someone informing me if any clerk in my counting office was embezzling from me. And even if the threat is not as serious as you suppose, I think Mr. Hunter is extremely fortunate to have such a loyal lady friend as you to come and warn him, so that he can at least look into any irregularities."

Clementina blushed, not only at the praise, but also because he considered her to be James's lady friend. Later, in her saner moments, she was daunted as she thought about the expedition she intended to make into the wilderness.

Clouds of dust billowing around the herds of mooing cattle and heavy draft horses pulling wagons on the busy highway rained dirt over the stagecoach and its passengers. It made Clementina's face feel gritty and her throat dry. Attempting to brush away the buzzing flies that were bothering her, she gazed out the coach window, fascinated to see the throngs of people, carts and animals moving steadily up and down the Great Philadelphian Wagon Road.

How she wished she'd not chosen to wear her heavy traveling gown in the sticky heat. Since early that morning — it was now late afternoon — she'd been jolted by the stage-coach going over the lumpy, stony ground. The coach's flexing leather springs did little to lessen the bumps. The experience made Clementina feel as if she were a skeleton being rattled around in a wooden coffin.

Despite her physical discomfort, she found an interest in the countryside west of Philadelphia. They passed thousands of tall pine trees, sunny agricultural land, farms with livestock, flour mills and highway inns. Farm workers were hard at work harvesting in the wheat fields they had carved out of the dense forests.

The stagecoach had to overtake slow convoys of red and blue Conestoga wagons that were covered with dirty white canvas, creaking and swaying along the road, taking new settlers with their few belongings, cows and chickens towards the heart of America. And there were all manner of wheeled carts driven by cigar-smoking, yelling teamsters. Bull whips cracked as the horses and mules strained to pull their loads along the rough road.

There were many amusing incidents to watch as people in buggies tried to dodge between the travelers and overtake slower vehicles. The stagecoach bugler demanded passageway for the stage as it went as swiftly as possible up the busy road. Clementina felt some satisfaction from knowing she was getting nearer Lancaster — and James.

The sun was slowly going down and the air became cooler.

"We're to take an overnight break here, ma'am," Hawkes, Mr. Redmarsh's decorous Indian servant, informed Clementina. His copper-colored skin, high cheekbones and narrow, observant eyes told of his proud race, which had mingled with the early settlers. He went on to say, "The Red Horse Inn is one of the better roadside taverns, my master thinks. It has a quiet parlor for you ladies away from the bar. I was instructed to make sure the landlord provides you with a comfortable bedchamber and some wholesome food." He patted his fat money pouch that Clementina knew would contain plenty of money given to him by Mr. Redmarsh.

Clementina said, "Thank you, Hawkes."

Clementina's Quaker companion, elderly Mrs. Cod, awoke from her doze. "Did I hear thee mention a stop at last? Mercy for that! This dreadful dust gets everywhere," she declared, brushing her grey gown to try and remove the film of dirt that covered her. "The chance to escape from this cramped, overheated coach will be welcome, will it not, Miss Willoby? Thee looks as travel worn as I feel, my dear." She strained to see out the window and recognized the tavern they were approaching. "Be assured, thee will be well cared for at this tavern. I've stayed here before when visiting my daughter in Lancaster."

She had informed Clementina earlier that she was making the journey to be with her daughter for the birth of her tenth grandchild, and was quite used to going up and down the highway because she had tended her daughter at each confinement.

Clementina smiled at her companion. She was tired and glad of the opportunity to stretch her legs.

Mrs. Cod had been instructed by Mr. Redmarsh to keep a close eye on Clementina, so they were to share a bedchamber. But Clementina didn't mind, because she found Mrs. Cod a kind-hearted and indomitable lady, who used the Quaker "thee" and "thine" in her speech and, like Mrs. Redmarsh, referred to Philadelphia as "Philly."

Hawkes helped the ladies out of the coach and escorted them into the tavern. It was a popular place. Coarse male voices and loud laughter coming from the inn's common room which was crammed with tired, thirsty teamsters, untraced and enjoying the landlord's home-brewed ale or cider as fast as the drawer could pour it into the great pewter tankards, made Clementina realize how protected she'd been, living in polite society.

She shrugged. If these were the non-gentlemen Mr. Redmarsh had warned her about, she was determined not to allow their exuberance to upset her. She was treading on their territory and had better be willing to accept them as they were. Mrs. Cod seemed to take their presence in her stride, and carried on as if they were no more than a roomful of boisterous children.

Seeing the sober Quaker lady unperturbed made Clementina feel she had nothing to fear from the workingmen, and she was grateful Mr. Redmarsh had arranged for her to travel with a sensible woman like Mrs. Cod.

Mrs. Cod was armed with an enormous basket of provisions, which she lugged with her into the quiet parlor. She explained she didn't want to find the contents of the basket gone in the morning. "My husband is a baker," she told Clementina. "He was up all night baking for our daughter's large family."

Hawkes joined the ladies in the parlor presently, informing them that their bedchamber was ready when they wanted to retire. He had ordered an "ordinary" for them, which was an inn meal, and that the waiter was coming to take their order for drinks.

Clementina was grateful for Hawkes too. Like all good servants, he anticipated their needs.

Clementina and Mrs. Cod tucked into their meal of roast goose stuffed with boiled peanuts and sweet potatoes, and had a fruit pie for dessert. They finished it off with a small peach brandy, which Mrs. Cod informed Clementina she needed to help her sleep well.

In a pleasant state of feeling satiated Clementina stifled a yawn. She was ready for bed. Going over to the window she looked out on the setting sun. Tomorrow she would be with James.

A muffled scream escaped her lips.

"What is it, child?" Mrs. Cod rushed to join her at the window.

Clementina was unable to reply for a moment or two. "I fear I have just seen two sailors. You can tell them by their rolling gait. And one of them, I swear, is Mr. Hugill. And if it is, he is after me!"

Hawkes came silently to her side. "Where are they?" he asked calmly, looking out of the window.

Clementina swallowed. She pointed towards a big, heavily built man swaggering purposefully towards the inn's entrance. The other man was lithe, with a lean face. Both wore sailors' baggy trousers, and their hair was plaited in the nautical fashion. Mr. Hugill it was. Clementina was sure of it. She felt suddenly cold and deeply afraid. She muttered, "They are after me."

"Why?" asked Mrs. Cod.

Clementina's heart pounded. The realization that she had not imagined Mr. Millard spotting her in the shipping office was a blow. It seemed obvious to her now that he had. He would certainly suspect that she would try and warn James. Those two evil men had undoubtedly been sent to waylay her.

Clementina didn't know how much Mr. Redmarsh had told her companions about her mission, so she answered simply, "I fear those men are here to prevent me from delivering a message to Mr. Hunter in Lancaster. They, and others of the crew, have in mind to steal his ship. Naturally, they will not want me to warn him."

As she said it, her heart sank lower and lower. She had seen how cruel Hugill could be. And the other man was hefty. Hawkes would be no match for him.

Fearing the worst, she became aware that Hawkes had left them.

"What shall I do?" asked Clementina frantically.

"Trust in the Lord," answered Mrs. Cod promptly, "and go to bed."

"But, but will we be safe in our beds?"

"Hawkes thinks so. He plans to deal with them."

Clementina looked at the Quaker as if she was already condemned to death. "How?"

Mrs. Cod picked up her heavy basket, saying, "We shall see. As thee knows, God tests us from time to time. But He will look after thee. Come along to bed, my dear."

Clementina felt so frightened she decided only God — and perhaps Hawkes — could help her now, and resignedly followed Mrs. Cod upstairs.

CHAPTER NINE

Hawkes made sure the ladies had locked themselves in their bedchamber before venturing downstairs. He felt under his shirt to make sure the pistol Mr. Redmarsh had given him was still there, tucked in his belt, as he looked around carefully to see if anyone was watching him. He was satisfied that the other inn visitors were not taking the slightest notice of him.

Hawkes knew he had to avoid being seen by the two tough-looking sailors he'd watched coming into the inn earlier. He'd thought of a plan to delay them while he got Miss Willoby away safely the next morning on the stagecoach. He was now seeking the landlord to have a private word with him.

Before he'd left Philadelphia, Mr. Redmarsh had explained Miss Willoby's mission and predicament to Hawkes. Particularly he stressed her fear of being followed by those who might harm her, and of trying to prevent her from meeting Mr. James Hunter.

Privately, Hawkes, having served the charming but frivolous Redmarsh ladies for many years, doubted the English lady was in any danger, thinking it was typical of all ladies to imagine things.

Nevertheless, his master had tried to impress on him the need to be vigilant. "I know I can trust you, Hawkes, to do what is necessary to protect the lady," Mr. Redmarsh had said in the privacy of his study, so that his wife did not get wind of possible trouble.

"Indeed you can, sir," replied Hawkes. He was not unhappy to have to guard the English lady whom he and the other Redmarsh servants found most pleasant to deal with.

Hawkes had two other reasons to oblige. First, he was devoted to his master, who had taken him in as a starving lad of fifteen. And the second reason was that he was a countryman at heart. He liked living in Philadelphia well enough, but he yearned to see the forestlands he remembered from his childhood, before the white man came. For him the deer darting through sunny glades and the fragrance of the pines were his homeland. Rivers teeming with fish and sparkling clear water tumbling over the falls were more precious than the Redmarshes' fine Philadelphian furniture and Aubusson or Axminster carpets.

His father had told him that he had some Cherokee blood in him. A noble Indian race. It made him proud, and made him yearn to see his roots once more. To experience the excitement of hunting was his dream. Any fool servant could stay at home and powder his master's wig! It took a brave man to pit his wits and strength against other men.

"I should take that grin off your face, Hawkes," Mr. Redmarsh had interrupted his thoughts.

"Sir, I'm not smiling because I think what you tell me is not important. It's because I'm looking forward to seeing the forests I knew as a boy."

Mr. Redmarsh glared at him. "Just remember to keep your mind on what I have told you to do, Hawkes. I don't want you standing in the forest gawping at the trees or the muskrats, deer or badgers, for if you do, it might be you'll get a sailor's knife stuck in your back. Miss Willoby may too! Looking after Miss Willoby might be very dangerous if anyone tries to harm her. For that reason, I'd like you to take this pistol of mine. Can you use it?"

"Sir, my unarmed family was shot in a surprise attack by white men. The attackers were French trappers who thought no more of shooting us than the animals they kill for their fur. I escaped, and when I got the chance, I learned to use a barking iron. I will not let any trigger-happy sailors shoot me unawares."

Mr. Redmarsh looked thoughtfully at the keen-eyed Indian and nodded. "Very good then, Hawkes, see to it. I would escort Miss Willoby myself if I thought I was up to it. But I ain't. I'm too old for one thing. And I want to keep an eye on Mr. Hunter's agent here, for another. You have my utmost confidence in your ability to deliver Miss Willoby into Mr. Hunter's care. I trust you as I would my own son. But I beg of you to take the greatest care."

Hawkes's fine set of teeth showed as he smiled. He felt honored to be so well thought of by his employer.

Hawkes remembered Mr. Redmarsh's words of caution when he saw the seamen coming into the Red Horse Inn. It was unusual to find sailors so far inland and, especially after Miss Willoby had said she recognized one of them, he was suspicious they might be seeking her.

But his blood rose for the occasion. He, with his Indian skills, would be able to protect the lady who had been put in his care. Although he didn't like the look of either of those two seamen, the hatchet-faced man in particular appeared to him to be a bad man.

After seeing the ladies to bed, he would have liked one of those rum-and-beer drinks they called "flip." Mr. Redmarsh had made sure he had plenty of sovereigns in his purse before he set off. But he knew he needed a clear head and dare not drink even one.

Excessive drinking was commonplace, and sailors liked their rum, he knew. If he could, he would try to persuade the landlord to keep the two brutish-looking seamen sitting where he'd spotted them on the settle by the wall with their tankards full.

Mr. Redmarsh, Hawkes reckoned, wouldn't mind paying for their rum to get them well and truly drunk, as it would be for a good reason. More flies are taken with a drop of honey than with a ton of vinegar!

The landlord was of German origin and a hearty sort. His huge figure was wrapped in an enormous apron that almost reached the floor. He could carry four tankards in each mighty fist and laughed a lot with his bawdy customers.

Hawkes had to bide his time, keeping out of sight and waiting for the opportunity to capture the landlord's attention. Midnight approached, and many of the inn's customers consumed enough to make them intoxicated. As Hawkes worried the sailors had not drunk enough, he noticed the landlord leaving his riotous customers and waddling his way towards the inn's cellar to replenish a jug of beer.

With quick steps, Hawkes followed the landlord along the passage and went down the steps after him into the cold, dark underground cellar lit by only one light.

"Phiss, landlord," Hawkes called softly.

He startled the landlord, as if he were a rat who'd suddenly appeared. The landlord almost dropped his jug. *"Was ist hier?"*

"A moment of your time, if you please, landlord," Hawkes whispered, coming up to him.

Hawkes's courteous manner and clearly spoken English waylaid the landlord's fears. "You want *tricken,* ya?" he asked.

Hawkes shook his head. "Landlord, I need your assistance."

"Ah. You want a pretty woman, ya?" The landlord's laughter rang out in the underground room, making Hawkes wince at the noise.

Hawkes quickly put his finger over his lips. "I have no need of a woman," he hissed.

"So? What is it, young fellow?"

Hawkes had difficulty explaining he wanted the landlord to keep filling the seamen's glasses at his expense. Such generosity was unknown. But when Hawkes offered him several gold sovereigns, he accepted them readily and promised to make the seamen well and truly bumpsie.

"I'll watch you and see that you do," Hawkes told him.

Hawkes was pleased with his achievement as he observed the seamen swill down the drinks the landlord kept providing.

After a while, thinking his plan had worked well, Hawkes decided he would go and get some sleep. He would cover himself with a blanket and sit outside the ladies' room so that he could guard them from any danger that might occur during the night, and wake them early in the morning so that they could be on their way before the sailors awoke from their drunken stupor.

As he made his way along the passageway towards the ladies' bedchamber, something hit him hard upon his head. He felt himself sink helplessly to the floor.

Earlier that evening, Clementina had been ready for bed by the time Hawkes had escorted them up to their bedchamber. She had made sure the maid had brought them up a pitcher of hot water so they could wash.

Although tired, she couldn't sleep for the chilling fear of the two sailors, one of whom she was sure was Hugill, down below in the bar. Her intuition told her that seamen do not come inland for a good reason — and that she might be the reason!

"Mrs. Cod," she asked anxiously, "I know the door is locked, but do you mind if I push a chair under the door handle?"

"Why no. I consider that to be most prudent, Miss Willoby."

Clementina, reluctant to change into her nightgown, said, "I'm afraid those seamen might try to break into our bedchamber." She gave a shudder.

Mrs. Cod's rather concerned eyes regarded her thoughtfully. "I don't relish a visit from them either. However, Hawkes is outside to see that it does not happen. Thee and I shall say some extra prayers before we retire."

Clementina had to smile. The Quaker lady

couldn't have been a more comforting companion for her. Mrs. Cod hadn't been turned into a jellyfish with the possibility of the worst happening to them. She had backbone, as most settlers who'd braved the New World's terrors had. And Clementina took courage from her.

She knew she might be in danger because the seamen might well have been sent to stop her from reaching Mr. Hunter. They might succeed. But she wasn't caught yet. She must show character, and be as level-headed as Mrs. Cod. Having reassured herself, she removed her tight stays, put on her nightie and got into her side of the big four-poster bed.

Whatever was the normal length of Mrs. Cod's nightly prayers? Clementina wondered. For on that evening, Mrs. Cod was on her knees for what seemed to be a full hour. Divine intervention was most certainly being requested, and even if it turned out not to be forthcoming, she knew it would not be because of Mrs. Cod's lack of faith.

At last the good lady snuffed out the bedside candle, and clambered into bed. The two ladies were asleep in no time.

Some time later, Clementina awoke to hear a rattle, as if someone was trying to enter their chamber. She thought sleepily that it was probably only Hawkes checking up on them and drowsily turned over to resume her sleep.

Then she heard it again. The wooden chair propped under the door handle was being pushed as if whoever it was had unlocked the door and was now determined to get in. She went rigid with fright.

"Mrs. Cod!" whispered Clementina urgently. "Wake up!" She gave her companion a none-too-gentle poke.

"What ails thee, child?" Mrs. Cod sat up. Her eyes peered from under her nightcap frill in the moonlit room.

"I heard someone trying to get in our chamber."

"Shush!"

They both sat and listened in silence. After a few minutes of suspense they heard the chair groan and shift slightly, then the unmistakable sound of someone trying to twist the handle to open the door. This was followed by a couple of heavy thuds, as a powerful shoulder heaved at the door from the other side.

"Get thee under the bed," Mrs. Cod told Clementina quietly. Then she planted her two bare feet heavily on the hooked rug by the side of the bed and trundled to the door.

"Hawkes, is that thee trying to get in?" she enquired loudly.

Coarse laughter told her it was not.

Standing in her voluminous nightgown she shouted, "Whosoever thou art, battering at my bedchamber door, get thee gone! Or the Angels of Heaven will strike thee with their swords!"

Clementina couldn't help giving a chuckle, wondering if the good lady could possibly make the heavenly angels appear in all their glory to save them, or — her smile vanished. The bluff wouldn't shoo the seamen away. She felt quite sure it was Hugill, as if she could smell the fiendish seaman, outside in the corridor.

A muffled, drunken man's voice sounded from outside, "Ma'am, I'm looking for Miss Willoby. That is, I must speak with her. Urgent like."

Mrs. Cod was up to his tricks. "Do I sound like her? Thou art full of wickedness to be waking a respectable lady at this hour of the night. If thee do not remove thyself from my door, I shall scream for help!"

"No, no ma'am, it will not be necessary for you to call. We'll find her in the morning."

This slurred speech was followed by heavy footsteps walking away down the corridor.

Mrs. Cod pressed her ear against the door for a full minute. She then crossed the room, looked under the bed and said, "Thee can come out now, Miss Willoby. They've gone."

"You were truly brave, Mrs. Cod," said Clementina, crawling out from under the bed and brushing the dust off herself. "I thank you with all my heart."

"Let's get back into bed and rest a while longer." Clementina could barely see the lady give her a conspiratorial wink. "Thee knows, friend, villainy and impudence tend to go together, and those two seaman have more than their fair share of both."

Clementina was recovered enough to smile.

Mrs. Cod, satisfied she'd done enough for one day to earn the generous amount of money Mr. Redmarsh had provided her to accompany Miss Willoby, soon settled down to sleep and was snoring gently.

Clementina could not sleep, however. The night was warm. Too disturbed to lie still, and afraid her tossing might disturb Mrs. Cod, she rose and silently paced the room. As she passed the casement window, a movement outside caught her eye and she stopped to take a look.

She saw two men carrying something

heavy and long in the darkened yard. Fascinated, she watched them staggering along, wondering if they might be carting a drunken comrade from the bar back to their wagon to sleep off the effects of excessive drinking.

Sleepy at last, she felt the overwhelming desire to creep back to bed and sleep. Which she did.

"Five in the morning is an uncivilized time to rise," grumbled Clementina, after Mrs. Cod nudged her and told her it was time to get up as the stagecoach left very early.

But the worry of knowing the evil seamen might be lurking around the inn brought urgency to the situation, and Clementina leapt out of bed when she saw the daylight already spilling through the window.

"What shall we do about the seamen?" she asked with a frown as they dressed.

Mrs. Cod replied briskly, "Thee shall stay here, while I find Hawkes and make sure the coast is clear for you to ride the coach."

Opening their bedchamber door gingerly, Mrs. Cod didn't find Hawkes on sentry outside. "I'll go and find him," she said to Clementina. "Bolt the door till I get back and I'll knock for thee to let me in."

As Clementina packed her cloth bag, she

waited apprehensively for Mrs. Cod to return.

Soon her footsteps could be heard walking smartly along the passage, and Clementina flew to open the door.

"Why, Mrs. Cod, what's wrong?"

"Hawkes is nowhere to be found, Miss Willoby."

"And the seamen — have you seen them?"

Mrs. Cod made a face. "Indeed I have. They drank too much. The landlord told me he'd put them in the barn overnight. And by the looks of them, it will be many hours before they come to. We should be away on the coach by then."

That was indeed good news. Clementina was concerned about Hawkes though. "It is only twenty minutes before the coach leaves, Mrs. Cod, and it waits for no one. We must find Hawkes. You go and take your breakfast while I search for him."

"But Miss Willoby, thee must have something to drink before thee goes. Thee knows how hot and dusty it is on the road."

"Yes, I do know, Mrs. Cod, but pray, don't concern yourself about me. I must find Hawkes first. If you pour me out a cup of coffee I'll be along directly to drink it."

As she left Mrs. Cod having her breakfast, Clementina hoped she would have time to eat something, too. Stepping outside cautiously, she wondered if James Hunter was worth all the worry he was giving her.

The early risers were harnessing their wagons for the day's travel. Clementina stopped and gazed about her, wondering whom she should ask if they had seen an Indian servant. The trouble was, there were so many carts, chaises, wagons and buggies.

Ignoring the sharp looks she got from some of the teamsters as she flitted about, desperately looking and daring to glance inside some of the covered carts, Clementina began to despair of finding him. Where could he have got? The time was ticking by.

She asked some travelers in a boat-like wagon, with its front and rear cover higher than the middle part, if they had seen him. But they only spoke German and didn't understand her.

Looking under one wagon, she set a dog barking, and seeing people accusingly stare at her, as if she were attempting to steal something, she rushed away and tripped.

"Oh my, ma'am, whatcha rushing for?" A kindly, older teamster helped Clementina up onto her feet.

"I've lost my Indian servant," she puffed, "and the stage leaves in a few minutes." Clementina felt like crying with frustration.

"I don't know if he be the one you want, ma'am, but there's an Indian a-sleepin' in my friend's cart."

"Where?"

"Come, I'll show yer."

Clementina was led to a covered cart and when the cover was thrown back she saw Hawkes. Asleep. "Hawkes! Wake up, we must be on our way," she cried, but he didn't move.

"Hawkes!" An icy fear that he was dead made her cry out again, "Hawkes!"

In the distance she could hear her name being called, "Miss Will-o-bee!"

Mrs. Cod came hurrying to her side, "Hurry, Miss Willoby, we must take our seats in the coach."

The teamster rolled Hawkes over and they saw why he didn't reply or move. He'd been trussed up with neat sailor's knots, and a gag covered his mouth. Thankfully, Clementina saw his eyes moving and knew he was alive. With the help of the teamster's knife, they unbound Hawkes.

Mr. Redmarsh's servant was full of apologies as he rubbed the red welts where the rope had bitten into his flesh. "Someone hit me from behind," he said, tenderly stroking the bump on his head. "They've stolen my master's money."

The bugle blared, calling all the stage-coach passengers.

"There is no time to explain now. We must run and get the coach."

It was only later, when they were aboard the coach, that Clementina discovered Hawkes had not only lost the purse of cash Mr. Redmarsh had given him when he was attacked, but also his master's gun was missing!

CHAPTER TEN

Lancaster, carved out of forestlands, was no longer a new frontier town. As soon as Clementina arrived, she noticed its booming industry. The people she saw lacked the refinements of the higher echelons of society, for they were simply dressed, according to the work they were doing. Innkeepers and shopkeepers, shoemakers and tailors, bakers, butchers, carpenters and barbers, all had plenty of custom in this expanding hinterland town.

The solid brick and stone houses of Philadelphia were not to be seen, only timber constructions. Deeply pitched roofs, gable ends, clapboarding with second-story overhangs, seemed typical of the dwellings.

As the stagecoach drew into the market square, shouting barefooted boys ran after it, men in the street stopped their conversations, while the women on the sidewalks shopping looked with interest to see who was arriving in their town all the way from Philadelphia, the City of Brotherly Love. Clementina could tell the arrival of the stagecoach was an exciting weekly event. It was probably the citizens' only contact with the outside world, apart from commercial wagons delivering goods or passing through. If you were surrounded by wild countryside, any contact with civilization was of interest.

"Hawkes, will you find Mr. Rogers and tell him of our need to contact Mr. Hunter as soon as possible?" Clementina had only that on her mind as she clambered down from the coach onto the dusty earth road, although she would have loved a drink.

"Yes, ma'am," Hawkes replied, looking around earnestly. His life, as well as Miss Willoby's, was now under threat. In fact, he knew he was lucky to be alive. His pride had received a knock when the rough seaman had caught him. He was now determined to take care not to be trussed up like a chicken again. Without Mr. Redmarsh's pistol, he felt vulnerable. He was anxious to deliver Miss Willoby into Mr. Hunter's hands as soon as possible.

The sound of delighted voices, squeals and laughter made Clementina turn around. She saw Mrs. Cod being greeted by her many grandchildren, who hopped around her and tried to peek into her big basket of cookies for the gingerbread men their grandfather always made for them. Mrs. Cod's pregnant daughter looked bright with health and happiness at seeing her mother.

"I wish thee God speed to find Mr. Hunter," Mrs. Cod said, kissing Clementina goodbye.

Soon Mrs. Cod was on a crowded wagon being driven away to her daughter's farm. Watching her go, Clementina, who had appreciated the Quaker lady's company, felt lonely.

Mr. Rogers was a sedate gentleman dressed in a plum-colored, square-cut coat. He was more pleased to see his case of Madeira safely arrived than he was to see a dust-blown young lady who was demanding to see Mr. Hunter without delay.

Hawkes managed to make him understand how urgent it was for them to get to the sawmill, and Mr. Rogers was able to inform her that a supply wagon was leaving for the camp that very afternoon. "If you insist on leaving immediately, Miss Willoby, the supply wagon is the best way of getting there. I regret it is not a comfortable mode of travel for a young lady. It is a considerable distance — and there's no cover on the wagon."

The day was hot, and Clementina was

afraid that, her skin being fair like many English ladies, she would burn easily. But that was not the only reason she felt increasingly apprehensive about the quest she had undertaken. In the orderly city of Philadelphia it had seemed noble to undertake a quest to inform James Hunter of the rogues who were planning to steal his ship. Out here in the rough township, even a glimpse of it told her she'd been rash to come. She hadn't listened to Mr. Redmarsh's warning that it was not a place for young ladies, but she remembered that now. Uncertainty made her struggle to control the urge to take the next coach back to Philadelphia. But she knew she must conquer her fears.

Beleaguered with doubts, Clementina nevertheless had the strong sense that she had to continue what she'd begun. She had come so far; she was not going to give in to fear. Her head ached as she thought with distress that her Indian bodyguard was useless, and she still had to find the lumber camp. But she wanted to help James Hunter if she could — and it was possible he might be grateful and even reward her by giving her the shop in Bath.

"Sir," she said urgently to Mr. Rogers, "I'm anxious to see Mr. Hunter as soon as possible. How I travel is immaterial."

They were brave words she was to regret as she sat on a big wagon driven by two sturdy drivers who were not keen to give her a ride. Clementina was squashed, surrounded by goods: beer barrels, sacks of suet, salted beef and pork, wrapped-round cheeses, as well as tools and the other necessities for camp life.

It was hard to concentrate on the beauty of the forest glades when the sun was beating down on her. She was aware of the country fragrances, but could not enjoy the herd of whitetail deer that stopped grazing and eyed her suspiciously. Squirrels scurried about the forest but went unnoticed by her.

Her corseted costume felt uncomfortably tight, and her head throbbed. She was also very thirsty.

As they progressed tortuously slowly, they came to ravines where there were roads constructed by logs laid side by side on trestles. These washboard surfaces jarred her unmercifully, until she felt like crying out for the corduroy road, as it was called, to end. Her spirits sank lower than the snakes that slid along the forest floor.

Jolted and bumped about, she wondered if her discomfort — nay, suffering — was worth it. She wished now she'd heeded Mr.

Redmarsh and let Hawkes take a message to James instead of going to Lancaster herself. But then she reminded herself that if she had not come, Hawkes might still be tied up in a cart and trundling along the wagon road to God knows where if she hadn't found him!

She had by now a tongue swollen from thirst, and she was perspiring in her clothes. Her posterior was bruised from the jars she was getting as the two draft horses dragged the wagon along the seemingly endless bumpy road. Clementina eventually fell into a reverie as she tried to escape her discomfort.

When at last the wagon reached the camp, she felt a great sense of relief. Hawkes helped her aching body out of the wagon, and she stood swaying, looking at the vast area of land that had been cleared. In the clearing many log huts and huge stacks of timber were to be seen. A river ran by.

Men, stripped to the waist, were working everywhere. Felled trees were being trimmed of their side branches, and in another area, bark was being removed. Sawpits, where sawyers were using long pit-saws with one man standing higher than the other and holding the tiller while the man under held the box, were being showered with sawdust. Clementina watched the to-and-fro movement and her nasty headache made her feel as if her head would split.

What she didn't observe at first was that some men spotted her. They stopped work and came over to gape at the little mantua-maker from Bath as if she were a strange wild species of animal. Soon encircled by jeering, catcalling lumbermen she was appalled and felt trapped. Rugged, wide-eyed men goggled at her. Uncouth, unshaved men with sweaty chests pointed and sniggered at her.

Finding her voice was difficult. "I've come to see Mr. Hunter," she managed to say, and wondered why they thought that so amusing and made coarse remarks. Was James not here? Was this the wrong camp? Then a daring man crept up behind her and slapped her bottom. This resulted in howls of laughter from the men.

While they guffawed and some of them shouted out lewd remarks, Clementina's heart began to palpitate. The male stench of their closeness in the heat made it difficult for her to say anything more, or even to breathe.

Hawkes, who should have been protecting her, was not to be seen. But then, what use would one servant be against this loud mob?

Had they frightened him so that he ran off? Or had they beaten him up or dragged him off and tied him up, as Hugill had done? She could understand why they were suspicious of Indians, since she'd heard the camp had been raided recently.

She hid her face in her hands, confused. Was she having a bad dream?

"What the hell is that woman doing here?" A deep, ringing voice resounded.

Silence descended upon the crowd as the tall man strode towards the crowd.

"What the devil?" Recognizing James Hunter's voice, Clementina felt instant relief. He sounded very angry, however.

"Who's responsible for bringing this female here? Any man who had anything to do with this petticoat will lose his job! I made it quite clear to you all when I hired you that I don't want camp followers."

A voice from the crowd answered him. "Mr. Hunter, she says she's *your* woman."

"My woman? Impossible!" James elbowed his way through the onlookers and came up to Clementina.

"My God, it's Miss Willoby!" he exclaimed, and the men howled with laughter.

At that moment, Clementina's knees gave way. She sank gracefully to the ground, unconscious.

■ ■ ■ ■

James Hunter shouted at his men to get back to work, and scooping Clementina up in his arms, he stood there wondering what to do. Hearing guffaws of laughter amongst his men, he glowered at them and they soon dispersed.

He was furious. He could not deny he knew this woman. She was a female he had once respected enough to think of courting, and had even considered marrying! The brazen little hussy of a dressmaker was after his shop in Bath, probably because she'd not heard about his decision. So she'd decided to come after him. She'd come into the camp unchaperoned. Most unseemly behavior for an unmarried lady!

James wondered if he was perhaps being a bit hard on her. He couldn't help but admire her audacity. She was a little like him, with a pioneering spirit, determined to achieve her aim despite the discomfort. It was also typical of a woman to be impatient. He carried her towards his cabin. Where else could he take her in this camp full of men? Fortunately she was light to carry, as his cabin stood apart from the others.

He looked down at her pale skin. There

was a smudge on her cheek. Her crumpled and dusty clothes were a disgrace. And her curly locks coming from beneath her bonnet looked untidy, but he had to admit he liked to see the strands of silky hair falling around her slender neck and shoulders. And her closed eyes were attractive too — as was her rosy-lipped mouth.

But he was angry with her at that moment. She'd made a fool of him in front of his men. Women! He decided he would be far better off to remain a bachelor. For a moment, Clementina's eyelids and lips parted as if she were trying to wake up and say something. But as he looked down on her questioningly her head fell back and she seemed unable to speak. The stupid girl had made herself ill from the sun. England didn't get the heat and the long hours of hot sunshine they had in America.

It crossed his mind that it seemed strange Mr. and Mrs. Redmarsh, who seemed kind and respectable folks, should have allowed her to come all the way from Philadelphia by herself. Very odd!

The end of the working day was approaching. James regretted her intrusion into the camp. It had taken him away from his work, and he was already behindhand. The job was quite important.

The introduction of his wind-powered sawmill would speed up timber production enormously. Mechanical designing fascinated him. He'd conceived the idea from similar sawmills used in Holland and Norway. He'd played with the plans he'd got hold of from immigrant sawyers; he wanted to get it right for his purposes, and he'd been practically two years constructing it.

Then, as it was almost finished last month, a raiding party of Indians attacked it, destroying the saws and frames. So James and his men had to repair the damage before the mill could start. The last thing he wanted was anything else to delay the work — like Clementina Willoby, who'd appeared out of the blue. He'd reached his cabin and stood before it, unsure how to open the cabin door, when an Indian in colonial clothes appeared and opened it for him. "Who are you?" James demanded.

"Hawkes, sir. I accompanied Miss Willoby. I'm Mr. Redmarsh's manservant. I have her carpet bag here."

So she had not come alone. James carried his burden into the cabin, saying, "Where's Miss Willoby's maid?"

"Sir, Miss Willoby traveled with a Quaker lady we left in Lancaster. I was sent to protect her."

"You? Alone?"

James detected Hawkes looked a little shame-faced. What had happened? Had the Indian been telling the truth? Was there any point in questioning the man further? He'd better wait and hear the true story from Miss Willoby.

He lowered Clementina gently onto his bearskin-covered bed. Clementina's eyes flickered and she groaned softly.

"Here, man, take this pitcher and go down to the creek and get some fresh water."

"Yessir."

As Hawkes sped off, James looked down at the still-unconscious young lady. He had to admit she was attractive, despite her travel-worn state. Once she'd had a drink, a wash and a rest, she'd probably be fine. People reared in orphanages tended to be tough; they had to be, or they wouldn't survive.

As he waited for Hawkes to return, James took off his own sweaty shirt, and using water from a bucket, splashed his face, his hairy chest and his underarms, then dried himself with a less-than-clean towel. When Hawkes got back, he would tell him to go to the stores and get a clean towel. He couldn't offer his soiled one to prim Miss Willoby!

Rejuvenated after her rest, Clementina came round and opened her eyes, then shut them again quickly, hoping to retire back into blissful, nonfeeling sleep. Her body was sore and ached when she tried to move.

Her lips were moist. Her mouth was no longer blisteringly dry. Someone had given her some water. In fact, she vaguely remembered waking earlier and finding some gentleman there, supporting her head with strong hands and saying, "Drink a little . . . take a sip only." She'd licked her lips gratefully and sipped the cold water.

Then she remembered. When she arrived at the camp, James had come and shouted at the men. He must have been the one who'd saved her from those loud, jeering workers and brought her to this quiet, cool cabin. She opened her eyes, and raising herself on one elbow, looked around, finding herself in a starkly built, hand-hewn wooden structure — a crude one-room dwelling.

It was empty, and strong sunlight shone through the one small window. The walls were unpainted logs, and there was a fireplace, a storage chest, a roughly made table and chair. It was a man's room, with no feminine touches such as curtains at the window, or a cloth on the table. It contained nothing but the bare essentials of living.

This was James's cabin, she was sure. He lived, presumably, just like his lumbermen, although they probably had to share cabins. That was something to admire about James. He was interested in his work and was prepared to live simply for months, years even, working on a project he was keen on. It showed initiative, determination and a mannishness she admired. There was a certain similarity between his hard years of toil and her own long, hard apprenticeship in dressmaking.

In a rush, she recollected why she was there, and knew she must get up and find him. But she was as weak as a newborn, and was unable to rise. She laid her head down again and fell asleep.

She must have woken later. The room was still empty, but the evening light poured through the window. She sat up and found she was recovered. A mug by her side contained water, and she drank it thirstily.

She was ready to speak now, and wished James would come back. But she dared not go outside to look for him with those vulgar men about. Sitting on the bed, she looked around the cabin again, seeing a long rifle propped up in a corner, a lantern hanging from a hook on the wall, a leather saddle and bridle. Her eyes moved farther around the room, and she saw his clothes hanging on a peg rail. And on the table were a candleholder and tinderbox, a few books, playing cards and a chess set.

Her eyes rested on what looked like linen hanging over the back of the chair. Puzzled, her eyes remained looking at it, thinking it was familiar, but what could it be? It didn't look like one of his shirts.

"Oh!" she squealed. She recognized what was hanging over the chair. It was her stays! Her hands slid down her body. Oh yes, she was clad only in her shift. Her boned stays, gown and hat were on the chair.

At that moment the door opened and James's tall silhouette filled the opening. Seeing her sitting up, he came in, carrying two platters and a long roll of bread tucked under his arm. As he kicked the door shut behind him with his foot, he remarked, "So you've recovered, Miss Willoby. I've brought you some grouse stew from the cookhouse."

Embarrassed by the thought that he'd probably undressed her, she felt like crawling under the bearskin. But what was the use? If he'd stripped her, there was nothing she could do about it now. And knowing that most men were well acquainted with naked women by the time they were much younger than James, there was no point in being missish about it.

"Mr. Hunter," she said tremulously, "I've come to tell you something vitally important."

"Well, I hope you've not made an idiot of me for no proper reason," he muttered, then almost shouted at her, "What is it?"

It was horribly difficult to look up into his hostile eyes. But she'd managed to overcome Princess Amelia's barking at her, so why not his? "Your shipping agent, Mr. Spear . . ." she said with a gulp.

"Yes, my shipping agent is Mr. Spear. So what?"

"Mr. Spear intends to steal your ship."

His mouth twitched. He placed two bowls and spoons on each side of the table. "Eat," he ordered, "before the grub gets cold."

"Mr. Hunter!" Her voice rose in panic. "You must do something immediately or you will lose your ship."

His expression was skeptical. "I'm going to do something. I'm going to eat my supper," he said, and ploughed his teeth into a hunk of bread that he'd torn off the loaf, and chewed it hungrily while he said, "I suggest you eat yours too. It's quite edible. Our cook ain't at all bad."

"But sir —"

"Eat!" He threw a menacing look at her, so she got up and sat at the table.

It was ridiculous, her sitting with him in her shift. Her reputation as a respectable dressmaker was quite gone.

She had compromised herself to warn him about his ship and he wouldn't listen! A tear threatened to roll down her cheek and she brushed it quickly away.

The food looked good and she was hungry. Since he was spooning his up and ignoring her, she picked up her spoon and tried a little of the stew. Mmm. It really was good. She had no difficulty finishing her bowlful while he sat chewing the rest of the loaf.

In a more relaxed mood after his food, he got up, stretched, and then went to rest on his bed. "Well, Miss Willoby, what have you to say about your disgraceful behavior?" he said, looking over at her.

She gave him a frosty look. "I'm sorry if my coming here appears hoydenish," she began stiffly.

"Hoydenish? It's downright lunacy, ma'am! Surely you are old enough to know that my men could have raped you?"

Her face turned scarlet, telling him she did know what he meant.

He went on, "Indians around here could have scalped you! And why? All because you want to know if you can have my aunt's shop, eh?"

Stung at getting nothing but ridicule for her trouble, Clementina smarted. After all the uncomfortable hours of traveling she endured in order to warn him about his crooked agent, the only thanks she was getting was incivility. No wonder he'd been sent down from Oxford. He was uncouth. He thought the worst of her too, believing she'd come all this way just because she was greedy and wanted to make sure he would give her the shop. It was too bad of him.

She felt an anger that even her training in self-restraint didn't quell. How was she to have known that women were not permitted in his camp? Neither Mr. Rogers nor the wagon drivers had told her. And how could she have foreseen that the timber men would see her as a woman of easy virtue?

He would not believe her. He seemed determined to humiliate her.

Another tear ran down her cheek. She gave a sniff. She wouldn't have minded his offhandedness, if she'd been at fault. But all she'd done was to think of his welfare, not her own. Rebelliousness made her snap back, "Perhaps you should listen to what I have to say before you decide who is the idiot!"

There was a moment's silence. Then he gave a mighty laugh that must have been heard by the men in the camp. It scared the wits out of her. She was in so much pain in mind and spirit, and all he could do was to laugh at her!

"You are priceless, Miss Willoby. Quite priceless. Now, perhaps you will light the stove and make us some coffee, then you may chatter away to me all night if you wish. Only I might fall asleep . . ." He closed his eyes and seemed ready to go to sleep, while she looked at him, aghast.

A shiver went through her body. Was he expecting her to spend the night with him? Sweat bedewed her brow. She was indeed a fool to have got herself into this dreadful situation.

Chapter Eleven

Clementina suddenly decided she had nothing more to lose if she were to be quite blunt with James Hunter. It was difficult for her at that moment to think rationally. Why had she thought she was in love with him? He was nothing but a hunk of male stubbornness, who would not take her seriously because she was only a dressmaker — a girl his aunt had taken from the orphanage to work in her shop, and who had showed she had no sense of decorum.

Except, of course, she still found him physically attractive.

Having finished his meal, he'd stood up, walked over to his bed and thrown himself on it, as if he were exhausted after his long, physical day's work, and had immediately fallen sleep.

He fascinated her, especially as she had never seen a man asleep before. In repose, his peaceful expression softened his rugged looks. His hair, which had turned darker with age, was tied back with a black thong. He'd washed after his day's work and changed into a clean shirt, but owing to the heat of the evening, he'd not done it up and she could see hairs on his broad chest. His breeches and stockings looked clean too. He'd left his work boots outside.

She wondered if he had changed from his dusty working clothes for her benefit. Or was he deliberately trying to make her feel inadequately dressed?

But that did not impress her at all. Her lack of dress and of modesty weren't her fault. He had undressed her when she was unconscious.

Taking a deep breath she said, as severely as if she were speaking to an errant girl in the shop, "Wake up, sir! Before you go to sleep, I think you should know I have good reason to believe your shipping agent in Philadelphia, Mr. Spear, is deceiving you." Her voice rose an octave. "*I insist* you listen to me, Mr. Hunter."

His body jerked. His eyes opened in a flash.

Her golden brown eyes glared at him as she spoke. Her severe, schoolmarm tone seemed to fascinate him.

"I believe, sir," she continued in a sharp

manner, standing erect out of habit as if she were wearing her stays, "if you have any sense, you'd better get back to Philadelphia before your agent absconds with all your assets!"

He glowered at her. "I should have thought you'd have been too busy with your stitchery to meddle with my affairs."

She wished she had been, and temporarily closed her eyes. A prim and proper businesswoman she was supposed to be.

But now that she'd come, she was determined to make him listen. She opened her eyes and saw him eyeing her shift-clad body, from her hair falling loose about her shoulders, to her bare feet. Infuriatingly, he was grinning, being completely unresponsive to the urgent message she brought. She felt strongly that she had made a mistake in coming. He might never believe her. She should have remained in Philadelphia and kept her dignity and reputation intact.

She frowned as she heard him chuckle. Lowering her head, she moved it slowly from side to side, wondering how she could convince him.

"Miss Willoby, I think you should understand I've known Nathaniel Spear since I came to America as a stripling and started up in business. I can assure you, I have always found him perfectly trustworthy. In fact, I went to see him after the Governor's Ball."

Clementina's mouth twisted cynically. "I know you did. And a useless visit it was! However trustworthy you found your Mr. Spear in the past, I am convinced he is not honest now. For one thing he has disobeyed you."

James's expression changed. He sat up. "He has?"

"Yes indeed. I regret to have to say it, but you are an appalling judge of character, sir. I overheard a man, who I'm convinced was your agent, Spear, talking to Mr. Millard. And I can tell you that your shipping affairs are leaking like a sinking boat."

James rubbed his chin. "What proof have you?"

"Well, for a start, he sent Mr. Millard back to England for another cargo of indentured servants —"

"What?" James's roar made her jump. "I dismissed Millard."

"You thought you did! But it seems quite clear to me they have been cheating you while you've been out here in the forest. I've spent my life in business, sir. I can smell a rogue, and that agent of yours has become one. I would swear on it. I heard them discussing the sale of some indentured servants they had just shipped over from England in your ship."

Clementina got no joy from dealing him these blows. She kept silent for a while as he raged around the cabin, kicking his rifle over and thumping the table so viciously that the spoons in the bowls rattled.

After his temper had subsided somewhat, she suggested, "Here, have some coffee, it might soothe you. I don't want to have to tell you the rest while you are raging like a wild animal in a china cabinet."

He towered over her. "What else have you to tell me?"

She could tell he was beginning to take her seriously. She said calmly, "Drink your coffee then I'll tell you." She realized she had the upper hand now but did not relish baiting him. The situation was too serious for funning.

He took the mug of coffee she offered him and she watched him drink it down in two or three great gulps. "Well?" he said, banging the mug on the table and wiping his mouth on his sleeve.

"Mr. Redmarsh would have come to tell you himself, Mr. Hunter. But he reckoned he was too old for the journey. He tried to prevent me from coming . . ."

Her mention of Mr. Redmarsh made James stare at her. Mr. Redmarsh was an upright Philadelphian wine merchant whom James respected. So the wine merchant knew about this affair, too, did he?

Clementina stopped only long enough for Mr. Redmarsh's name to register. Then she continued, "Mr. Redmarsh is keeping an eye on Mr. Spear. He has to go down to the wharf occasionally to see about his shipments of wine, and he will try to find out more about what is going on. But it was I who overheard their plans to steal your ship and take it to the Caribbean to sell to pirates. They may sail away with it any day. That is why I came to tell you in such haste."

"Good God!" He struck himself on the forehead. "Is this true?"

"Indeed it is, Mr. Hunter. I give you my word I am telling you what I overheard," Clementina said dryly. "And you may well need God to help you."

"Why didn't Mr. Redmarsh send a messenger post haste?"

"In a way he did. As soon as he knew Mr. Spear's plan, he sent his trusted servant, Hawkes. But from what little I saw earlier, your men were treating him roughly because he is an Indian. Where is he now? Has he been fed?"

Disconcerted, James turned his back on her. He frowned. "Hmm! I must do something immediately." He strode to the door.

"Wait, I haven't finished yet."

He swung round, his eyes beating down on her. "Well?"

"Unfortunately, when I was at the shipping office and overheard them talking, Mr. Millard recognized me from the time I was on the *Heron.* He and Mr. Spear were anxious I should not contact you. They sent two sailors to prevent me from reaching you."

James put his hand over his eyes for a moment. "This gets worse by the minute. Go on."

"They followed us to the Red Horse Inn, on the wagon road, and Hawkes managed to get them drunk." She didn't think it necessary to relate that Hawkes had ended up bound and gagged in a wagon. "So we went off to Lancaster in the morning leaving them behind. But when I arrived at Lancaster I had to take the first available transport here, which was the supply wagon, as I don't ride — they didn't provide children with horseback riding lessons at the orphanage."

"So," he said, guessing the next part,

"those two sailors may still try and prevent me from getting to Philadelphia?"

"Yes, I fear they might, Mr. Hunter." She gave a little shudder when she remembered they had Mr. Redmarsh's pistol, too. "And I have to tell you —"

"Good God, woman, what else?"

"They've stolen the gun Mr. Redmarsh gave Hawkes."

His eyes narrowed. "What do you mean?"

"I mean, sir, that those seamen are armed. They may attempt to shoot you if you set off for Philadelphia."

A groan escaped his lips. She could see his temper rising and felt suddenly defeated. She couldn't take any more of his battering. She was weary. Exhausted. She'd done her duty and told the full story to James, and now she felt drained.

Her reputation and successful career were in ruins! She'd compromised herself by coming to the camp like this, and the supply wagon probably wouldn't return until next week. She was stuck in the camp with a hundred or so unfriendly men.

And James hadn't even thought about giving her the gown shop in Bath, had he? All he cared about was getting his wind-powered sawmill going. Even now he didn't seem to be totally convinced about the warning she'd come such a long way to deliver.

All at once everything seemed too much for her to bear. Too painful for her to think about. Her lips trembled as she sank slowly down on a chair and rested her elbow on the table, supporting her bowed head. Unwanted tears trickled down her face. She didn't care. All the fight had gone out of her and she just wanted to cry and cry.

Alerted by her sobs, James looked keenly at her. At first he couldn't believe that bold little Miss Willoby could actually cry. She'd been trained to hold back her feelings because his strict aunt hadn't expected her to have any feelings at all! He was seeing a prissy spinster, whose no-nonsense talk could keep men at bay, melting like a block of ice.

It was extraordinary. Except for that time when he'd kissed her in the parlor, he doubted if she knew what passion was. She was a tough little lady. Look what she'd been through to get here. Then he looked at her again and realized he was being very unfair. She'd suffered, trying to get a warning to him. And all he'd done was add to her sufferings. Now he'd made her cry, and he felt remorseful.

Before he could act on the dastardly information she'd given him, he had to comfort her. Show her he appreciated her efforts to help him. He came softly to her side and knelt down, taking her hands away from her face. He cupped her tear-stained face tenderly in his hands. "Oh, Miss Willoby! I've been uncivil. You've been so brave coming all this way from Philadelphia to warn me. And I've made it difficult for you. Forgive me. I am an ungrateful beast. I admit I am at fault. I should have known what was happening onboard my ship and kept a closer eye on those I left in charge."

This set the tears streaming down her face again, and she turned her head away from him, ashamed to be weeping and unable to speak. It was true he had been rude to her and neglectful about his responsibilities. But hearing him admit his failings only made her love him more. He used his hand to gently take her chin and turn her face towards him once more. Her eyelids fanned over her cheek as his finger gently stroked the tears away. She gave a shuddering sob. She had ruined her reputation, and she had lost her livelihood, and nothing he could do now would repair it.

But his words, spoken gently, helped ease her spirits. "Miss Willoby — Clementina —

you have every right to be angry and upset. I should have believed you straight away. My aunt thought very highly of you."

"I'm not angry," she said weakly, trying to pull herself together. She barely recognized her own voice.

"Look at me."

It was a request rather than an order. She forced herself to look up and blinked at him, thinking even in the fading light that his eyes were as beautiful as stars. Finding her voice again, she said sadly, "I suppose I shouldn't have come. It's probably too late anyway. Even if you rode all day and night, you might not be in time to stop them taking your ship."

He leant forward and gently kissed her wet cheeks, first one and then the other. Then he kissed her small straight nose and finally her quivering lips. He put his hands around her and hugged her close. With her head resting on his chest he rocked her for a while, like a child in a cradle.

"Oh Clementina, Clementina!" he said lovingly, "don't cry. A ship is only a ship, when all is said and done."

Clementina was comforted, yet alarmed, as her heart began beating with the passion he was kindling within her. With only her cotton shift and his open shirt between her body and his, she could feel the strength of his wide chest against her tender breasts, giving her a delightful sensation. But the thundering sermons of the waywardness of men and the sins of the flesh, hammered into orphans by church ministers, pounded into her mind also.

"Oh, don't kiss me. Please don't," she cried, yet wanting him to continue embracing her forever. She loved being crushed in his strong arms. A joy greater than this she'd never known. But she feared that if he did not stop stroking and kissing her, she would be begging him to make love to her. "Stop!" she repeated desperately.

"Why, Clementina? You didn't mind my kissing you in Philadelphia."

So he had treasured the memory of that earlier kiss too!

"That was entirely different circumstances," she said with a sniff, trying to regain her normal composure and pushing him away.

"Of course, I will stop if that is what you want."

Disappointment was written on his face as he stood up and walked to look out the window. She wished she hadn't turned him away so abruptly. She really wanted to be in his arms, giving herself to him and not thinking of the consequences.

But his mind had already leapt ahead. "You are right. We mustn't spend the night in each other's arms . . ."

She blushed to know his mind had contemplated their lovemaking too. The strong love she felt for him — and thought he had for her — overwhelmed her. The revelation excited her heart and filled her mind with happiness.

He did want her.

But he didn't want her at that moment.

He muttered, "I must go to Philadelphia. Set off tonight. There might just be a chance I could get there in time to prevent those thieving rogues from absconding with my ship."

She came out of the clouds and down to earth. She was pleased that he believed her now, but fear like a draught blew over her. She didn't want to be left alone in a camp full of men without him to protect her.

"May I go with you?"

"But you can't ride."

"I can't stay here by myself either. Think of the scandal."

His eyes rose towards the ceiling. "It's a little late to think of that now. You and I are meant for each other, are we not, my little mantua-maker?"

She got up and walked to him, and he held out his hand to take hers. They stood side by side and he looked down at her and said, "You will have to learn to ride as we go on our way, my darling Clementina, because I'll take the short Indian track. We can't take a cart that way."

"I will manage," she said.

He kissed her then, clasping her tightly. His lips were hard on hers until she panted for breath. She was aware of his hands touching her breast, and then her small round backside. He grasped her body close to his. She desperately wanted to give herself to him.

But they must not make love now! They hadn't the time. James mustn't delay getting to Philadelphia. Every minute counted. He should take action without delay. She must be strong and drive him to go.

Hard though it was, her schooling to control her feelings, to abstain from what she wanted, took over. "James, you must go, right now," she whispered urgently in his ear.

"Yes," he said hoarsely. "Another time we will continue this." He kissed her tenderly as he released her. "My love."

Joy filled her and she wanted to sing. He did care about her. He was not going to forget her. He intended to take her with him. To make love to her later. He took it for granted that she was now his to protect.

The mantua-maker from Bath had come a long way: over the ocean and miles to this hinterland camp. She'd lost much — but gained a lover.

And having James was all she really wanted.

Earlier that morning, Hugill had kicked Big Jack's sleeping form as they lay in the Red Horse's barn. "Wake up!" he roared at the snoring sailor. "Heave out or, by Jasus, I'll see to it you'll never get up again."

"Get orff!" snarled Jack, whose head was throbbing.

Hugill was in no mood for insubordination as he took Hawkes's pistol from his belt. His head ached too, and his mind was still befuddled after all the rum he'd drunk last night. But one thing was clear in his mind: if that Willoby woman got to James Hunter and he raced back to Philadelphia before Hugill had dealt with him, his dream of sailing off to the Caribbean with Spear was lost.

"Up. Up, you brute," he yelled, giving Jack another vicious kick, which made the seaman grimace with pain.

The daylight outside the barn told him how late they'd slept. Hugill's plan to kidnap Miss Willoby, tie her up, and put her in the cart with that Indian servant was impossible now as the cart and the stage-coach would have left early.

But all was not lost. There was more than one way to kill a cat.

He thudded his boot into Big Jack's posterior once more and the man groaned again and sat up, snarling. "You do that again, bos'n, and I'll murder yer!"

Hugill didn't lack audacity, although his head pounded. "I'll do more than that, you great lout. Get on your feet."

Jack held his head in both hands. Painfully, he rose at last. "What's ado then, bos'n?" he growled.

"We've got to go after that Willoby female. Fast. Stop her from seeing Mr. Hunter, see?"

Big Jack rubbed his hands together. "Shouldn't be difficult now we've got her servant. Got him, didn't we? No trouble at all! That crafty Indian thought a few drinks would put us out flat, but we sailors are used to grog, and we overpowered him like he was naught but a fairy."

Hugill almost choked with rage. "But it weren't the servant we were sent to get, were it, Jack? It were the wench. And we got ourselves well and truly in the tankards later last night, didn't we? And we didn't capture the Willoby woman, did we?"

Jack's mouth opened wide as he shook his great, pigtailed head.

"So 'ere we are, stuck on the highway, miles from anywhere. The stage left hours ago, didn't it? And the wagon we got a lift on here has moved off too. Now, Jack, you try telling that to the capt'n when you get back. He'd have you flogged, that's wot."

Jack's face fell. Then it brightened slowly. "We got the Indian servant's purse, as well as his firearm, though, ain't we, bos'n? We've got enough money in that purse to hire us a couple of mules, ain't we?"

Hugill's eyes narrowed. "Aye, lad, you've a point there. But instead of going to Lancaster we'll go directly to Hunter's sawmill."

Later, as the pair rode along together, another idea came to Hugill. He mentioned it to Jack and the pair's vindictive laughter could be heard half a mile away.

Clementina remained in a state of bliss for a while after James had gone in search of Hawkes and to get the horses ready for the long trek back to Philadelphia. Then, having washed and slipped on clean underwear from her carpetbag, she decided her travel gown would be the best to ride in. Although it was warm now, the night could become cold.

Inside she felt a strange sense of peace. She and James were in love. Whoever would have thought it? But she knew love was a fickle emotion. Love didn't always lead to marriage. Women were especially vulnerable when their hearts led them into love affairs with no prospect of permanent relationships. As an orphan herself, she wondered if her mother had been unfortunate with the man she'd loved. Had Clementina been the child of a servant girl whose master had taken advantage of her?

With these mixed thoughts, she lay down again on James's bed. There was a long ride ahead of her, which she didn't relish. Even if it meant she was going with James.

She'd never ridden a horse, and the more she thought about it, the more she was scared of being perched up high on a horse's back. It would be a long way to the ground when she fell off — which she was sure she would.

Unable to eliminate the burden of her coming ordeal, she decided she would at least rest until James returned for her.

It was sunset when she awoke from her slumber. She was aware James had come back to the cabin and was lying with her on the bed with his arm around her.

He seemed to sense she was awake and said, "I didn't like to disturb you. But now that you have rested, the sooner we get started the better, Clementina."

She asked, "How will you know the way in the dark?"

"There is a moon tonight, and I know the trail through the forest. I've been up and down it many times during the past few years. Some men will accompany us as far as the Forbes Road."

"Is it dangerous?" she wanted to know, picturing the glittering eyes of coyotes and bands of renegade Indians.

"Here in the backwoods there are always dangers, yes indeed. But we are unlikely to meet any city footpads!"

She smiled wryly as they rose and hurriedly prepared to leave.

CHAPTER TWELVE

When they were preparing to leave the cabin, Clementina with her carpetbag, and James carrying his saddle and rifle, a loud explosion shook the ground. They looked at each other questioningly. After a moment's silence the camp dogs started barking.

"What the hell was that?" James cried as they rushed out the door.

"Look," said Clementina, grabbing James's arm. "Over there." She pointed to the sky, which was glowing orange. They saw columns of smoke rising like ominous ghosts into the air.

"Fire!" They both said the dreaded word together.

In the distance the yells of men and screaming horses gave them more fatal information. A fire was burning the mill and could easily spread to the cabins and stables — and even into the forest. Fire was the worst disaster that could overtake a wooden settlement. The long hot summer had made the entire countryside as dry as tinder.

James looked devastated for an instant. "Not those Indians back again!" he groaned. Dropping his saddle and running with his rifle, he called back, "Get to the river, Clementina. I'll send someone to take care of you."

Leaving her stunned, he tore towards the scene that she could now see was a raging fire. Huge billows of purple smoke rose up as eerie orange lights lit the sky, illuminating fast-moving clouds. The pale moon glowed down upon the bright red, yellow and white flames as they engulfed the wood stacks in the lumberyard.

Clementina broke into a trot as she saw the flames leap higher. Shouting men were spilling out from their log cabins and racing here and there, trying to assess the situation as James tore up to them, giving orders and getting his men armed and ready for action.

Clementina could feel the heat and smell the burning. The men seemed as puny as Lilliputians before the inferno.

She gasped. The leaping flames and sparks had engulfed the new sawmill! James's pride and joy was alight as she watched helplessly. With a sinking heart, she thought how catastrophic it must be for James to see his years of hard work destroyed before his eyes.

Heartbroken, Clementina suddenly realized this fire would result in casualties. Instead of standing and watching it, she should go and see if she could help. Men might be burned.

Then, as a great blast of heat met her going down to the river, she saw James's tall figure silhouetted against the flames, dragging a body from a cabin.

She hesitated, unsure whether she should race up to help James. But he was carrying the man down to the river, so she followed. On the riverbank she saw other men were seated, and she knew already there had been casualties. Lying by the riverside were several injured men. She strode down to see if she could help them.

Then an amazing sound greeted her ears: a fire bell.

Looking round, she saw a fire engine drawn by four horses. Men scrambled around it, forming a human chain down to the river so that water buckets could be passed from one man to another to fill the engine and then pump water on the fire. James had foreseen the possibility of fire, and had brought this engine all the way from Philadelphia in case of emergencies. And then she saw another fire engine coming to join the fight to quell the fire.

She realized James had not neglected safety here. The sawmill had been built so that it was near the river, and the trees behind it had been cut down to prevent a fire from spreading into the forest. Many of the log cabins and stables, too, were grouped together with fire gaps between them.

The plan was quite effective but, alas, it was unable to prevent the fire from engulfing James's sawmill. Huge flames could not be put out, and they burnt the wooden structure with ease. Soon rafters stood out like ribs against the red sky, or came crashing down to the earth.

A sudden scream reminded Clementina that she must tend the injured. She looked up and saw a man with his clothes on fire running towards the river, and went speedily after him. He fell before he'd managed to get into the water. Clementina rushed up, and scooping river water with her hands, doused the flames.

The man's cries were pitiful. She did what she could to remove the burnt clothing, using the cold river water to cool his skin as she tried to reassure him that the flames were out and that his burns, though painful, would heal.

Her calm manner and reassurance was of

some comfort for those men whose hands and faces were burned. She fetched water for them to splash over the injuries and gave them water to drink.

Hawkes was by her side. "Miss Willoby, are you all right, ma'am?"

She brushed a curl of hair from her damp forehead. "I am, thank you. What about you and Mr. Hunter?" she asked, sitting back on her heels. She had been tending another casualty.

"I'm going down to the water to drink and bathe my hands. Mr. Hunter is still trying to put the last of the fire out."

"Have the Indians gone?"

"There were no Indians, Miss Willoby."

"Then what happened? Was it a cookhouse fire?"

He looked at her sorrowfully. "I've been keeping sentry on the road. Out of sight. Expecting to see those seamen who captured me. And this evening I saw two men approaching on mules and recognized them. Their furtive manner alerted me to the fact they were planning to fire the place. But they started their evil deed so quickly, I had no time to do more than warn the men and help take the horses to safety." He looked downcast. "I'm sorry, ma'am. I saw them do it, but I couldn't stop them setting off an explosion and starting the fire."

"Oh Hawkes, you shall not take the blame. You did what you could."

"I have been no use to you, Miss Willoby."

"On the contrary," she assured him, "you saw who was responsible for lighting the fire and causing the damage." She gave a little shudder. "And where are those wicked seamen now?"

"I saw one scarper. I don't know about the other one."

Fear made her shiver. What other wickedness might they get up to? James could try to capture them if he knew where they were. But where was he? She looked around, seeing devastation everywhere. The loggers and sawyers were in disarray or injured.

Stunned to think men could deliberately start a fire in a logging camp, she bit her lip. But on second thought, she realized a man like Hugill would think nothing of putting men at risk. He wouldn't hesitate to do something spiteful like burning down Mr. Hunter's new sawmill. He was truly evil. She gazed over the riverbank to see men in groups, resting on the ground or propped up against the trunks of trees, nursing their injuries. How brutal life could be! How cruel it had been to James Hunter tonight. And because Clementina loved him, she felt his pain as if it were her own.

She had no medicine for burns. All she could do, with Hawkes's aid, was to comfort the groaning, shocked men as they came down to the cooling river, some with swollen, red-and-grey burnt areas of flesh and charred skin.

"Thank you," breathed one grateful man, grasping her wrist. "You are a wonderful lady."

A lady she was not, especially after coming to the camp. But she was a changed woman, no longer scared of touching a man or feeling a man grip her. She no longer recoiled at these fellows' unshaven chins and gruff ways. She felt she had lost the wall of English respectability she'd built around herself. She was now an ordinary woman who could cry when she fell down. She could look after the sick and those in pain and do whatever she could to help them. She could show her distress and let tears fall.

She had learned to love a man, too. But James would not offer her a permanent relationship, the kind she wanted. Being someone's mistress was not her ambition. James would not want a woman with a ruined reputation.

She sighed. No matter what she did, her

fate was sealed. She was an orphan and had no standing in society. She'd chosen to throw away the respectability Mrs. Hunter had given her, and there was no getting it back.

But Clementina was not the kind of woman to bemoan her lot. She never had been and she wouldn't start now. There was always hope. She'd survived quite well until her twenty-sixth year, and she would continue to survive.

As she tied back her loose hair, she thought that she had to think about those less fortunate than herself — those poor men who'd been injured. She looked about her and saw men tending their comrades and was amazed and gratified to see men could be tender towards each other.

Next she saw a man leaning against a tree trunk, looking as if he'd been badly injured. His clothes were torn and singed. He was moaning in pain and his head tilted to one side. He looked all in.

Coming up to him she gave a sharp cry. "James!" For James it was.

He seemed lost, dazed, as if he hadn't heard her.

"James?" she said, coming close and seeing the burns on his face and his hands, and she could have wept. Going to the river, she brought some water in her cupped hands for him to drink and bathe his face with. But for a while he did not seem to even notice who she was.

He was exhausted. He closed his eyes and she let him rest for a few minutes.

"I am a ruined man," he said suddenly. "My sawmill is burned to a cinder."

"Oh, I wouldn't say that!" Clementina retorted — although she did know how he was feeling. Occasionally a gown she'd made was not a success, and after all the hard work she'd put into it, it made her want to weep. But she never did. She just unpicked the stitches and made it up again until she and the lady buying the gown were satisfied. She said, "You'll just have to build your sawmill again."

He replied bitterly, "For it to be burnt down again?"

"No. Disasters rarely happen. Didn't you know Hawkes saw the seamen starting the fire?"

Clearly he did not. "Did you say someone started this fire deliberately?"

"I told you some seamen from your ship had followed us here. Hawkes spotted them. He told me he saw them start the explosion and then fire the wood stacks."

James gave an agonized cry. He seemed to

sink back into inertia.

Clementina knew she had to impart some of her fighting spirit to restore the pioneering character that had brought him out to the backwoods in the first place. Although he was suffering from the pain of his burns, in the long run she knew he would suffer more from the loss of his sawmill. With the loss of his project, his pride and his confidence were at stake. Knowing she had to spur him into action again, she said firmly, "Now, James, you are not to give in. I won't have it — and neither would your aunt if she were here."

He looked faintly amused. "And what do you suggest?" He said bitterly, "Have you a magic wand to set it aright?" He pointed to the pall of smoke hanging over what was once one of the finest sawmills in Pennsylvania.

Not crushed by his cynicism, she replied briskly, "You'll have to catch Hugill. Have him arrested for arson. And rebuild."

"Yes. Yes, I will." Then his spark of determination died out. He gave an agonized moan. "I deserve this suffering for my stupidity. I can't race Hugill back to Philadelphia. They'll take my ship next. All my assets are gone. I'm a broken man, Clementina."

"Rubbish!" she said decisively. "When I was in Bath I saw people come to the spa who were in desperate need of the water's cure. But you're a healthy man — although in great pain with those burns, I grant you." She took a ragged breath in. "But there's nothing wrong with you that won't heal."

"You sound like my Aunt Elizabeth," he said, trying to smile, but it obviously hurt him to do so.

"I wouldn't be surprised if I do sound like her. She taught me to pick myself up after a fall and get going again. And I dare say that is what she said to you when you came to see her years ago after being sent down from Oxford and turned away by your father."

"It was." He looked at her and again he tried to smile.

She went to get some more water for him in order to give him time to think about what she'd said. When she returned he drank a little. He perked up and said, "Do you think I should start off for Philadelphia now? Is there still a hope I may catch him?"

At first she was amazed that he should ask her advice. Yet, as a businesswoman, wasn't she used to making decisions for others? She replied, "I don't see why not. You can but try to apprehend the villains. It will be uncomfortable for you with those burns, whether you travel or stay here. It is necessary for you to keep out of the sun, so making the journey at night is preferable to riding during the day."

He drew his brows together as he looked around. "I don't like to ask any of the men to accompany me. They are all tired out."

"It won't be necessary. I won't be able ride fast with you, but neither will you feel like galloping all the way there."

"Oh, I wasn't thinking of taking you," he said quickly. "I'll get Hawkes to take you to Lancaster, and put you on the stage."

Clementina scoffed, "Travel with Hugill?"

James gave a chuckle. It was a poignant moment. He was back to thinking about his responsibilities. He was trying to make up his mind on the best course of action. Rising to his feet, he surveyed the scene of devastation. He recognized a man walking away from the scene of the fire and called him over. "Is the fire out?"

The man came towards him. He'd obviously been one of the lucky ones who escaped from being burned. "Yes, Mr. Hunter. We've been trying to salvage what we could."

"All the men found?"

"Most of the men are down here by the river, sir."

James gave a swallow. "Any killed?"

"Only one was caught up in the blaze. A great big fellow. Not a man from this camp — and not an Indian either."

Clementina knew who he was. One of the seamen. He deserved his fate. "That would be the big seaman I told you about," she said.

"Ah, yes. Now I want you to find the foremen and ask them to come and see me. I need to go to Philadelphia immediately, and some arrangements must be made for while I'm gone."

"Yessir," the man touched his forelock.

Clementina was overjoyed to see James return to his former assertive self. She nodded at him approvingly. "You will suffer on the journey, James, but you would suffer more if you stayed and attempted to do nothing to bring justice about."

He looked at her and her heart went out to him when she saw his singed body and hair, his sore face and hands. How much it must hurt him!

"Yes. I shall go, and I'd like you to come with me, Clementina," he said softly, as if he really did want her.

Her heart beat fast as she looked deeply into his eyes. He was a bit like a child who had hurt himself and had run to his mama for comfort. But soon he would be away, tumbling with his playmates again.

"Yes indeed, I'll go with you," she said, looking into his eyes and wanting to say *I always want to be with you,* but she said instead, "It will be a gamble, but I would say I've been more than a little rash during my life recently."

"Clementina," he said, patting her shoulder, "you are a wonderful lady."

She was sure he would have kissed her, only his lips were too sore. So she stood on tiptoe and kissed the side of his face that had not been burned.

He wanted to smile but mouthed, "Thank you." He smelled of wood smoke and it made her feel she would remember that moment all her life.

Hawkes decided he would take the stagecoach back to Philadelphia. He would spot Hugill if the man appeared. And with only one villain to deal with instead of two, it would be easier for him to avoid being captured again. Then when he got back to Philadelphia, he could go and report to Mr. Redmarsh and tell him what had happened — in case Clementina and James didn't manage to get back to Philadelphia alive.

They walked back towards his cabin, which had been untouched by the fire.

Before James picked up his saddle, which he'd thrown down when the fire started, he turned, slipped his arms around Clementina's waist and drew her towards him. Even if someone saw them together in the moonlight, what did it matter now?

She knew it was not a physical passion that made him want her. It was the need to be comforted. He was sobbing. But soon the anger in him flowed out. For several minutes as he held her close, she felt his gasps of anguished rage, and she knew he had to have time to get over his acute disappointment and loss. So she put her head on his chest and let him stroke her head until his frustration died down.

He slowly released her, and she saw his natural air of command had returned. Straightening his wide shoulders, he said between clenched teeth, "Damn those villains." Then he said with icy calmness, "I will catch that swine Hugill if it kills me!"

That fighting spirit was necessary. Vengeance was rightfully his.

When he picked up his saddle, she was reminded that she should be carrying something. But she had no idea what had happened to her carpetbag as he strode down towards the stables and she trotted after him. And she didn't want to delay him by saying she had to look for it in the dark.

A man was looking after the horses. All of them had been rounded up and put in a fenced-in area. They had been frightened, but they had been watered and calmed, and now only appeared slightly jumpy after the disaster.

But to Clementina, they looked like huge, ferocious beasts that were wide-eyed, snorting and skittering around, and tossing their tails and manes in a disturbed manner. She longed to cry out that she could not — would not — mount one, let alone ride one all the way to Philadelphia!

With the help of the stable hand, James managed to find his horse that came whinnying to his master, as if pleased to see him.

"He ain't come to no harm, sir," the stable hand said. "Should get you to Philly in a wink."

They placed the saddle on the horse and James swung himself up, while Clementina backed away into the shadows.

"Will he take Miss Willoby too?" James asked almost as an afterthought.

The stable hand looked Clementina up and down. "There ain't much of her," he commented. "I don't think your horse would notice the difference."

"Throw her up then," said James.

At that moment, Clementina's hands pricked with fear. Her mouth went dry. Had her feet not been unable to move, she might have made a run for it. But before she'd had time to protest, the stable hand had hoisted her up behind James.

"Hold on to me," he said. She thought she would expire with fright.

The stable hand opened the gate for them, and the horse moved slowly forward.

Clinging on desperately, terrified she might fall, Clementina rode out of the camp with James, unaware that several men looked on, but none jeered to see the little dressmaker riding with their master. By the time they had gone a few hundred yards she began to feel the swing of the horse's body and adjusted to it. Fortunately, she didn't look down, but concentrated on sitting as comfortably as she could as the horse swayed forward. And she clung tightly to James.

Hawkes was waiting to receive his last orders, which James gave him.

"Take care," James said finally, giving him some money, as his horse turned round abruptly and almost unseated Clementina.

"And you take care too, sir. And you, ma'am." The Indian grinned to see strait-laced Miss Willoby perched precariously on

the horse's backside, clinging onto James as
if her life depended on it.

CHAPTER THIRTEEN

Being physically close to James as they rode together, Clementina, although still scared of being on horseback, felt comforted. Deep in the dark forest they were passing through, she experienced a strange sense of reality. Her love for him infiltrated her innermost being, and that gave her extraordinary happiness, yet she asked herself if it was a dream. Would it last?

Perhaps her doubts troubled her because she was tired after the whirlwind of experiences she'd had in the last few days. Or perhaps she knew that without him she would be lost in the forest, and she had to cling to him. She also felt in communion with the nature, with the wildlife she could not see in the darkness, but knew must be around her.

Becoming accustomed to riding, she noted James was taking care not to unseat her, and she forgot any possible danger they might encounter. She drifted into a doze, resting her head on his back.

When she awoke, she was acutely aware not only of James's beating heart, but the calls of the wild. What these cries of the forest signified she didn't know, being someone who'd spent all her life in a city. But a strong primitive urge inside her told her she shouldn't fear them. Elks, bison, coyotes, bluebirds or woodpeckers, she'd heard of them all, but never seen them. Every living thing had the same right to live in peace as she had. Tranquility closed over her like a blanket.

Dreaming perhaps, she felt as if she'd died and gone to heavenly paradise. The Garden of Eden was everyone's destiny. Except of course for wicked men like Hugill who would not be welcome there.

"Are you awake, Clementina?" James asked suddenly.

"Yes," she replied. She didn't like to ask how he was. She knew he was in pain. Only a man accustomed to ride would tolerate what he was going through. He was so brave to ignore so much pain and continue with his quest.

He stopped his horse for a while, and she saw they were on a rise. Between the trees, she saw a great expanse of the sky. The sunrise in all its glory shone before them. Reds, yellows and purples streaked across the lightening sky, and around them in the trees birds began to sing. James told her to listen as an elk bugled, as if awakening the morn. It was a moment of utmost joy.

"The beauty of it all makes me feel insignificant," said Clementina humbly.

"You are not insignificant to me!" James retorted.

Not knowing if he meant he loved her or she was a burden he had to carry, she kept her mouth shut. They continued riding for a while. She understood his burns would make him fractious.

It was full daylight by the time they descended towards the highway and to the Forbes Road tavern. They'd reached the edge of civilization. Clementina rejoiced, thinking they'd got over the most dangerous part of their journey. Yet part of her balked at the thought of having to return to civilization and resume her role as a fashionable dressmaker.

Mmm! The aroma of the tavern's coffee was wonderful. And the freshly baked pies and corn bread tempted her as they rode past the kitchen and towards the stables.

Clementina was aware that the ostlers regarded them oddly as the tired horse ambled into the yard. And was it surprising? The Queen's Horseshoe Inn was used to seeing weary travelers with dust on their clothes and dirt on their boots. But they probably weren't accustomed to the sight of a tousled-haired man in a torn and burnt shirt with his face red from burns riding an exhausted horse. The bedraggled woman who rode behind him wore a lady's gown, but it was ripped and stained. Her glorious auburn hair was in disarray, as if she had long ago lost her hat — as well as her dignity.

"Have you been attacked by Indians?" the groom asked, coming up to take the horse's bridle so the riders could dismount.

"No," replied James, "it was a white man who set fire to my sawmill. Take my horse and rub him down well and have him well stabled."

The groom recognized a gentleman of authority, despite his rags, when he saw one. He quickly did as he was told.

James lifted Christina down from the horse and she stood rubbing her posterior that ached after sitting for hours. Her feet were numb. But knowing James was feeling worse than she did, she didn't complain.

"We've been riding all night. Nip into the bar and get me a tankard of beer and a coffee for the lady," said James, tossing a young stable lad a coin. "Quick, mind, and the rest of the shilling will be yours." The boy sped away.

The knowledge that their journey was not over yet and that she had to continue riding made Clementina's heart sink. But when a steaming jug of coffee was brought out and a cup placed in her hands and when she could drink the delicious liquid, it made her throat feel silky, and her mind shook off its despondency. The waiter had brought out a platter of freshly made muffins.

"I need to get to Philadelphia. Fast," James said, in between swilling his beer and chewing a muffin.

"Our horses are all out," the older groom explained. "Anyhows, we ain't got anything of the likes of yours. He's a beauty, ain't he?"

James squared his shoulders. His frown prevented the groom from any desire to engage in chitchat. "Nothing, you say?" He strode around the yard as if he didn't believe his bad luck. Entering the stables, he viewed the horses in the stalls and asked, "Do all these mounts belong to travelers in the tavern?"

"Yes. None are available for you to ride, sir. I allus speak the truth, sir."

Clementina could see James's temper begin to boil. She bit her thumbnail and watched him pace about with clenched fists.

He wandered off, giving time for Clementina to finish her coffee.

"Yippee!" She heard him give a joyful cry after he'd disappeared around the corner of the tavern.

Hearing no more, Clementina put down her empty coffee cup and went to see what he'd found.

She stared. She couldn't believe her eyes. There, by the side of the tavern, was parked a beautifully turned-out-two-wheeled racing gig. The ostentatious equipage with its spanking bright yellow paintwork and silver trim was intended to impress because it had been designed for a gentleman fop. Matching creamy white horses were already in harness, waiting for their owner to finish his refreshment in the tavern and continue on their drive.

"This is just what I want," called James, already seated on the high perch with the reins in his hands. "With a bit of luck we could be in Philadelphia before the day is out."

Clementina couldn't deny the carriage would assist his speedy return to Philadelphia. There was one problem, however; it didn't belong to him.

"Who owns this rig?" he shouted at the groom.

"Mr. Richard Wakefield, of Philadelphia, sir."

James gave a short laugh as far as his sore face enabled him to. "Richard Wakefield, eh? I know the young shaver. That young man's got nothing better to do than race around the countryside. Well, you tell him that Mr. James Hunter has borrowed his fancy cart, will you?"

He put one hand into his pocket and grimaced with the pain of his burnt fingers as he withdrew a gold coin from his pocket and tossed it at the groom. "Here man, catch. Now tell Mr. Wakefield I am in a great hurry to get to the city. I'm obliged to him for the use of his rig. He has my word that I will return his carriage unharmed."

"You can't take it, sir," the groom said, alarmed. "Get down, I beg of you."

But James ignored his entreaties and turned the horses, ready to leave. He yelled above the horses' snorts and neighs, "Clementina, will you get up on the rig right now for heaven's sake!"

Appalled that James could even contemplate taking the carriage without the owner's permission, Clementina gaped at him. She was sympathetic with James's need to get to Philadelphia quickly and could see here was the means for him to do it, but it was wicked to steal. Why, you could get hanged for stealing!

James, of course, had probably stolen money as a student, so he hadn't the same horror of the crime as she had.

"It's against my principles to steal," she said primly, and then gave a little gasp when she remembered acquiring the drawing of James by Thomas Gainsborough. Indeed, she was not as worthy as she should be either.

Blushing, she hesitated. "James. . . ." she began.

"There's no time to argue, woman! Get in, or get out of my way," he shouted, brandishing the long chaise whip he had armed himself with.

Perhaps it was the devil himself that lifted Clementina up into the carriage. It certainly wasn't her usual common sense. Feet she didn't recognize as her own swept her up the steps, and she fell back into the leather seat beside James.

This was madness. Sheer madness. She had gone against all the goodness the orphanage and Mrs. Hunter had drummed into her for years. She'd impulsively given in to temptation to steal — again.

And so had James. They were both wicked thieves together.

But as James flicked the reins and the team moved forward, the shouts of the grooms didn't seem to penetrate her ears. The thrill of riding in this luxurious rig was only more exciting the faster James drove the horses.

She was not surprised James could drive a team. He'd probably done some racing himself before he got the idea of building a sawmill in the depth of the forest.

The Forbes Road was a major highway, and on this fine morning it was perfect for racing. The road surface was hard and dry and the wheels of the carriage whirred at such a speed they frequently leapt into the air.

Clementina held on for dear life. But she felt a surge of blood in her veins. It was thrilling, tearing along like this. The chaise was a superb example of racing craftwork carriage makers in Philadelphia made and gaudily decorated. Many young gentlemen who could afford such carriages in that prosperous city liked to show off by racing around the Colony.

Wary travelers on the road moved their wagons and carts aside and herded their flocks as the pounding horses raced by. They cursed the young bloods who liked to charge around for their own amusement, often scaring honest folk going about their lawful work.

The road was straight for the most part. Villages built on or near the road sometimes slowed them down, and James wanted to regulate the horses so they could have a time to rest at the trot before they set off galloping at top speed once more.

He turned to give her a tortured grin on one occasion as they were going over a bridge very slowly because a herd of cattle was coming the other way. That grin set Clementina's mind to thinking he had enormous audacity to steal the carriage and then grin about his criminal behavior. But who was she to criticize James? Had she not also been reckless lately? Light-fingered too?

James had got the horses to race again. The wind sent her hair flying behind her and she laughed with enjoyment.

After more miles, they'd reached an open plain of farmlands. A wind came up. The oppressive feeling of a storm coming made Clementina sense danger. She viewed the heavy-looking clouds with misgiving.

"Look!" James shouted, pointing to the sky in the distance where a strange black and purple vertical column could be seen. "Damn, it's a twister!" He tried to settle the horses that'd become uneasy.

Clementina had heard of these American summer storms. Nancy had told her about the time she'd come home from the shops with a few packages containing a new fan, some kid gloves and some hair ribbons, when a tall twisting cloud had come out of the wind, moving fast, like a spinning top. She was warned by a householder to come in and shelter until the twister had passed. But Nancy said she hadn't far to walk and continued on her way. And that, Nancy told her, was all she remembered, until she came round and found herself lying on the ground with people looking down at her asking her if she felt all right.

Nancy had told Clementina she never did find her packages. They were, she said, probably taken from her hand by the tornado and scattered miles away.

Remembering the tale, Clementina sobered and eyed the twister with terror.

"We may be lucky, or unlucky, either way," remarked James. "It could turn in any direction."

Clementina knew a twister could turn, and that any man, beast, tree or barn in its path could be struck. She didn't scream.

She felt in her heart that she and James deserved to suffer for their wrongdoing. This was the wrath of God.

James didn't see it that way. He didn't say a thing to suggest he was at fault. Perhaps, Clementina thought, he had no conscience. But that was not true. He had shown remorse when he'd heard Millard had used his ship against his wishes and brought over another crowd of indentured servants. And indeed, he had apologized to her on more than one occasion.

He was a curious man: a gentleman and a rugged pioneer rolled into one. He was part boy still in some ways with his go-ahead, assertive nature. Hadn't he come to America with nothing as a lad? But he'd got things done and achieved many successes as he'd overcome difficulties. Wasn't that the spirit needed in this new land? Not all men were foppish and wanted to attire themselves in silks and strut around town for all to admire them.

Yes, deep in her heart she admired and loved James, despite all his faults. She was convinced he had many admirable qualities.

As he drove the horses fearlessly onwards, steadying the nervous creatures, the animals seemed to gain the courage from him to trot on regardless in the storm. And indeed, it wasn't long before they were out of the worst of it.

But the going was hard. Clementina's enjoyment of the ride was over, and she was drenched with rain and clung to the wet carriage seat. She caught a glimpse of a signpost that read Philadelphia — fifteen miles. So near and yet so far, it seemed in their present condition. Her weariness made her sigh. Tearful, she checked herself; she would not give in to the vapors when James was suffering far worse than she. If it was necessary to suffer, then suffer she would.

Then they became aware of another noise behind them, the steady beat of a horse galloping up fast behind the carriage. James slowed the team and steered them to the side of the road to allow the galloping rider to pass them.

Something made him glance over his shoulder.

She could hear his sharp intake of breath.

"Jupiter!" he cried, horrified.

"What is it?" Clementina mouthed.

James swore. "It's that young buck whose carriage we've taken!"

She went cold inside.

"He's hell bent after us. Richard's got more bottom than I'd thought!" Bottom referred to gumption. And James should know; he had plenty of it.

She asked, trembling, "What shall we do?"

Knowing they were so near the city — so near to being able to prevent Spear from stealing his ship — James flourished the whip and set the horses going from a canter into a gallop.

On they raced, covering the ground with alarming speed.

But so did their pursuer.

The carriage horses, foaming at the mouth, were fine racers and did their best, but they were tired creatures, and James was unwilling to ruin good horseflesh by forcing them to race until they dropped, although his need for speed was dire. He'd recognized Richard Wakefield was riding his own horse, too, and didn't want to lose his horse through misuse either. He began to slow the team.

"Whoa," he cried, reining in.

The horses weren't expecting to be stopped in full flight. Even the rider behind them went racing on. In the confusion James didn't see a boulder on the road and a carriage wheel bumped against it, rocking the light vehicle alarmingly.

James's cry, and the neighs of the bewildered horses as they swerved out of control, resulted in the carriage tilting. Although

Clementina attempted to cling on, she found to her horror that her grip was slipping. Desperate and unable to hold on, she screamed.

Frightened by her scream, the horses danced about so that the light carriage swung violently from side to side. One horse reared.

Clementina found herself in the air, flying, until she thudded onto the hard earth. It flashed through her mind that this was her just deserts. It was her punishment for disobeying God's commandments, she told herself. Then she knew no more.

At the same time, the young buck had come racing back to the toppled carriage, and with the feat of a performing rider, had stood up on his horse and leapt on James like a cougar attacking its prey.

When Clementina came to her senses, she winced, feeling her bruised body and aching head. Sitting up, she became aware there were men panting nearby and shouts that sounded like expletives. Looking around she saw a knuckle fight going on.

CHAPTER FOURTEEN

Clementina must have drifted off again. The next time she became aware of anything, she noticed she was lying on long fragrant grass at the edge of a meadow. She could hear the rustle of an oak tree's leaves overhead and saw a row of curious, dribbling cows who'd ambled up to see what all the commotion was about.

Then she heard the horses nearby snorting, whinnying and pawing the ground. She forced herself to sit up and looked around.

The shiny carriage was lying on its side.

And then she saw something else that made her forget her pains. The two men were still sparring. They cursed, groaned, puffed and panted.

"Steady on now, Richard," she heard James say breathlessly. "Put up your cuffs and I'll explain the matter."

Young Mr. Richard Wakefield felt right was on his side, and he was doing his best to teach James Hunter a lesson — without success, as James was a far stronger and more experienced fighter.

After watching for a minute or two, wondering what she should do to stop them, Clementina came to the conclusion that James was trying to hold the pimply youth off, not only because he was suffering from burns, but also because he didn't want to hurt the lad. Young Richard was springing about like a mountain goat, doing his best to avoid James's guard and land a blow. But he was getting more and more furious as he wasn't able to land one. The contest ended when Richard lost his footing and spun backwards, falling into a muddy pool of water, which did nothing for his bright orange-striped breeches.

James quickly offered him a hand up. "There, man, hit me if you must, but please listen to what I have to say first."

Sobered by a wet backside, Richard grunted, "I don't want to hear your excuses, Hunter. I just want to have my carriage back."

"And so you shall. I only borrowed it. And knowing you to be a kind-hearted fellow, I thought you wouldn't mind. Any damage done to your equipage will be paid for, I assure you, Richard. But I think no harm's been done, it's only toppled over."

The younger man stood mopping his brow and catching his breath, looking to Clementina as if he was ready to begin fighting again at any moment.

She tried to stand, but her ankle pained her, and she cried out.

Richard's head turned quickly towards her. "Your pardon, ma'am," he said with a bow. His red wig, which had become unlodged during his exertions, fell on the ground.

James picked it up, intending to give it to Richard, but stood and looked at the hairpiece disapprovingly and said, "You shouldn't be wearing a red wig, Richard." Then he tossed it over towards the inquisitive cows that looked down at it suspiciously. "Wigs are going out of fashion, m'boy. Everyone and the pieman wears the tatty things! They ain't smart any longer. Only older men, the army and the British like 'em, but not American men of discernment."

Richard scratched his cropped head.

James continued, "Miss Willoby here comes from the fashionable resort town of Bath, in England. She's a royal mantuamaker. Makes gowns for Princess Amelia. She knows what the best young gentlemen wear and it ain't wigs. Is it, Miss Willoby?"

Clementina, catching the drift of James's subterfuge, immediately replied, "Indeed. I would say a fashionable young gentleman like you, Richard, should have a good barber, and show off your hair. Ladies like to see a man with a good crop of hair. And you should learn to make an art of your cravat, sir. That is the latest fashion."

Richard bowed, clearly impressed by this latest fashion tip.

"Now," said James, coming up to Richard, as he no longer feared he might be attacked, "you must allow me to pay for a new suit of clothes for you, too. And may I suggest my tailor in Oak Street, who has, I think, the best cloth and cut of any tailor in town, and certainly won't make you another pair of those hideous orange breeches. We can't have Richard looking like a countrified dowdy, can we, Miss Willoby?"

Richard looked at James and then at Clementina, opening and closing his mouth like a landed fish.

"We're going to see a change in you, Richard Wakefield. Make a man of you!"

While Richard stood open-mouthed, James and Clementina nodded to each other, trying not to laugh. James then continued, "But first I have an important job for you to do. We are in a jam, you see. Have to get to Philadelphia before my agent runs off with my ship. He intends to sail it abroad and sell it. My agent is intending to ruin me, so I must get there fast and put a stop to his evil scheme."

"Oh, I say!" exclaimed Richard, looking concerned.

"He's already sent a man who burned down James's sawmill," added Clementina, anxious to assist James, whom she could see was in great pain and dying to be off.

"Oh, no, not your fine sawmill!" Richard exclaimed.

"Yes, indeed, old chap. Look at my burns. That's why I need your help. I have to get to Philadelphia as soon as I can. Only you can save me now. And you wouldn't let down an old friend, would you, Richard?"

Clementina was managing to stand on her sore ankle with difficulty. She brushed back her hair, wishing she was as well-dressed as she usually was. Shaken, it was difficult for her to feel confident. She looked beseechingly at Richard. "You can see, I think, that we have survived the fire. But James is in grave danger of losing all his assets. Can you imagine what you would feel like if your house went up in a puff of smoke?"

Richard looked at her and bit the inside

of his mouth. "I would not like it, ma'am."

She continued, "I think you were rightly angry. We shouldn't have taken your fine chaise —"

"Without asking your permission," added James gravely.

"But," Clementina rushed on, "if you knew someone in Philadelphia planned to run off with your valuable ship, wouldn't you do something that perhaps you shouldn't do, out of desperation?"

Not giving Richard time to think of an argument as to why they shouldn't have taken his carriage, James said hurriedly, "I apologize for taking your chaise, Richard. Now would you be so good as to allow me to continue?"

It was a tense moment, and it might have been Clementina's lovely smile that made James relent. "Very well," he said. "It's all dirty now and nothing to boast about. I was only out for a run in it anyway."

Clementina gasped at the amount of money James agreed to pay the young man for any damage to his rig. Surely, after losing his sawmill and perhaps his ship, too, he wouldn't be able to pay that huge sum?

"Let's upright the barrow," suggested James, and Richard gave him a hand to set the carriage on its wheels. They then adjusted the horses, who were by now quieter.

Richard noticed Clementina hobbling towards the carriage. "Why, your lady has been hurt, sir!"

Clementina was flabbergasted to be called James's lady, as she had been when Nancy called him her beau. She was about to deny it when James cut in.

"May I ask another favour, Richard? May I suggest you take Miss Willoby to the Redmarshes' residence in your rig and explain she's had a carriage accident, while I will ride my horse at an easy pace to the shipping office?"

Clementina was at once alarmed to think of James riding alone to try and stop his swindling agent. After being so close to him for twenty-four hours, the parting seemed abrupt and painful. It tore at her heart to think of him leaving to tackle those robbers without help, when he was the one who needed help. If she had not been convinced of his bravery, his intelligence and ingenuity to see him through, she might have tried to stop him. But sensibly, she could see that it would be for the best. It would save time, and she could explain her tattered appearance to the Redmarsh ladies as a simple carriage accident.

But how dreadful she felt when she saw

James mount his horse. Both man and animal were very tired, but had to plod on. James was muddied as well as bleeding and bruised, and his burns looked red and weepy. She wanted to be able to tend those awful wounds. She longed to rush over and kiss him goodbye, but she couldn't rush anywhere with her sore foot. As their eyes met, their pain was shared. She knew the situation was too critical for any more delay.

"Obliged to you, Richard," James called from his horse. "Miss Willoby, I will be in touch." Saluting them both, he turned his mount in the direction of Philadelphia and set off at the fastest pace his horse could manage.

"God bless you, James," she prayed. It worried her that he seemed so confident, so sure he, one man against a crew, could do something to save his ship even at this late stage.

When he'd gone loneliness stuck her. Even Richard's pleasantries and gallantry did not make her feel better. Determined to keep a tight control over her feelings so as not to embarrass the young gentleman who was doing his best to escort her back to the safety of the Redmarsh home, Christina still fell into a deep chasm of gloom.

She feared most that which James faced

as he rode off alone. But selfishly she thought of her own predicament, too. She was just as ruined as he. She had no bright future to look forward to, not even the shop she'd gone to such lengths to acquire. She tried to comfort herself with the knowledge that she'd done all she could. She would have to explain that to the girls when she got back to Bath. And then look for the best job she could find with some other dressmaking establishment.

As for falling in love with James, that was something she would never admit to anyone. Her love would be buried deep in her heart and treasured there. It was better, she thought, to love James, although it would come to nothing, than have no love in her life.

Sadness engulfed her. But Clementina shrugged her slight shoulders. Life had always been hard for her. She did not regret what she'd set from England to do. Although she'd failed, she gained in some ways. She liked America, and the people — with the exception of Hugill — had been very nice to her. They'd been most hospitable. She would go home with good remembrances.

It was just as well the young gentleman driving his racing gig regarded her silence as a sign of fatigue and did not expect her to hold a lively conversation as they approached Philadelphia.

In Philadelphia's shipping office, Nathaniel Spear was trying not to show his exasperation with the wine merchant, who was being very charming, but who was delaying him. It would seem odd if he refused to do business — a very lucrative shipment — with Mr. Redmarsh. If that reputable Philadelphian gentleman required him to ship some cases of wine and he refused, people might ask why. And the last thing Spear wanted at this time was for anyone to be asking questions about the next destination of the *Heron*. Mr. Redmarsh had sailed back from England on the *Heron* after his visit earlier that year. He always chose a reliable shipping line for himself, his family and his wine. Spear had to appear interested, although he knew the *Heron* would be sailing nowhere near the British Isles.

If only the big American gentleman wasn't so garrulous. He was genial, and his anecdotes were amusing, but they did waste so much time. And time was running out. From his office he'd seen the *Heron*'s captain signaling he wanted to get going on the high tide. Spear had had to hurriedly find another disreputable captain when Captain Millard could not be found, and the bos'n, Hugill, had not returned from the hinterland. Agitated, Spear had to sit and listen to a deal that was taking all the afternoon when it would normally take an hour. Most of Ralph Redmarsh's chatter had nothing to do with the shipping arrangements. Spear could have sworn Mr. Redmarsh was trying to delay him on purpose. But for what reason?

He knew that meddling English dressmaker, Miss Willoby, who'd complained about the indentured servants and sent Mr. Hunter down to his office to find out what was going on, was staying with the Redmarsh family. But he need have no worry on that score, for she was well out of the way in Lancaster. Hugill had sent a message to say they were going to dispose of Mr. James Hunter and that English wench. They intended to burn his valuable sawmill down to the ground.

But when news of the fire reached Philadelphia and Mr. Hunter's estate had to be wound up, he had better not be around. Spear knew that, while his swindling might have fooled that young Mr. Hunter, it probably wouldn't fool an accountant's more thorough examination. Indeed, it was necessary to wind up his fraudulent stewardship as soon as possible.

The thought of his coming retirement in the Caribbean made him completely oblivious to what Mr. Redmarsh was saying. He wriggled with excitement on his counting house stool as he contemplated all the joys to come. His coat pocket would be bulging with gold coins. The delights of what he could spend his fortune on would be endless . . .

If only he could think of a way to get rid of the gabbling Mr. Redmarsh and join the ship where his belongings were already stashed. The suspense was making him nervous.

He used the only excuse that came to mind. "Excuse me, Mr. Redmarsh," Spear said, sending a shower of spittle over the merchant's papers, "I am anxious to complete our business right now. I have a family matter to attend to. My wife is enduring a difficult lying-in. Her first child, you know."

Mr. Redmarsh murmured his sympathies, but knew Spear was not telling the truth. Mr. Redmarsh doubted if the defalcating little shipping agent was married. And by no stretch of the imagination could he believe his first child was due to be born that very day. What Spear really wanted was for him to leave his office. How much longer he could prevent the *Heron* from sailing by keeping the shipping agent talking he didn't know. But, Mr. Redmarsh reasoned, every second would give James Hunter more time to return.

Mr. Redmarsh realized he had no proof of any irregularities to report to the Harbor Constable that might keep the ship in dock. If he could get rid of Spear for a short while, he might take a quick glance through his ledgers and find a few solid pieces of evidence.

"My pardon, Mr. Spear," he said, "for keeping you. I suggest you pay a quick visit home to see your wife while I stay here and complete my paperwork, if you don't mind."

Mr. Spear did mind. But what could he do to get the genial American merchant out of his office? He'd planned to take the ledgers with him and throw them overboard. But now he knew he had no choice. If he wanted to sail on the *Heron,* he would have to leave behind the ledgers and Mr. Hunter's undelivered mail. But what did it matter? He knew he'd be safely out of reach, sunning himself on a foreign beach, by the time a summons could be made for his arrest.

Spear's squat figure rose uneasily. He

hated making quick decisions. A calculating man, he'd thought out every last detail of his deceptions with the utmost care. He couldn't stomach this last-minute problem he hadn't envisaged. No way did he want to leave evidence that would incriminate him. But neither did he want to miss the tide. They might sail without him if he lingered any longer.

He wanted to wring Mr. Redmarsh's neck! Especially when he saw him take out his pipe and begin to fill it with tobacco, settling down for a smoke before he got on with his paperwork. "Good evening to you, Mr. Redmarsh, and thank you for your custom," he managed to say, holding his temper in check.

"Good evening to you, Mr. Spear."

Ralph waited until Mr. Spear was halfway down the passage when he went to the door and called him, "One moment, if you please."

Nervously, Spear turned to face him.

"I only want to wish that you find your wife progressing well," he called cheerfully, noting Spear's annoyance.

"My wife?" Spear asked, puzzled for a moment, quite forgetting he was supposed to have one. "Oh, yes, my wife."

"Another mouth to feed, eh?"

Spear was foxed. What was Mr. Redmarsh playing at? Without thinking he said, "Oh, no, sir. We dote on our little ones."

"How many children did you say you had?"

Spear looked totally lost. His face had become crimson as his fists clenched. He turned and ran down the stairs, almost tumbling on the steps.

Away at last, his face changed to an expression of relief. Walking as fast as his short fat legs allowed, he made for the *Heron,* and panted as he rushed up the gangplank.

He had got away.

Within a few minutes the ship, too, had sailed.

Meanwhile, James Hunter was still walking his exhausted horse towards the shipping office. His suffering body was not as tortured as his mind when he failed to see the mast of his ship at his quay.

CHAPTER FIFTEEN

Mr. Redmarsh looked out the window of Spear's office and saw him departing. He then pulled down several large, heavy ledgers, which were arranged on the shelf behind Spear's desk.

Opening one up, he leafed through the pages. His experienced businessman's eyes soon detected discrepancies in the recorded goods transported from England. On the date he'd returned to Philadelphia earlier that year, there was no mention of the indentured servants onboard. He looked at another recent page, which showed the ship full of cargo, but it named goods, which, owing to the law preventing importation of those commodities by the colony, would not have been shipped.

"Harrumph!" he exclaimed. "The rascal has made a large profit from dishonesty!"

Realizing he had probably only found the tip of the iceberg, but at least enough evidence to put Spear in prison, he clutched the ledger and rushed out of the shipping office, hotfooting for the Harbor Constable's office. Fortunately, since he had frequented the harbor for years, Ralph Redmarsh knew the Chief Constable, which made it easier for him to see him without delay and to show him what he'd found in the ledgers Spear kept for James Hunter.

Being a Quaker, the Chief Constable had a particular dislike of the practice of selling indentured servants. Selling human beings conflicted with his belief that all men were equal in the sight of God, and any form of slavery was abhorrent to him.

He jumped at the chance of nabbing the shipping agent, Spear. For some time he'd been concerned that the likeable Mr. James Hunter was too trusting of that agent. The Constable had been on the lookout to warn him — but Hunter was never at his wharf.

"Friend, I perceive thou hast evidence enough to charge Nathaniel Spear," the Constable declared, pleased.

Mr. Redmarsh shook his head sadly. "Alas, I could not detain him long enough for Mr. Hunter to return. I can see from your window the *Heron* has already set sail this evening. It would not surprise me at all if Spear is onboard."

The Constable watched the fine sailing ship heading out to sea. "Don't despair, friend. If thou wilt take my advice . . ." He proceeded to inform Ralph about a fast schooner for hire, with a captain well used to chasing rogue vessels and boarding them.

It took time to find the captain, John MacPherson of the *Jackal,* who was a prime sailor as well as an adventurer eager to be commissioned for such a task. MacPherson was expensive to hire, but Ralph assured them he was willing to pay for Mr. Hunter's ship to be brought back, because he was keen to see justice done.

The Chief Constable, Ralph and Captain MacPherson were discussing matters, and the Constable had just remarked that he hoped the magistrate would be rigorous with Spear if the chase was successful, when he caught sight of a man on horseback riding up to his office.

"Who can that ragamuffin be?" asked the Chief Constable. All three men watched the rider almost fall from his exhausted horse and stagger into the office.

"Why if it isn't James Hunter himself!" declared John MacPherson. "He ha' turned up at the nick o' time to go ahunting his-self."

But Ralph was alarmed to see the state

Mr. Hunter was in. Apart from being so fatigued he could hardly stand, red raw burns covered his skin and his dirty clothes showed signs of being scorched and blacked by dirt and soot.

Exhausted, James had difficulty explaining about the fire in Lancaster. He mentioned to Ralph confidentially that fortunately Clementina had not been burned, but that after a slight carriage mishap on the road, she had gone back to Ralph's house.

"She needs rest," he told Ralph.

No one, however, could persuade Mr. Hunter to rest, or to go to a pharmacy for treatment for his burns. James insisted on joining John MacPherson and the crew of the *Jackal* immediately, to begin searching for his ship.

Mrs. Eleanor Redmarsh, genteelly nibbling her sugar lump and sipping coffee from one of her gilt and rose English china cups, was surprised when her maid barely knocked loudly on the door before bursting into the drawing room.

"La! Martha, what is it, pray?"

"Ma'am, you'd never guess . . ."

"No, I don't suppose I would, girl, so you'd better tell me at once."

"Ma'am, Miss Willoby has arrived — and

you should see the state she's in! She says she's suffered a carriage accident."

Mrs. Redmarsh popped the rest of the sugar lump into her mouth and crunched it hurriedly as she put down her precious china cup with care. Whatever was the world coming to these days? All the talk in Philadelphia these last few months was about dissension with the British. And being of English parentage, she didn't like it. Not that she understood it all, as her husband Ralph seemed to. But the last thing she wanted to hear was about something else disagreeable.

"Martha," she said, swallowing the last of her sugar, "don't just stand there. If Miss Willoby has had an accident, she'll need a tub, clean towels, some lavender soap, and possibly some balm. Go and see to it."

"Yes, ma'am."

Nancy, who'd been playing the harpsichord, came tripping into the room, wondering what was making the servants raise their voices. "My, what a babble is going on, Mama," she exclaimed. "I can't concentrate on my music with all the racket. What has happened?"

Her mother explained all she knew, which wasn't much, so both ladies went to find Clementina.

"Heavens! Poor Clementina!" cried Nancy upon seeing an unbelievably crumpled ragamuffin instead of the well-groomed little dressmaker she knew. "Are you badly hurt?"

"Shall I call for Dr. Blumen?" enquired Eleanor.

"No, no, thank you," Clementina assured the ladies, whose eyes showed they were horrified to see her in such disarray. "I'm not badly injured. Nothing a wash and a spell in bed won't cure. Although if my ankle has not cured itself in a day or so, then a doctor might be able to advise me."

"Tell us what happened," Nancy requested excitedly.

"Would you mind if I tell you later, Nancy, for I am all done in?" Clementina had resumed her role as a politely mannered tradeswoman. She was glad to be back in women's company though. She relished the thought of a bath, washing and dressing her hair, wearing clean clothes — and having a good night's sleep.

"Of course you must have time to recover, my dear," said Eleanor kindly. "But I hope you are soon well again so that you may tell us what occurred on your travels. Did you see Mr. Hunter?"

Clementina, who was now being helped

upstairs, tripped and almost fell at the thought of what was happening to her poor burned man. "Oh yes, indeed, I saw him," she said, wondering how she was going to explain everything that had happened. "May I explain it all to you later . . . that is, when I'm more myself?"

Eleanor, who stood in the hall looking up the stairs as Martha and Nancy helped Clementina mount them, called after her, "My dear, I can see you need to rest now and get over your ragged nerves. When you are better, I shall quiz you about your escapade in the wilderness. Oh, and Clementina, you are much in demand for making gowns. Mrs. Norris says she loves the one you made for her, and wants two others, and Mrs. Sidaway had heard of your skill and would love you to make a gown for her. Then you have two other orders from . . ."

No more was heard because the door closed behind Clementina. She was so glad to be back in her room. She was tremendously thankful she'd been so warmly welcomed back into the Redmarsh household — her safe haven — and swore she would do the same for anyone who ever came to her needing comfort or help. She was also glad to hear the American ladies liked the gowns she'd made for them, and wanted more. So many orders had given her the chance to save some money for her passage back to England.

Clean and comfortable in bed, with the draperies closed to shut out the daylight, Clementina lay wondering how James was getting on. She had a physical yearning to have his muscular body near her. She wanted to recover quickly and to hear him chuckle again. And she hoped sincerely he would have something to be joyful about. Before she could consider all the difficulties he might be in at that moment, she'd gone to sleep.

Hawkes returned on the stagecoach the next day and went straight into Mr. Redmarsh's study to make his report.

"Well, Hawkes, I'm sure glad to see you back safe and sound. And Miss Willoby, too, although she was exhausted and has slept the clock round."

Hawkes was also glad to know Miss Willoby was safe. He was aware he had to be discreet about what he told anyone — especially about Miss Willoby sharing Mr. Hunter's cabin. But as his master already knew Hugill was a villain, he could relate most of what happened during the last couple of days.

Mr. Redmarsh let him recount his story in his own way and in his own time without interruption, glad his wife wasn't there to butt in with her chatter. "You've done well, my man," Ralph declared. But he was concerned when he heard his pistol had been stolen.

Hawkes, in his turn, was sad to hear that Mr. Hunter had arrived in Philadelphia too late to prevent his ship from getting away, and was now on the high seas in the *Jackal,* in pursuit of the *Heron.*

Finally Mr. Redmarsh asked Hawkes, "What do you think has happened to the bos'n, Hugill?"

"That I do not know, sir. His partner was killed, so maybe he also suffered burns and died."

Ralph rubbed his chin thoughtfully. Indeed that could have happened, but it could be that Hugill was now running free, as he might not have reached the *Heron* before she sailed. That was a worry. What was more alarming was the possibility that the arsonist could be carrying the gun he gave Hawkes.

Nancy and her mother could hardly wait to hear all about Clementina's hinterland expedition next morning.

"I saw Mr. Hunter," Clementina said, sitting up in bed and drinking some hot chocolate as the two ladies sat on chairs by her bedside. "Only . . ."

"Yes?" said both rapt ladies together.

"I was there when a fire started and, of course, he had to rush off and help to put it out."

The word fire made the ladies raise their hands in horror. Fire was a major disaster and caused the destruction of much property, and fire sometimes took lives, too. That was why the city of Philadelphia had fire engines.

"I hope it was not too terrible," Eleanor said in a strained voice.

"I'm afraid it was, ma'am. The fire took hold quickly, it being summertime and the wood dry. Men were burned. James, too, and his new sawmill was completely destroyed."

Her listeners put their hands to their mouths as they listened about this tragedy. They didn't notice Clementina use Mr. Hunter's first name.

"What will he do?" asked Nancy.

"He'll rebuild it, of course."

"Where is he now?"

Clementina wondered about that too. She just prayed he was safe. She hadn't had the chance to see Mr. Redmarsh and to find out what he knew. So she answered, "He planned to come to Philadelphia. To see his lawyer, I suppose. That's why Richard Wakefield kindly brought me home."

It may not have been the whole truth, but it was not a lie, and Clementina was glad when the questioning stopped as Eleanor said, "That reminds me. Mr. Percival, who is a lawyer in town, sent you a letter a few days ago. Run downstairs and get it for her, will you, Nancy? It's in my bureau."

Clementina had never received a letter in her life. She wondered why a lawyer would bother writing to her.

Nancy gave her a dimpled smile as she handed her the envelope. The ladies made no attempt to leave her bedchamber. Clementina thought it was because they were just as anxious to know what was in the letter as she. She smiled. The Redmarshes had been so very kind to her, giving her a home that she could not fault. Even their feminine failing of wanting to know everyone's business did not distress her.

Clementina opened the sealed letter and read it through quickly.

Dear Miss Willoby,
    Mr. James Hunter has authorized me

to tell you that he would like you to have the late Mrs. Elizabeth Hunter's house and business in Bath, England. He believes it was his aunt's wish that they should be yours. I have now written out the official documents for you to sign. If you will call in at my office one day, I will arrange for you to sign the papers which will put the premises and the business in your name.

I remain, yours faithfully,
Arthur Percival.
Philadelphia, 1st September, 1774

Embarrassingly, Clementina found it impossible not to weep.

James had given her the shop weeks ago when he knew he couldn't come back to see her immediately and tell her. And when she went to Lancaster, she'd presumed, as he was busy with his sawmill work, that he was delaying making a decision about the shop. Not knowing she'd been given it, she hadn't thanked him. In the short, eventful time she'd been with him the matter hadn't been discussed. So now his late aunt's shop was hers, and she was crying because she was overcome to think James had generously given it to her even before they'd declared their love for each other. Her mission to Philadelphia, to obtain the little shop, had been successful, and Miss Brush and her seamstresses in Bath would be overjoyed, too.

The Redmarsh ladies thought at first the news must be bad, since Clementina was weeping. But with watery eyes, she smiled and handed the letter to Eleanor as she stemmed her tears. "Read it," she croaked.

Nancy rushed round the bed to look over her mother's shoulder, and both squealed with joy when they knew Clementina's wish had come true.

Noises of the crying and screams of delight brought Mr. Redmarsh upstairs with Martha to see what was wrong. "What is it, what is it, Eleanor?" Ralph demanded, standing at the doorway.

The ladies soon enlightened him and he beamed. "I would like to speak to Clementina when she is up," he said before going downstairs again.

So the ladies departed, leaving Martha to help Clementina dress.

Clementina wanted to run down the street singing that she was the proud owner of a shop in Bath. She couldn't wait to get back to England and tell the seamstresses. In her excitement, it was difficult for her to sit still and have her hair brushed.

Still, she hadn't forgotten James's quest and was dying to get downstairs and hear what Mr. Redmarsh had to tell her about him.

Neatly attired, as became a shop-owning mantua-maker, and submerging her natural instincts that had surfaced in the past few days, Clementina went down the staircase — with a little difficulty as her ankle was still sore — to Mr. Redmarsh's study.

Ralph rose politely as she came in. "Ah, Clementina, come in do. You are none the worse for your expedition, I trust?"

"I am recovered. Thank you, sir."

"Close the door and sit down," he said quietly, and she suspected that whatever he had to tell her, he didn't want his wife to overhear.

"Can you tell me, was James Hunter able to save his ship?" she asked anxiously.

"He arrived at the harbor, but his ship had sailed."

"Oh, no!" Clementina's hand flew to her mouth. Despite her efforts to repress her emotions, as she had been disciplined as a child, now that her feelings had been let loose, it was impossible for her to control them as well as she used to.

"All is not lost," Ralph said promptly.

"What hope is there for him?" she asked

miserably, acutely aware of the despair James must be suffering.

"He hired a ship and has gone chasing after the *Heron.* John MacPherson, the captain of the privateer he is on, has a good reputation for bringing back the ships of those sailors who thought they could evade the law."

Clementina started to hope. She sat up rod-straight, her head giving the quick movements of a watching bird. "But he was burnt," she said with feeling.

Ralph leant forward. "Yes, I noticed he was. But a man of his calibre can overlook physical pain when set on a goal. James Hunter is such a man. He may have lost his sawmill, as Hawkes informed me when he arrived yesterday, and rascals might have purloined his ship, but is he going to sit in the hospital and bemoan his lot? You betcha he's not! No, ma'am. Like you, he'll fight his corner." Ralph beamed at her. "And probably win, as you have done."

Clementina swallowed, not sure now if she had really got what she wanted. The shop in Bath, yes, she had wanted it. But wasn't her heart telling her she wanted something else? Something she desired even more than the shop. "Have you heard anything more from James? Where is he sailing? Has he had any success in finding the *Heron*?"

Ralph put up his large hands to fend off the battery of questions. "No. Naturally I've heard nothing yet. It is early days. It may be some time before Mr. Hunter's ship is seen on the high seas. The Chief Constable at the harbor is a friend of mine, and he will inform us as soon as anything is known."

Mr. Redmarsh was too kind-hearted to say it, but Clementina knew they were both worried that the *Heron* might never be found. The ocean was huge. It would be difficult, almost impossible, to follow a ship when you didn't know where it was going, although they hoped Captain MacPherson, who had a nose for sniffing out rogue vessels, would locate it. But even if the *Heron* was spotted, an attempt to board her might not succeed. The weather might present difficulties. Many disasters happen at sea.

"Oh dear, I do so hope James will be all right!" Clementina's cry from the heart touched Ralph, who came and patted her on the shoulder. "I believe he has a good chance," he said, giving her as much comfort as he could.

He returned to his chair and regarded her thoughtfully until he felt she was properly composed and ready to listen. "Now, there are several other matters to attend to. First you must go to Mr. Percival's office and sign the documents as soon as possible."

"Will not James require the shop in Bath now? I mean, as he has lost everything. Won't he need the money from the sale of the shop to start up his business ventures again?"

Ralph chuckled. "My dear young lady, James Hunter is a very wealthy man. He's not going into debt because he has lost a couple of assets, valuable as they are. No, I believe James Hunter could afford to buy two more ships if he wanted them!"

Clementina was staggered. She sat, stunned, for a moment or two. "Oh, well," she said at last, blinking fast, "then I needn't worry about taking the shop."

"No, indeed."

She sat as if in a dream, then said sadly, "I suppose I should return to England . . ." Then an urge from her heart made her add, "But I'd like to wait a while and make sure James is safe and well before I go."

But was she wise to delay? She was devastated to learn any lingering hope she had that she and James were meant for each other had vanished. He was a very rich man, which made him completely out of her range. He wouldn't want to marry a poor mantua-maker.

Feeling sorry for James's predicament was a waste of time. It was her own future that needed settling.

Ralph interrupted her thoughts. "Which brings me to another important matter. I think I mentioned there was going to be a meeting of the Continental Congress in Philadelphia in September?"

Clementina, with her thoughts on her dilemma, was uninterested, but she nodded politely.

"Well, I regret to have to tell you that when it was held, the congressmen decided they would stand up to the British government. They will not trade with Britain any longer — until Parliament removes the unfair taxes they have been heaping on us colonists. The truth is, many Americans want to be independent from Britain. We are now capable of ruling ourselves."

Clementina's interest became acute. "Oh, dear me, that has set the cat amongst the pigeons."

"Oh, indeed, it has. I foresee a head-on clash before long. You may have trouble finding a safe passage home if you linger here much longer."

Bowing her head, Clementina gave a sigh. "That is right, sir, I ought to leave soon," she said. Indeed, she must go before hostilities between her country and the country she had grown to love broke out.

But although she'd talked herself into leaving America, she couldn't feel enthusiastic about returning to her shop and her hardworking life in Bath.

CHAPTER SIXTEEN

The stiflingly hot weather of summer was over. The leaves bore touches of red and gold, signifying the start of the fall. Clementina knew her time in Philadelphia was drawing to an end.

Clementina had seen Mr. Percival, James Hunter's lawyer, signed the forms, and now the shop in Bath officially belonged to her. She felt sure Mrs. Elizabeth Hunter would have approved and commended her nephew for his generosity. And the shop girls, too, would rejoice when they received her letter to Miss Brush telling them their jobs were secure.

Now she hadn't any reason to delay any longer and would have to leave America — wouldn't she? She asked herself that question several times a day but never answered it.

Before she fell asleep each night, she looked at the pretty blue and rich cream *toile de jouy* printed wall fabric decorating her bedchamber. The pastoral scenes showing a shepherd and shepherdess in idyllic rural surroundings made her think of James and herself. But she now knew how vast, wild and beautiful the American countryside was. Not at all as romantic as the attractive French illustrations depicted the countryside. The pictures didn't show the hard existence of living in a log cabin — of having to survive the freezing winters, heavy drifts of snow and howling winds.

Being in love was not an ideal state, either. It made her feel light-headed at times, as if her feet were not really on the ground, yet at other times she felt the pain of knowing her love might never be hers. And leaving America would definitely put an end to her romance.

She tried to think of a reason to stay. One reason would be that she'd really like to thank James personally for giving her the shop. That was why, she told herself, she'd been delaying making up her mind to sail. Also, her sewing work was booming. She'd had to find two girls to help her with all the orders she was getting for gowns for the Philadelphian ladies.

"Clementina, my dear," Eleanor had said one day. "One of the shopkeepers in town is moving to Canada because of discontent with English rule here. I was wondering if you could use that empty shop, as you must find it very crowded working in your room."

"Oh, dear me, am I being a nuisance?" Clementina said immediately. She pursed her lips and then said, "I realize the maid can't get in to clean my room for all the stuff around, and the ladies coming here for a fitting are tramping up and down your stairs all day long."

"No, my dear, those customers of yours don't bother me. I like to see them and hear all their gossip. I was really thinking that as the weather becomes wintry, your seam-stresses won't be able to sit outside on the veranda to sew. They will need a warm room in which to work. And the bales of material you require to show your customers keep growing, and they can't be kept in the outhouse as they'll be in danger of being spoiled . . ."

Eleanor took a deep breath before chattering on. The beautiful fabrics that were imported from France flashed though Clementina's mind. British merchandise was not permitted to be imported, but the French stuffs were, and they were very fine indeed. Clementina enjoyed working with them. No way did she want to see them spoilt. "Indeed, ma'am, I would not want any harm to come to those expensive fabrics."

Eleanor went on, "Quite so. Ralph and I thought, as your business is so successful, you might like to take over the little shop in Silver Street. The present owners are anxious to sell the property quickly and want very little for it. So what do you think?"

Oh, my. Clementina's head spun. "Ma'am, I, er, I can't. I mean . . . I will have to think about it."

"If you are concerned about a down payment, I'm sure Ralph would be willing to make that for you. Why, with the amount of work you have, and you are so quick at it, I'm sure you would soon be able to pay him back."

Clementina thought so too. If she wanted to stay . . . did she want to stay? How unbearably difficult it was for her to make up her mind. Perhaps it wouldn't matter if she waited until the spring before she sailed for England. There was a lot of talk about the growing conflict with Britain — but nothing had happened as Ralph had predicted. Maybe the two sides would come to their senses and would become friends again. Most American colonists were as anxious as she was to see any trouble blow over. But the British were so stiff-necked and the Patriots so hotheaded.

If only James Hunter would come back. With or without his ship, she longed to see him again.

She knew Ralph went down to the harbor daily hoping to see the *Jackal,* and even visited The Anchor Tavern in case he might hear some chance remark by sailors about sighting the *Jackal* or the *Heron.* But each time he returned, he had to shake his head sadly when he met Clementina's inquiring eyes.

One day he did come back with a letter for her though. A ship from England had brought it over.

It was from Bath. She hurriedly tore it open. It was from Matilda Brush. Surprisingly the date was quite recent, the fifteenth of November.

Honoured Madam,

I trust you are in good health. Your long absence has made me take some decisions concerning the shop merchandise. I trust you will approve. French silk is prohibited, so I have taken the liberty of accruing a good stock of silk from Spitalfields. Fashionable ladies have taken to wearing their hair very high on their heads in the French style. Adorning it with fancies such as flowers, feathers, ribbons and bobbin lace . . .

Clementina smiled when she read that and was glad most American ladies were not as vain or as impractical as their British sisters.

. . . I have been asked to advise them on the design of these fancy headdresses to match their gowns. Consequently, I have added embroidered nets, beads, gauze, extra ribbons and laces to our stock to accommodate this latest mode . . .

Clementina had no doubt Miss Brush would be able to cope with this latest fashion exceedingly well, as it was her forte to mix and match fabric, colors and textures. In fact, Clementina was quite glad she wasn't there and had to tell the ladies how fine they looked with all that superfluous finery balanced on their heads. Miss Brush ended the letter:

The shop trade is excellent. The order list keeps us busy all day long. The girls are content, but I fear have too much

work to do. May I engage another seamstress?

My kindest respects to you,
Miss Willoby.
Matilda Brush.

Clementina folded the letter thoughtfully.
So the shop in Bath was doing very well
without her. Miss Brush was doing better
than coping; the business was thriving.
Reading between the lines, Clementina
detected that Matilda Brush had gained
confidence and was as capable of running
the shop as she was. There was no mention
of Princess Amelia, but then, if Miss Brush
had not been able to pacify the awful lady,
what did it matter? The business seemed to
be doing quite well without royal patron-
age.

Therefore, she could stay until the spring,
couldn't she? She would write a reply to the
letter and tell Miss Brush that the shop in
Bath was now hers and ask Miss Brush to
continue running it as she thought best. In
the meantime she would take the opportunity of having a shop of her own in Philadelphia over the winter months.

Not only Eleanor and Nancy, but Ralph
as well, welcomed her decision to stay. "You
have a home here as long as you want it,"

Eleanor assured her.

Days went by pleasantly and Nancy's wedding was soon occupying the Redmarsh household's minds. Nancy's wedding dress had been a particular joy to make, yet, as Clementina made other garments suitable for married ladies, a little nagging pain of jealousy had to be dispelled. Clementina would have loved to be marrying her beau, just as Nancy was marrying hers.

A carpenter was hired to make Nancy a Pennsylvanian bridal chest ready to be filled with household linens. "It's traditional in Pennsylvania to have a 'Dutch' chest like this," Nancy explained, caressing the large wooden box painted with bright colors. "Dutch means German, of course."

It didn't seem logical to Clementina, and she laughed. However, they had fun buying and making items to fill the chest. It struck Clementina, though, that she would miss Nancy when she was married and went to live with her husband, Henry Fisher.

The wedding gifts began to arrive and crowded the small parlor: a Staffordshire dinner set; baluster-stemmed wine glasses and a lily pad—ornamented decanter; a silver chocolate pot and Monteith punch bowl. And a glittering canteen of solid silver knives, spoons and forks.

A number of elegant furniture pieces were ordered for Nancy's new home, to be made by Affleck, an American cabinetmaker with the highest standards. Since she was an only child, Mr. and Mrs. Redmarsh's daughter was very fortunate to be set up so well for her future married life.

Ralph told Clementina he thought it best Nancy should have the wedding over and be settled in her new home before any hostilities with the British began. As he told her confidentially, it was sure to happen soon. The local militia was asking for volunteers. They were arming themselves and practicing to fight when the British weren't looking.

Some Americans insisted the quarrel would soon blow over and continued toasting the king. Others saw themselves as Americans, and said they didn't want to continue living under unfair British rule. Clementina was too busy to notice any signs of a revolution, and Ralph didn't want to spoil his daughter's wedding by repeating the alarming reports he'd heard about of outbreaks of revolt in the colonies.

It was the day before the wedding and Clementina was coming back from her dressmaking shop via the Callowhill Market.

It was a little later than she would normally walk back alone, as she'd had some tidying up to do. Night was falling and the street lamps were being lit. After sitting sewing most of the day, she felt she needed to stretch her legs, so she walked quickly.

She was humming a little tune to herself and wondering if her gown of floral peach was the best to wear for tomorrow's celebration. She was very conscious nowadays of having to be punctilious about her own dress, as an advertisement of her skill as a dressmaker. It was so rewarding to see the painted sign, *Clementina Willoby, Mantua-maker,* over the door of her establishment in Silver Street, and to have gained a fine reputation in Philadelphia as an excellent dressmaker. Here in Philadelphia, she was looked up to as a professional business-woman, not simply as a skilled trade worker, as she was in England. Attitudes were so important. And in Philadelphia she was looked upon favorably.

Shouts from a distance became louder, and she noticed a crowd of boisterous youths approaching, but she didn't realize they were racing down the street towards her until it was too late to avoid them. Her mood changed to one of anxiety.

It was evening, and men who'd been

drinking too much after work were capable of loutish behavior. Clementina stopped walking and tried to shelter in a doorway as the stick-welding mob came nearer.

Listening to their loud taunts was even more frightening. "Drub the British!" some were shouting. "Let's get the lobsters and boil 'em."

Clementina knew they were referring to the red-coated British soldiers. She was shocked. She was aware of the disagreements between her country and the colonies, but she'd had no idea there was actual *hatred* for the British. Ralph had hinted at a revolt by some who called themselves patriots, but this was the first time Clementina had witnessed such behavior.

Calling, shouting and threatening, the crowd pushed by her. To her relief, they didn't seem to notice her crouched in a doorway. When they'd passed she was trembling, frightened by their loud, threatening behavior. She was a loyal British citizen and wished she were back in England.

Now she desperately wanted to get back to the safety of the Redmarsh house and began to hurry up the street, only to be met by another group of lads whose coarse language and rough appearance made her heart quicken and her neck hairs prick with fear. How was she to get past them? Would they guess she was English or think she was an expensively attired Tory lady of the sort these young men ridiculed? What would they say or do to her in their openly aggressive state?

Just as her fear was preventing her from thinking straight she felt firm hands take hold of her. She screamed. Whoever was holding her practically lifted her off the ground and hustled her into a side street.

Then, to her alarm, she realized the gentleman holding her was in no hurry to let her go!

"Clementina." She heard the rich timbre of a familiar voice that sent an orchestral sensation of delight through her.

"James!"

Indeed, it was James Hunter. She found it difficult to believe that the man who had occupied her dreams for weeks, the man she loved and who loved her, was back safe. She clung to him with gasps of joy.

He continued to hold her, firmly, protectively. Her body relaxed, knowing it was he. She glanced up at his face. He looked stern, but not at the mob that was passing.

"Are you hurt?" he asked when the noise of the demonstrators faded.

"No. Not at all. I was merely frightened."

He did not smile at her. "You are exceedingly foolish!"

Staggered to hear his rebuke when she wanted to say how pleased she was to see him and expected him to say something similar, she stiffened. "I was walking home from work. I didn't know those ruffians were about."

"At this hour, it is asking for trouble for a lady to walk the streets alone. Especially as elegantly dressed up as you are."

This made Clementina wince. "I don't walk the streets. As a rule I come home earlier. I just happened to have been a little late today," she said in a prim, disappointed voice. He'd come back with a dictatorial attitude; his mouth had hardened. He certainly wasn't the loving man she'd expected him to be.

She heard him draw in a deep breath, and she wondered what else he found wrong with her. This was a fine homecoming, wasn't it? She'd waited for him, and now that he was here, all he could do was criticize her. "I couldn't help meeting those American louts!" she said.

"They are not louts. They are men put out of work by the British government's insensitive treatment of the colonists with their stupid taxes."

"Everyone has to pay taxes," she snapped back. "No one likes it."

He ignored her tart remark and took her arm, walking her fast towards the Redmarsh residence.

It was unfortunate they'd met again in a difficult situation. But a far worse fear now struck Clementina. James was obviously fit and well, and she needn't worry about his well-being nor whether he'd found his ship. She knew he was rich enough not to be debt-ridden even if he'd lost it. But he was showing her as clearly as the mob did that he was a patriotic American! And she was not. She was an Englishwoman to the bone.

She hadn't in her wildest dreams expected Mrs. Elizabeth Hunter's English nephew to support the American side of the conflict. And yet she should have. He was an American now, wasn't he? He'd lived over here for years and did not plan to return to England.

But she certainly did intend to go back now. She liked the Americans and they'd been very good to her, but she wasn't going to be disloyal to her own country and take the American side in this dispute. It broke her heart to know she still loved James, and at the same time she also loved England, the land where she was born, and whose people she knew.

As she strode along with James, her heart was thumping. Winter was approaching and she couldn't contemplate returning to England until the weather was calmer. The Atlantic became less ferocious in springtime. It seemed a long time to wait until next year. But she would have to wait, as she had missed her chance to go earlier. Disappointed and upset, she prayed James would go away and rebuild his sawmill and leave her to continue with her mantuamaking.

They were almost at the front gates. Clementina decided that, as Nancy's wedding was to take place in the morning, she had to be diplomatic with James. She wouldn't spoil Nancy's big day by showing how upset she was. An iron resolve to hide her feelings took over.

"Did you find your ship?" she asked in a friendly voice.

He seemed to understand that as a guest in the house they were approaching, he shouldn't show any dissent between them either. "Yes," he said, becoming a charming gentleman again. "We caught the *Heron.* Wily Captain John MacPherson in his fast-running *Jackal,* was soon on the *Heron*'s heels, and without Hugill there to sail the ship, the *Heron's* captain hadn't a chance. We brought him and Nathaniel Spear back in chains. They are now in prison."

"Oh." Clementina found it was a lot to take in, as they were about to enter the house. There was so much she'd like to know, so much she'd like to ask him.

But she detected that he'd changed. His boyishness was gone. In the last few months, he'd acquired maturity. He seemed to her to be more attractive as an older man. She paused by the door to ask, "What happened to the bos'n, Hugill?"

"We don't know."

Clementina's teeth pressed her lip thoughtfully. "Well I suppose it doesn't matter what happens to him. You got your ship back."

"Yes, I did, thanks to you." He was looking into her eyes deeply and smiled. She blushed.

Annoyed to think he had such power over her, she turned her head away, and saw Nancy running downstairs with Henry in tow to greet them. Her dimpled smile was genuine as she cried, "Clementina! James! It is lovely to see you both together again. I thought you would find her, James, when I suggested you walk towards her shop. And you must be tired, Clementina, after such a long day at work." She rushed up and kissed them both, saying cheerily, "You're just in time for dinner."

It was not necessary for Clementina to tell her of the mob in town. James didn't mention it either. It was Nancy's wedding day eve, and both she and Henry were young, in love, and no one should spoil their happy day.

Clementina felt a moment of envy. Nancy's love for Henry was so straightforward, so uncomplicated. She envied them. Her love for James was in a tight coil.

CHAPTER SEVENTEEN

They assembled for dinner in the Redmarshes' fine dining room. Glass and silverware sparkled on the highly polished mahogany table. Six starched white napkins awaited Nancy and her betrothed, proud mama, Clementina, and her beau, the ruggedly handsome gentleman, James Hunter.

As soon as they sat down at the table, Ralph came hurrying in. He looked relieved to see Clementina and then smiled at James sitting beside her. "I'm glad you found Clementina, and brought her safely back, Mr. Hunter. I heard from Hawkes there was a riot in town this evening."

"Oh, I wouldn't have called it a riot, sir," said James quickly, "although I daresay the British might call it that. There were just a few lads marching about with sticks in their hands complaining about losing their employment since Congress told us to stop trading with Britain."

This explanation seemed to placate the Redmarsh ladies, but Clementina paled. She'd been in the thick of the riot and she didn't consider it to have been just a few lads marching about with sticks! Something far more sinister had surfaced in the hearts and minds of those men. Some had been shouting words like "Liberty," although they looked like free men to her. They were certainly free enough to shout their curses, opinions, and slogans.

"Harrumph!" Ralph sat down at the head of the table. Everyone knew it was bad manners to talk politics or to make a guest feel uncomfortable, so he let the matter drop and said to his daughter pleasantly, "Nancy, my dear, I'll drink a toast to you because tomorrow you will be not only my dear daughter, but also a wife. To Mrs. Henry Fisher . . ."

He got no further as tears began to run down Eleanor's face. Clementina got up quickly to put her arm around Nancy's emotional mama.

"Oh, how could you remind me that I am losing my daughter, Ralph?" Eleanor said as she pressed her handkerchief to her watering eyes.

"She's my beloved daughter too, Eleanor. And the sooner you get used to your little chick leaving the nest the better, my dear. Nancy ain't crying."

Nancy giggled. "Oh, Mama, don't upset yourself. Henry and I will be living very close by and I can visit you any day."

That seemed to pacify her doting mama, whose quivering mouth curved into a smile, and the meal was served.

Unfortunately, Clementina found it difficult to enjoy the feast. She had no appetite. Sitting next to James was a joy — but an agony, as well.

Having him back was wonderful. He was in good health, too. His burns had healed. But she had a dilemma. James had returned from his journey a different man. A boy had left Philadelphia, but an older and harder man had returned — a gentleman totally opposed to Britain, the country to which she was loyal. Perhaps he'd held those opinions for some time, but she hadn't known his views. It was so disappointing. She had not envisaged that they would be at loggerheads when they met again.

She was convinced he still had a *tendre* for her. But somewhere in the chase after the ship, he'd lost his love for her — or so it seemed to her. She felt like a trapped English mouse, sitting amongst all the hearty Americans who were laughing and talking as if they didn't have a worry in the world.

Ralph caught her eye and she wondered if he guessed she wasn't enjoying the meal. Nancy and Henry didn't notice her unhappiness, being too wrapped up in their premarital bliss. Clementina considered it right that they should be happy.

But why shouldn't she enjoy happiness too? Hadn't orphans a right to be contented, just as richer folk were? She shook herself. Self-pity was not something Clementina usually indulged in. She reminded herself that she had a successful business. In fact, by goodness, she owned *two* fine dressmaking shops at the moment!

She turned to James and said softly, as the conversation continued on the other side of the table, "I'd like to thank you with all my heart for giving me the shop in Bath." His eyes met hers. Such wonderful eyes he had; she could gaze into them all night.

He replied with a little lift at the corner of his mouth, "I'm pleased you appreciate it. You might like to know the Harbor Constable raided my former agent's office and found some letters from my aunt that Spear had not delivered to me. One of them said she wanted to leave the shop to you. So you would have got it anyway."

"Nevertheless, I do thank you," she repeated, knowing he'd kindly given her the shop before the missing letters were discovered. She added, "And I'm sure the seamstresses would thank you just as warmly if they were here. It was just as important for them not to be thrown out of work."

"So now do you understand why those lads in town were in a rage this evening?"

No, Clementina did not. "My seamstresses would not have caused havoc in Bath even if they had lost their jobs," she replied tartly.

"Yes, the English are inclined to be a bit straitlaced," he rejoined.

"Well, Mr. Hunter, being an Englishman, you ought to know!"

"Miss Willoby, I wouldn't call myself an Englishman now, any more than you would call yourself an orphan. We might have been born in those situations, but I have made my home here in Pennsylvania, and although the beautiful gowns you make and wear do you credit, you would look quite out of place in an orphanage I think. Eh?" His eyes questioned her, as if he were a teacher demanding a pupil to give him an answer she had to puzzle out.

He was reasonable. Clementina gave him credit for that. He was polite. But he was not loyal. She pursed her lips, trying to decide how she could answer him.

At this point Eleanor's voice broke into their quiet *tête-à-tête*. "And what are you two talking about, pray? Or shouldn't I ask?"

She clearly expected them to be having a lovers' whispered conversation. But Clementina didn't blush as everyone looked at them. James casually picked up the biscuit platter and passed it to Clementina. "I was about to tell Clementina about how we caught my crooked agent."

"Oh, yes, do tell us the story," begged Nancy.

"Do you want all the gory details, Miss Redmarsh?" James was funning her as he took a sip of wine.

"Indeed I do, Mr. Hunter. Every one of them."

He laughed and took a mouthful of bread, chewing it slowly as if he were teasing her by keeping her waiting. Then he swallowed it. "And you, Miss Willoby, have you a desire to hear it all?" He turned to her and winked.

Her heart soared. He wasn't intending to keep up a quarrel with her.

"Yes, indeed. I'm just as curious."

Clementina thought immediately how proud she felt of James. He was a man who had tremendous energy for physical work and the endurance to overcome pain. He could sail to the West Indies and back, as easily as she might walk to her shop and return in the evening. And now he'd revealed that he was taking up the challenge of resisting the British laws Americans viewed as unjust. She might think he was wrong to do so, but she was impressed by his conviction that the colonists were in the right. He was a man of ideas who could act on them, as he had done by creating his sawmill. And she could understand why Nancy's sparkling eyes were fixed on him, because as well as being a man of action, he could be a charming ladies' man, too, when he wanted to be.

She didn't envy Nancy her nice but solid Henry. She was sure Henry would make Nancy a fine husband. But compared with James, he seemed an insignificant man.

James was powerful and dashing. He was a man she respected, although she had a difference of opinion with him. When she was with him, as she was now, he made her feel complete. When he kissed her, there was nothing in the world she wanted more. And when he was not with her, she was lonely.

While the others listened avidly to his account, it was his voice Clementina enjoyed listening to. "When we set sail on the *Jackal,* we were behind the *Heron* by some days. We thought he would be making for the Caribbean, so we sailed in that direction. I was unwell for many days, but MacPherson knew the route. His fast schooner made good progress and the captain, not expecting anyone to hunt him, was in no hurry."

James began to eat again and Nancy cried out in suspense, "Mr. Hunter, you cannot eat in the middle of such an exciting story."

Everyone chuckled as James dabbed his mouth with his napkin and said, "You must appreciate, Miss Redmarsh, that I have been living on salt beef and ship's biscuits for the past two months. Do not deny me an excellent meal."

Nancy said of course he could eat, but would he please be quick about it.

Everyone laughed. Even Clementina enjoyed his showmanship. His recent travels had seemingly given him the chance to take a rest from his physically demanding job in the backwoods, and time not only to form his opinions about the ideas that were afoot, but also to enjoy a little acting, which showed he hadn't lost his sense of humor.

He went on, "When the captain discovered we were on his tail, he led us a pretty dance. We lost him at one stage, owing to the difficult winds and tides around the Caribbean. And when we finally caught up with the *Heron,* MacPherson boarded the ship and put the captain in irons. He confessed he'd dropped Spear off in Barbados. So, leaving a crew of experienced sailors to sail my ship back to Philadelphia, we went on to hunt Spear there." This time James made a great show of drinking his wine, telling his host how delicious the wine was, which led to his glass being filled again, keeping his audience in suspense.

Clementina was enjoying the fun and was so intrigued by James's account of what happened that her appetite returned. So she ate and enjoyed her meal. She turned to James and said laughingly, "I'm not at all surprised you found Nathaniel Spear led you a merry dance — he'd been doing it for years!"

James's eyes glinted, and he then gave her a flirtatious wink that shocked her into silence. He then continued, "We caught him by accident. Spear has rotten teeth and has an unfortunate habit of spitting as he talks. One evening when Captain MacPherson and I were walking by a market stall we heard a big Negro trader complaining loudly about his well-laid-out vegetables and fruits being spat on."

"Oh I sympathize. I've been sprayed on by him myself," remarked Ralph, grimacing.

"Ugh!" exclaimed Nancy.

As all eyes were fixed on him, James finished his meal and sat back, saying, "The spitter was a squat gentleman who wore a new-looking suit in gaudy colors that bespoke wealth rather than fit or good taste. The stupid fellow began to abuse the trader in angry tones, attracting attention to himself. I suddenly realized who it was buying a hand of bananas."

"Spear!" said Nancy, entranced.

"Yes indeed, and he wasn't pleased to see me, I can tell you! We collared him easily, as he was too amazed even to try and run or fight."

After seeing James fighting with Richard Wakefield, Clementina was not surprised to hear Spear had given in easily. "What excuses did he make?" she asked.

"Poor Spear had words tumbling out of his mouth to protest his innocence. But even he knew the game was up. He was furious to know that his new life of luxury was over. Mind you, it's my opinion he wouldn't have lasted there for long anyway. His attitude towards the natives was such that they would probably have tipped him into the sea to feed the sharks before long!"

Laughter rang through the dining room. The atmosphere was as joyful as a pre-wedding occasion should be. Everyone, including Martha, who was serving, enjoyed a chuckle.

As the dessert was served and the nuts and fruit were placed on the table and Ralph ordered an especially fine wine to toast the couple about to wed, Clementina heard Eleanor ask James what he intended to do now. Her ears pricked up.

"Well," he drawled like an American, "I guess I'll need to give it some thought."

Clementina found her fingers curling around a tendril of hair falling by the side of her face. Would she figure in his future? Pride and frustration prevented her from asking him.

After-dinner coffee was served in the drawing room. While they drank it, Nancy entertained them with some charmingly played pieces on the harpsichord.

Clementina noticed that James and Ralph chose to sit together and were holding a lively conversation. She wanted to hear what they were saying. She imagined they were discussing the colonies' worsening relationship with Britain. And because she noticed them glance at her once in a while, she guessed they were discussing her, too.

In fact, James and Ralph were discussing the political dilemma, as well as the attractive little mantua-maker sitting across the room. "I can't continue my shipping business with the Bristol and Philadelphia trade route at a standstill," James complained. "I can use the *Heron* to take passengers to England, because many want to go right now. But I doubt if many Englishmen will want to come to Pennsylvania at present."

Ralph nodded.

James said angrily, "The British have taken to commandeering our ships. I met several American seamen in the West Indies who told me they'd been left stranded in Barbados because they refused to sail under the British flag. I brought a number of them back with me to Philadelphia, but merchantmen jobs are hard to find at present."

Ralph said quietly, "I know the city fathers are concerned about so many men being out of work. Some of the jobless are joining the militia, which I regret, as I feel sure if we arm ourselves it won't be long before we are fighting the British."

James drained his coffee cup. "I guess that's what I'll end up doing. I can't bring myself to go into the backwoods and rebuild my sawmill at a time when there is so much unrest in the country. And my privateer can be used to harass British shipping; it's faster than a man-of-war —"

"Keep your voice down," hissed Ralph, "I don't want the ladies to be alarmed. I belong to the Philadelphian Society where we discuss issues of importance, and I sense the building up of determination to defy the British. There is a strong feeling our colonies should unite and form one nation. A proposal will be put to the next Congress. But the British are going to object. So I suppose we'd better prepare to fight."

"We'll have a long, bitter struggle on our hands if it comes to war. But we'll have to do it, or forever be like marionettes on strings with the British using us to dance to their tune."

Ralph shifted in his chair. "I regret it has come to this. By the way, I notice you keep glancing at Clementina. What will you do about her?"

James made a rueful face. "That I do not know. I will admit to you that I hoped she would marry me, but I believe she is strongly loyal to Britain. She's a staunch English lady."

"Yet she seems to have settled down here very well. She is well liked, and has no relatives back in England."

"That is so, Ralph. And I daresay if I were prepared to keep my head down in this coming conflict and return to rebuild my sawmill, she might consider marrying me. But I do not intend to take a back seat. I want the conflict settled in our favor, so I must do my best to help the cause."

"And Miss Willoby?"

James sighed. "I would not wish any harm to come to her. If she is unwilling to change her allegiance then, alas, she will return to England and I will lose her."

"I hope it will not come to that."

James stood up and prepared to walk over to talk to Clementina, "So do I. Therefore, if you will excuse me, I will waste no time in trying to persuade her that her future is with me in this developing country."

Ralph smiled. He knew Clementina Willoby would not be easy to win over. But then, neither could he see James Hunter on the losing side of any fight. That young man had matured and was one of a new breed of Americans. He'd help to forge a new country that would rule itself.

Clementina started when she saw James approaching, but could not help giving him a smile. He looked so handsome and she yearned to get up and rush to embrace him.

He brought up a chair and sat by her. "Clementina," he said quietly, "I would ask you not to walk around alone in town."

Her smile faded. "Do you think I might meet another mob?"

"It is likely. You must know these are unsettled times. Tempers are rising. The American colonies are in a state of ferment —"

"You mean some of the colonists are becoming rebels."

He gave a short laugh. "View it as you like. I say they are preparing to stand up and fight for their rights. And I have decided to help them."

This blatant statement of fact shook Clementina. Her eyes blazed as her mouth formed a tight moue. "You can't do that — fight against your own people!"

"May I remind you that there was a civil war in Britain during the last century? The king's men fought Cromwell, remember?"

Clementina felt he had dealt her a mortal blow. All hope of them ever joining in matrimony — which had never been certain — had blown away like dandelion fluff. But she was not going to show him how distressed she was. Whatever he believed in was no concern of hers now. She'd decided she'd go back to England.

He looked at her pale face, her downcast eyes, and sighed. He knew it was going to be a difficult task to make her change her mind. Perhaps he never would. But he didn't feel the despair she did. He thought he had plenty of time to make her understand why he was going to fight for the Americans. And it was likely to be a long time before she could return to England even if she wanted to.

"Clementina," he said, wanting to take her hand but afraid she might snatch it away, "Clementina, listen. I want you to know that I do appreciate how you're feeling. I don't scorn your loyalty to Britain. I find it admirable. Many people here think as you do." He tried to make her smile. "I just hope you will come to understand how I feel. I have reasoned that America, which is so far from England, should be allowed to settle its own affairs."

James might have said more, but he could see it was not the right time to try and woo her. Despite her iron self-control, she looked as if she might burst into tears — and that would never do at a pre-wedding party.

CHAPTER EIGHTEEN

A shaft of misty autumnal sun shone through the bedchamber window and high-lighted Nancy's figure in her bridal gown, making her appear as ethereal as an exquisite flower.

"You are absolutely beautiful, Nancy," exclaimed Clementina, who was kneeling on the floor adjusting her hem.

Breathless with happiness, Nancy stooped and kissed Clementina's cheek. "Thank you for making me this wonderful gown. I feel like a princess."

Clementina chuckled, having known and dressed crotchety Princess Amelia. She stood and looked at the bride in her white and silver gown reflected in the fretwork looking glass, and hid a sigh. Henry, she thought, was a fortunate man to have such a beautiful bride. And Nancy was lucky to be marrying a good man.

Caught up as she'd been in the excitement

of the wedding preparations of the last few weeks, all traces of jealousy had long left Clementina. She had accepted she would never be a bride, but wanted to enjoy Nancy's happiness. And she was enjoying it.

Nancy's wedding dress, even by Clementina's high standards, was a masterpiece, made with all her skill and loving care. Clementina was proud of her handiwork. "I'm thrilled you love your dress, Nancy," she said, smiling.

Nancy's dimpled smile thanked her. "Henry tells me he's wearing an embroidered white waistcoat and white breeches. So this ribbed white silk should make us a pair," she purred as she stroked the folds of her long gown and lightly fingered the low, square frilled neckline and the ruffles of silver edging lace on the cuffs of the slim-fitting sleeves.

Clementina walked around the bride, adjusting the curls of her dark hair, and the headdress wreath of lily of the valley and ribbons. She lightly pulled the gown's long train out. Then she said, "There, Nancy, my dear, you are perfect." Satisfied her expertise was no longer required, she stood back, ready to open the door for her friend.

It was a poignant moment Clementina shared with Nancy, as the virgin bride stood looking wistfully back at her bedchamber. Perhaps she was remembering her happy childhood before going forth to meet her bridegroom and the next stage of her life.

The magical moments were disturbed by the bride's mother, who came bustling into the bedchamber in her blue silk, striped gown. "Ah, you look divine, just divine, my darling Nancy," she said, kissing her daughter with pride.

Clementina, fearing the lady might shed a few tears, stepped up to fuss around Mrs. Redmarsh's dress.

"Now this is for you," Eleanor said, handing Nancy a small, flat leather jewel case. Nancy opened it and exclaimed, "Mama, these sparkling stones are just beautiful!"

"They are real sapphires and a present from your papa and me."

Nancy's eyes were shining as brightly as the sapphires as Clementina clasped them around the bride's slender neck. For Eleanor had asked her to put them on her daughter as she declared, "I am too nervous to do anything today, my dears."

Clementina was delighted to see how well this surprise wedding gift from her parents gave the final touch of beauty to the dazzlingly attractive bride.

"Now we must start off for the church

straight away. Papa is waiting downstairs, pacing the hall like a wild animal in a cage. I fear his tailor has made his new velvet suit a little tight for his paunch, and he says that if we do not hurry, the minister will be standing waiting, thinking perhaps he has come to perform the ceremony on the wrong day!"

Nancy giggled a little nervously.

"We'd better go then, before the groom thinks so too," Clementina said, catching up the bride's train and carrying it as the three ladies promenaded down the stairs.

A little girl relative came forward, dressed prettily in a miniature mantua made by Clementina, and with a curtsy and a shy smile, she handed the bride a bouquet of white roses.

The servants stood at every door and window, eager to catch a glimpse of Nancy, who waved and smiled at them, before she got into the coach beside her parents.

"Clementina." She heard her name and gasped with surprise.

She hadn't expected to find James waiting to escort her to the church. He'd been visiting the Redmarsh house irregularly and had been occupied with his own affairs, which kept him busy.

Her smile was spontaneous. He was attired in a splendidly fitting navy jacket over his wide shoulders and sported cream breeches, which showed his long straight legs to perfection. He said, "You look most charming in your gown," and gave her one of his endearing smiles. "But then, you always do."

"Thank you, sir," she replied, blushing and giving him a little curtsy.

When she thought back to the time they spent in the backwoods together, those days seemed almost like a dream that never happened. They'd almost made love and had ridden companionably together on a horse overnight. Yes, indeed, she told herself firmly, it was a memory like a book that is finished and is closed.

But it seemed when he took her gloved hand and helped her up into his gig that he had not forgotten their previous closeness. His presence brought her physical need for him back so strongly, she felt vulnerable.

Before they set off, he turned and placed a leather-covered box in her hands. "This is for you," he said. "I bought it in Barbados to thank you for helping me save my ship."

Holding one of the few presents she'd ever received, Clementina felt as if she were in another world. "For me?" she gasped.

"Indeed, it is for you, and please hurry

and put it on because we have to get to the church before the bride does."

She couldn't say, *No, I will not accept a gift from you. Our relationship is at an end.*

As she seemed reluctant to open the box, he took it from her and opened it himself, revealing a silvery pearl necklace.

"Oh, James!"

"Don't you like it?"

"Naturally I do, but, they are too grand for me. A dressmaker can't wear pearls."

"Why ever not?"

"In England they will think I stole them!"

James gave a hoot of laughter, "Well, you're not in England now. Turn round and I'll fix them around your neck."

And he did. Clementina's hands went to feel the soft jewels. But the carriage horse leapt forward as James cracked his whip, and she had to hold on tight, as he was determined to get to the church before the bride. Her mind, which had settled on losing him, was now in disarray. She knew he wouldn't have given her this valuable gift if he did not care for her. She was delighted with the pearls, but embarrassed too. If he thought he could bribe her into staying in America and marrying him — a traitor — he was mistaken. It was an impasse between them. Hopeless love. But she was going to

Nancy's wedding and she had to smile. Graciously she turned to James and said, "I thank you for my pearls, which I shall always treasure."

His mind was on getting to the church on time but he replied, "And I shall always enjoy seeing you wearing them."

Not, she thought sadly, *for very long.*

The church ceremony over, the bride and groom and their guests went to the Assembly Rooms, where they feasted. A five-piece orchestra played for the guests to dance. Clementina, who had attended several dances during her stay in the colony, had become accustomed to the country dances and was able to enjoy the celebrations.

James was her constant escort, and she noticed that the company saw nothing to gossip about because he was accepted as her beau — although he wasn't.

Before Nancy set off to her new home, the bride made sure Clementina caught her bridal spray. Clementina looked down at it and smiled broken-heartedly, believing she was never to be a bride.

James seemed surprisingly buoyant, however. His engaging smile and constant attention seemed to indicate he didn't think she was lost to him.

Before James left, he explained, "I'm training a group of men in Chester County in the use of rifles, if you should ever want me."

"Why should I want you?"

His eyebrow lifted attractively as he grinned. "As an escort?"

Clementina thought about it for a moment or two. "Well," she said, hiding the fact she'd be pleased to see him anyway, "I suppose it might be a good idea for us to take Eleanor out to the theatre occasionally, or for some musical entertainment this winter to prevent her from becoming too downcast about missing her daughter."

He touched her wrist and sent excited shivers up her arm. "And you, Clementina? Don't you become downcast? About us being parted, I mean?"

He didn't know how hollow inside she felt. "I have my work to do," she said primly. "I haven't time to think much about how I feel."

They both knew that was a lie. He said, "It's not illegal for me to be training those recruits. The charters of the Royal Provinces of North America from earliest times have allowed us to have a militia."

"Not to fight the British," she snapped back.

His smile could have been considered boyish and irresponsible, as it used to be. But his amused look appeared knowing. He was confident he was right, just as she was sure he was wrong. "I hope the Pennsylvania Rifle Regiment will not have to fight."

They stood looking at each other. She longed to press herself close to his strong body, to have him kiss and stroke her. But there was an invisible wall called loyalty between them. He did kiss her though, tenderly, before he turned away and left her standing alone. Bereft.

After the gloriously fine autumn, the long winter months seemed bitterly cold. More snow than Clementina had ever known descended, and she had thick boots made to crunch through the drifts to and from her shop each day. Hawkes accompanied her, or sometimes Mr. Redmarsh took her on his sleigh.

The bitter cold kept the dissenters indoors, and there were no more signs of the patriots. But when Clementina saw some red-coated British soldiers marching about the town, she wanted to run up to them and warn them that some of the colonists were ganging up against them and they had better watch their backs.

She didn't, of course. She knew their enemies were invisible. Would this tradesman or that be on their side or the other? Perhaps in the spring they might know. She did have the strange feeling that she herself was being watched.

She asked Hawkes, whose Indian eyes were sharp, "Have you been aware of us being followed?"

Hawkes shook his head. "No, ma'am."

But Clementina couldn't believe that her hunch was not correct. When Hawkes was with her, perhaps the person spying on her took care not to be around.

She saw little of James over those winter months. But she was always glad to see him when he came to dinner or accompanied them to some entertainment. He became leaner and tougher-looking, as though the soldier's life he led had stolen the last of his youth.

She sighed when she took out Gainsborough's drawing of him occasionally and studied it, thinking Elizabeth Hunter wouldn't recognize her nephew now. She then asked herself if his aunt would be ashamed of him for turning against Britain, or would she understand that he now felt he was an American?

The spring of 1775 awoke the needs of the ladies for new gowns for their wardrobes, and Clementina became busier than ever. She had to take on two new seamstresses.

Now was the time she should go back to the shipping office and book a passage home — but she always seemed too busy and found an excuse not to go. Something inside kept telling her to wait a while. The shocking news from Lexington took everyone by surprise. Nancy came charging into her shop one late April day. "Clementina," she called excitedly. Clementina smiled to see her friend. But her smile dimmed when she noticed Nancy's agitation.

She left one of her assistants to finish ironing the gown she'd been showing her how to press, and walked over to Nancy, taking her arm. "Yes, my dear? You look a trifle overwrought." Clementina hoped Eleanor or her husband had not met with an accident.

Nancy drew Clementina out of earshot of the busy workers. There happened to be no customers in the shop. "Papa sent me to tell you, because he has been called to a meeting . . ." Nancy gasped for breath. "The news is that some minutemen up near

Boston have fired on some British soldiers!" Her eyes were wide, and the news seemed just as shocking to her as it was to Clementina. "And the soldiers fired back."

Clementina found a chair and sat down. "This is what your father and I have feared might happen for some time."

"What are you going to do?"

Clementina was lost in thought. Then she shrugged. "What can I do? They have been warming up for a fight for some time. Perhaps now that they have come to blows, things will be sorted out."

"Henry said he'll join the fight for freedom."

Henry, thought Clementina crossly, might do well to consider reconciliation before fanning the flames. Tears from nowhere sprang to her eyes. She turned away quickly and picked up a cotton reel that had fallen on the floor.

"Oh Clementina, you're crying. How thoughtless of me!" Nancy put her arm around Clementina.

"No, I'm not. I must have a cold coming on."

Nancy withdrew her arm and said, "Papa said I was to tell you you must not walk out alone. Stay in the shop until either he or Hawkes comes to collect you, because you are known to be an Englishwoman."

Clementina brushed a tear from her cheek and replied, "Your papa is most considerate. But you can tell him I will not paint a sign on my back that states that I am an Englishwoman. And I doubt very much that anyone would take a shot at me if I did. Nancy, don't look at me like that; I'll not do anything foolish to draw attention to myself. But I will not deny that I am English and proud to be."

"That's what Papa said you would say."

They both laughed. Then they embraced.

Nancy said, "I do feel for you. I can imagine how painful this conflict must be for you. And I have a little English blood in me. Mama is half English."

"I can think of someone else I know who is English through and through, although he won't admit it."

"James?"

"Exactly."

"But James has been living in America for years. I can understand he feels he is now an American."

Clementina frowned. "Well, I don't think, however long I stayed here, that I will feel like an American, as you put it."

"You won't know that until you've stayed for years. You might find your opinion alters.

People's opinions do change, you know."

Clementina chuckled. "You sound like your father, Nancy. Perhaps you are becoming wise in your married state?"

Nancy giggled. "Seriously, though, Clementina, do take care. Some Patriot hothead might decide to taunt you. When men become fired up about a cause, they can do dreadful things, which they justify by saying you are their enemy."

Clementina sighed as she nodded. "Yes, Nancy, you are becoming more like your father. And if all Americans were like him, I would have nothing to be afraid of. But, alas, I know what you say is true. Thank you for the warning. I will take care, but I doubt very much if anything will happen in this little dress shop. And I will wait, as your father suggested, for someone to fetch me home."

Satisfied that Clementina was not afraid and would do her father's bidding, Nancy left.

For the rest of that day Clementina was a little apprehensive. She didn't know why. She remembered the strange feeling that someone was stalking her and didn't like it. But she knew that a person without courage could die a thousand deaths before she was killed, and was determined not to allow herself to become a trembling idiot for no reason.

She would ask Ralph Redmarsh to book her a ticket home. Looking round at her spacious, sunny workshop and the excellent seamstresses she'd employed to help her with her full order of fine gowns, however, she did think it was a shame she had to leave her prospering Philadelphia mantua-making business.

CHAPTER NINETEEN

Clementina, having decided to return to England, was determined that while she remained in Philadelphia, she would conduct her dressmaking business as she normally did and try to ignore the increasing troubles. Mr. Redmarsh said he would look out for a ship's passage for her, but he did not seem keen to do so.

Clementina heard that the Siege of Boston in Massachusetts had followed the rebellion against His Majesty King George's troops at Lexington. This brought more accounts of deaths on both sides, all adding to the tension and unrest felt in the Colony of Pennsylvania, where those in sympathy with the rebels — who now called themselves Patriots — were condemned by the Loyalists. Consequently, an uneasy peace reigned in the city of Philadelphia, although life appeared to proceed as normal.

In her dressmaking establishment, Clementina continued to labor with her seamstresses to provide fashionable garments for the ladies of the "better sort," as they liked to be known, aping the costly attire worn by the aristocracy in Europe. She also sewed for a growing number of American middle-class ladies who required more practical garments to wear. It often required tact on her part to satisfy both types of customers.

One day when Clementina was facing a particularly exacting task — cutting a tricky section of a gown's bodice and trying not to waste the exquisite French silk, and matching the pattern on the material to another section — she heard shrill ladies' voices in the front of the shop.

"Oh dear!" she muttered, putting down the scissors, thinking she couldn't go on cutting the precious silk with that disturbance going on, as it would be easy for her to snip a bit she didn't mean to and make a costly mistake. Fearing the young girl she'd hired to receive her customers wasn't able to cope with some exacting ladies, she hurried out of the cutting room. She passed through the workroom where the seamstresses were occupied making up gowns that had been ordered and headed towards the front reception area of the shop. She recognized the affected voice of a prominent

Tory, Lady Standish, whose haughty manner echoed the attitude of some of the titled ladies back in Bath.

"I do not consider *any* benefit will come from the rebels' defiance," Lady Standish pronounced. "The British soldiers will soon crush them."

A sharp retort from another lady answered her. "Well, I and my friends are not of that opinion, Lady Standish. We consider it desirable for the British to respect our wishes and leave our shores."

Lady Standish gasped at the offensive remark.

Clementina felt her pulse quicken. The conflict had invaded her shop! She would have to put a quick stop to that. She made the effort to appear at ease as she confronted the prestigious lady. "Ah, good morning, your ladyship. I trust you are not finding the present cold spell too arduous?" It was not the best thing she could have said, but Clementina couldn't think of anything more suitable on the spur of the moment.

"Weather? What has the weather to do with the affair, Miss Willoby? I regret that, as a mantua-maker, your frivolous mind does not understand the difficulties we face from the rebels. They are nothing but ruffians and convicts gone wild!"

Clementina gulped. Such downright rudeness from a customer was not unknown to her — especially when she worked in Bath. But she did understand this lady's wrath. Her class's aristocratic power, which for centuries had ruled the masses, was being undermined. A new breed of Americans was being formed: tradespeople with democratic leanings.

But Clementina objected to hearing the rebel Patriots — and James was undoubtedly one of them — being described as ruffians. He was no saint, but she smarted at hearing him referred to as the lowest of the low.

"Oh, I wouldn't say that," Clementina protested without thinking. Then she rushed on, hoping to pacify the irate lady. "I do not think, your ladyship, that you should allow what is happening so far away in Boston to affect you."

The stony look Clementina received from Lady Standish was as insulting as the "direct cut" the aristocratic English were prone to give their inferiors. But Clementina had developed more confidence, more a sense of self-worth than she'd had when she was an orphan girl working in Bath. Her previous tendency to be cowed by a superior person had lessened.

For a full quarter minute both ladies confronted one another, Lady Standish no doubt hoping the mantua-maker would show subservience, and Clementina desperately trying to think how she could make this sudden confrontation fly away. Being a shrewd businesswoman, Clementina decided it would be prudent to play up to the conceited woman. She didn't want to lose a wealthy customer or her friends and acquaintances. So she said with a forced smile, "I do beg your pardon, ma'am, if I gave offence. Of course, you know better than I, and must excuse me as I am, as you say, only a dressmaker."

A flicker of approval in Lady Standish's cold eyes made Clementina go on quickly, "Now, you have come to see the new French silks, I believe. They are of excellent quality and very beautiful. And I am sure you will be interested to know I have some new fashion plates just arrived from Paris which I have not shown to any other lady so you will be the first to see them . . ."

As she talked smoothly on, Clementina was half aware of the other two ladies in the shop behind her huffing and complaining. She caught phrases like, "We came into the shop first, but the quality get served first here, you see," and, "She's buttering her up," and, "Of course, she's English. What can you expect?"

With a sharp ring on the doorbell, they stalked out of the shop before Clementina could appease them. Her little assistant shut the door after them without making a useful comment like, "I hope you will come again when we are less busy, ma'am," as Clementina would have done.

It took all her training in diplomacy to soften Lady Standish, but before she'd wished her good day, her ladyship had ordered another gown and was puffed up again, like a contented hen.

"I didn't know what to do, Miss Willoby!" wailed the assistant when Lady Standish had left the shop and clambered into her grand coach.

"Don't upset yourself, Betsy. It was a difficult situation, and you were not to know how to deal with those kinds of quarrels. I don't know that I dealt with it all that well myself."

Betsy thanked her for being so understanding, but when Clementina returned alone to her cutting room, she was shaking. The venom Lady Standish had shown was like that of a snake that had bitten her. She dared not continue with her cutting or her temper might make her hack the material to pieces.

She decided to do a job she enjoyed most, which was looking through the latest French fashion plates. The French made clothing an art, and she had an interesting task deciding which of the trends were significant for her customers and making a new fashion doll to put in the shop's bow-fronted window. So, thinking Betsy might still be feeling unhappy about the encounter too, she called the girl in to help her. The unpleasant confrontation was largely forgotten as they looked through the scrap material box in the cutting room for the stuff they wanted to dress the new doll. Their fingers were soon busily sewing up the small garments as they chatted about this and that.

A loud crash in the shop took them both by surprise.

"What was that?" Betsy's mouth and eyes rounded.

"I don't know," said Clementina, puzzled. Getting up, she shook the pieces of material from her apron. "I'll go and see. Fix this little skirt on the doll, would you, Betsy?"

Clementina tripped through to the front of the shop where the noise had come from, expecting to find that one of the heavy dress stands on which gowns were hung for the customer to examine had fallen over.

The seamstresses had stopped work and looked at her open-mouthed as she rushed by.

"Oh!" Clementina gave a sharp cry. There on the floor amongst the pieces of broken glass was a chunk of brick. Someone had obviously thrown it through a pane in her bow window!

Betsy and the seamstresses came running into the reception area when they heard their employer give a little scream. In no time, the room was filled with the seamstresses who came to find out what had gone amiss. They began chorusing exclamations:

"Part of a brick has broken the glass! Oh my!"

"Oh Miss Willoby, whoever has done that?"

Clementina held on to the freestanding long mirror for support. She was shaking as if she'd been personally harmed. Whoever had thrown the brick through the window, even if it had been a misbehaving child, had shown her how vulnerable she was.

"Who would want to damage your shop?" A seamstress voiced the question on everyone's mind.

"Look. There's a note with it." Another

seamstress stepped forward to retrieve the message.

"Take care you don't cut yourself on the glass," warned Clementina as the girl gingerly picked up the note. Since she couldn't read, she handed it to Clementina.

The scrawl read: *British whore go home.* It was signed: *Son of Liberty.*

If the note hadn't been so ridiculous, it might have upset Clementina more. A whore she was not, by any stretch of the imagination. It was certainly insulting, but it was not appropriate, because at twenty-six years old, Clementina was still a virgin! Who could possibly think she was a loose woman?

"Well," she said, reluctant even to read the note to her workers, "I think whoever attacked this shop may do so again. I think you should all go home until I have found out who is responsible and made sure they are not going to throw anything else at us."

The brave grin on Clementina's lips made the seamstresses look at each other and giggle. They did not mind being let off work for the afternoon, and one said, "May I take my work home and get on with it? Mrs. Camberwell will be in tomorrow expecting it finished."

Clementina smiled at her. "Yes indeed,

Ginny, and any of you who are able to work at home may do so. But take a sheet to wrap up your sewing so it doesn't become soiled."

Excitement bubbled up as the girls prepared to leave for the half-day holiday, which was an unexpected treat for them.

After they had all trooped off, Clementina felt like crying as she locked the door behind them and surveyed the mess of broken glass on the floor and the jagged hole in the window, which would be an invitation to burglars. She hardly noticed the tap on the part of the window that was not smashed, but when she did look up she found three grey-dressed ladies peering in at her. Going to unlock the door she found to her delight that it was Mrs. Cod with two other Quaker ladies.

"I see thee are in trouble again, Miss Willoby," said Mrs. Cod, peering through the broken window. "Would thee like us to help thee sweep the glass up?"

Clementina smiled her tears away and, "Mrs. Cod, come in do. I would love your help. You're an angel."

Mrs. Cod bustled in with her friends carrying their baskets of shopping. They clucked when they saw the mess of broken glass, and one asked, "Miss Willoby, show us where thou keeps thy broom."

Clementina was overjoyed to have their practical help, and their cheerfulness soon lifted her spirits.

When the good ladies had made the shop look spick and span again, and a rag was stuffed through the hole in the glass that the brick made, Clementina offered them a cup of coffee, which they accepted enthusiastically.

"It's most kind of you to help me," Clementina said. "It was quite a shock to know people will attack me for being English."

The ladies seemed sympathetic but not overly concerned.

"I don't know what to do about it." Clementina gave a long sigh.

Mrs. Cod put her coffee cup down on the table. "Put thy faith in God," she said, "and have the window mended."

One of the ladies said, "My husband can mend thy window. Shall I ask him to call?"

That did sound helpful. Clementina nodded and said, "Yes, if you would, please."

"Well, we must be on our way, my dear," Mrs. Cod said, getting up and picking up her shopping basket.

Clementina's expression must have shown her disappointment.

"Thou must not fear attacks. We all have enemies," one lady said to her confidentially.

"We will pray for thee."

Clementina didn't like to say she was a little afraid of being left alone, but she didn't want to delay the ladies, who probably had to hurry back to their homes with their shopping and cook the family dinner.

But someone else was at the door. A man of stature: James Hunter.

"James!" Clementina cried delightedly.

The joy and relief she experienced at seeing him made her run with outstretched arms towards him, not caring that the Quaker trio could see how thrilled she was at his arrival.

He wanted to draw her into his arms, but because of the visitors he held her at arm's length and looked her up and down. His deep voice was anxious. "I heard your shop had been attacked. You're not hurt, I trust?"

Clementina struggled to regain her poise. "No. Fortunately nobody was hurt. I sent the seamstresses home, and then these kind ladies came by and have cleared up all the glass fragments for me." She introduced the ladies.

James gave the sweet Quakers a bow and one of his endearing smiles, and they were clearly as pleased, yet as coy, as schoolgirls.

"We must go," Mrs. Cod said briskly. "But we can see we leave thee in good hands,

Miss Willoby. I'm not surprised thee went all the way to Lancaster to find him."

Clementina chuckled. "Thank you all. You've been so helpful. I don't know how I would have managed alone without your help."

"Thee is never alone, Miss Willoby. We Quakers know what it is like to suffer the ill will of others. But we do not despair. And neither must thee forget thy God is always watching over thee, my dear." Mrs. Cod instructed her in her usual calm manner and gave her a peck on the cheek.

Clementina was so touched, she could say no more, but she forgot her normal English reserve and hugged the three kind ladies.

James courteously opened the door for them and they glided out into the street. When they'd toddled off out of sight, James closed the door. "That was most neighborly of them," he said. "We will be needing a great deal of their sort in the coming struggle."

Clementina held her tongue. She wanted to say the rebels had a lot to answer for. But how could she say that, when she was so pleased to see this particular rebel?

"Is this the brick that was thrown through the glass?" he asked, picking it up and examining it.

"It was. And the paper that was attached to it is over there on the table."

James marched over to read it. He gave a grunt. "This is not the work of the Sons of Liberty, I can assure you of that. They are thinking men, not shop window breakers."

"Who then?"

"That, I do not know."

"A wayward boy out for a bit of a lark? Or perhaps it was . . ." Clementina went on to explain the incident in the shop earlier when Lady Standish had aggravated her other customers with her toplofty remarks.

James sat down and drew his hand wearily over his forehead and then over the back of his neck. For the first time Clementina noted he was attired in his militia uniform and looked out of place in town.

"The situation will get worse, I fear," he said. Then he added quickly, "And before you start accusing me of inciting trouble, I'll tell you straight that I give no backing to indiscriminate attacks on anyone. If our country is to be free, then it should be free for everyone. Tolerance is necessary on everyone's part."

"Fine words, James. But how can you prevent these acts of violence when you overthrow the law?"

He sighed heavily. "Of course I can't be

responsible for those who behave with thoughtless acts of bullying! But you must realize, Clementina, that nothing will improve unless men are prepared to try and make things better. We can't just sit back and hope the British will relent, because they won't. They've had plenty of time to make peace with us and they haven't shown they've wanted to."

Clementina could have protested about several things he'd said. But what was the use? She had her opinion and he had his. Their relationship was as impossible as two buck deer with their antlers entwined in a fight.

She sighed wearily. "The only thing I can do is to go home."

"I have my horse outside. I will ride you back."

"I mean," she said icily, "go home to Bath."

He chuckled. "I think dinner might make you feel better. I know a tavern near here that serves very fine meals. Shall we go there?"

That did sound enticing. Being in his company for longer appealed to her even more.

"I'll go if you promise not to try and convert me to your rebel ways."

He laughed. "That is a promise."

She glanced around quickly. "What about the shop? I'm expecting one of the Quaker ladies' husbands, who is a glazier, to come and fix the window."

"Don't worry. I have a local man watching your shop in case of trouble. How else do you think I knew about your broken window?"

He didn't mention what else he knew, not wishing to frighten her.

He'd really instructed his man to watch out for a possible arsonist.

A system of spies and informers often existed in wartime, and Clementina thought perhaps having a man keeping an eye on her property was a good training for one. It was a comfort to her to know someone was nearby. She smiled up at James. After a good meal, and after the shop window was mended, she was sure she would feel able to return to work in the morning as if nothing unpleasant had happened. In the meantime, she would bask in the happiness of having James's company for a while.

He smiled at her and offered her his arm as they walked out together into the street. Just like a respectable colonial couple.

CHAPTER TWENTY

The Tavern Inn in Philadelphia was a meeting place not only for those wanting good ale and food. It provided a place for men interested in social and cultural affairs to meet and talk.

And there was plenty of discussion going on when James and Clementina arrived.

For a moment or two when she saw the attention she drew, Clementina thought that she was the subject of their comments. She did not know that few women would come into a tavern. And an agreeably dressed woman with graceful movements and a pleasant expression would always draw male interest. But the drinkers were looking also at the commanding militiaman who was escorting her and protecting her. Soon, however, their conversation returned to the matter that mostly occupied their minds before the handsome couple came in: the British occupation of Boston.

Clementina overheard snatches of heated conversation and realized the underlying cause of it. However, she'd determined not to take sides in Britain's dispute with the American colonies; consequently she dared not open her mouth, except to eat and drink, in case some rebel heard her English accent and accused her of being a British spy.

James met several people he knew and some came over to question him about the situation, which made Clementina realize he was not just one of the rank-and-file soldiers, but a commander in General Washington's army.

Should we support the Patriots camped outside Boston? seemed to be the main question under discussion.

"Indeed, we should," growled an older man, who stamped his walking stick on the tavern floorboards, but Clementina doubted if he would take part in any action.

"General Washington has considered several modes of attack, but I am of the opinion we should wait and see if the British offer terms."

"The Port of Boston is still closed," lamented a merchant. Then he almost whispered, "We have had to start smuggling goods there."

Laughter rang out. But Clementina, eating her pork and corn meal, didn't laugh. She'd heard from Mr. Redmarsh that the British were hampering American shipping, and several American vessels had become privateers to harass the British. It wasn't the best time to sail to England, he'd advised her. Now the summer was upon them and before long it would be winter again, and Clementina would still be stuck in Philadelphia.

Amazed that she hadn't started insisting she wanted to go home, she asked herself why. She'd been busy with her shop, setting up a successful dressmaking business, and she was enjoying the work. She'd even become accustomed to the hot weather. The thought of a dull, rainy summer in Bath didn't appeal to her. And she'd got used to another set of seamstresses who worked just as diligently as her English girls.

"Clementina."

She became aware that James was talking to her and turned to him.

"Here's someone you know."

At first Clementina didn't recognize the man dressed in rough rifleman's uniform. When recognition dawned, she was delighted. "Richard Wakefield, I do declare," she exclaimed, returning his broad smile.

He looked fitter than when she'd seen him last, and now she felt he would be able to put up a better fight against James. His change of occupation had made a man of him.

"Yes, ma'am," said Richard with the slightest bow. "I'm Minuteman Wakefield, at your service."

"Do sit by me and tell me what has happened to your fine carriage and matching pair?" Clementina might also have asked about his orange-striped breeches but thought better of it.

"My carriage is at home on blocks in the stables. My horses were sold for two sturdier mounts, which are of more use to me in the militia."

Clementina didn't have to ask him about the change of direction in his life, because he volunteered it. "I got to thinking my life was going nowhere after I met you and James Hunter. Having been divested of my wig, I began to prefer a less flamboyant style of dress."

"Yes," said Clementina, nodding approvingly. "Gentlemen in England like to wear country-style clothes now, and ladies in France have adopted gowns copied from milkmaids. At least they have abandoned those really impractical wide hooped skirts that made them have to go through a door sideways."

They laughed at the memory of those gigantic skirts.

"Anyway," said Richard, anxious to tell Clementina more about himself, "when I heard about Boston, and the severity of the British blockade of its harbor, causing bloodshed and strife, I was angry. So when I met James again and he said more minutemen were required, he suggested I could help the cause, and so I have."

Clementina asked, "What did your parents have to say about that?"

"My papa is of the opinion I should make up my own mind. He wasn't sorry I left the band of young men whose main purpose in life is to pursue pleasure — racing, gambling and cock fighting. He never did approve of me spending my time doing that. But while I have chosen the path of a rebel soldier, Mama is all of a jelly, saying I will end up on the British gallows."

"And do you think you will?"

"Difficult to say, ma'am, which side will win."

James had just finished his conversation with a gentleman who'd moved off. He joined in by saying, "There is no doubt in my mind the British will lose this tussle eventually."

"Why do you say that?" asked Clementina nervously.

He drank from his tankard. "It stands to reason. America is a huge continent. Immigrants are coming in all the time and expanding the size of the colonies. Britain might be able to control the eastern seaboard, but the whole vast continent of America? Impossible! She hasn't the men to do it. She hasn't the supplies. We hold the countryside. And what is more, no Dutch farmer is going to care a fig about whether the British rule us."

Clementina could see James had worked it all out in his mind. And she had the strong feeling his logic was right. Giddiness made her lower her head.

James looked at her bowed head and said sincerely, "I'm sorry, Clementina. That is what I believe. I'm not trying to make you feel you are mistaken to believe the British will continue to rule this land."

"I know you're not."

"I think the colonies will unite and become a separate nation. And many believe that sentiment. By next year everything the people are thinking and saying will be drawn up into a document and presented to Congress for a vote."

"Ah," said Clementina, following the drift of what he was saying. It all sounded so traitorous to her mind. That he could say this boldly within yards of a group of Loyalists sitting enjoying their ale, was for her almost unbelievable.

But, of course, it was only talk. Opinion. Even James had admitted the struggle had just begun. It hadn't touched New York or Philadelphia. Or was she mistaken? Wasn't the Philadelphian man she loved already preparing to fight? She shuddered.

She was aware that James was watching her closely as she finished the last mouthful of her meal. Her gaze met his. Was she mistaken, or were his eyes questioning her? He'd presented her with what he thought were the facts of the cause he was fighting. Was he asking her to trust him and believe in them, too? Did he see her future in this new vast country of his?

She smiled at his impudence. "I think you are counting your chickens before they are hatched, Mr. Hunter. I think you will find the British are tough fighters."

His endearing smile made her detest the conflict that divided them. "We shall see," he said simply. "They make easy targets in their bright red coats. Our men call them lobsters."

Clementina bristled. "You were glad enough of their protection in the French and Indian wars, were you not?"

He acquiesced. "But times change, Clementina. We change with them. The British have overstepped their guardianship and become tyrants. You know the unfair legislation they are imposing on us. Indeed, we must make them see reason or kick them out. I dream of a free land in America."

"Oh, yes?" Cynically, she thought he had plenty of freedom to do as he liked as it was. She knew he would do his best to bring his dream about, and that he bore no ill will towards his fellow countrymen who chose the other path. But James was a good man. Many rebels were. But not all were honourable men — like, for instance, the one who'd thrown a brick through her shop window.

She just prayed the conflict, if it occurred, would soon be sorted out.

The time came for them to leave. Before Clementina left, she gave a quick motherly kiss to brave young Richard and wished him sincerely to take care.

"I will indeed. And if you are ever in Walnut Street, do call upon my mother, Miss Willoby. I know she would like to meet you."

Clementina promised she would.

Her leave-taking of James, she knew, would be far more emotional. James was now a seasoned soldier, a rifleman with an accurate eye. He was committed to fighting if it became necessary, and as soldiers' sweethearts know, their love needs to be passionate, as death might lurk around any corner.

He accompanied her back to the Redmarsh house and they dismounted, tying James's horse to the railings as they walked up the drive, hands linked. On the way up the drive he pulled her behind a shrub and held her close, so that she could feel the beating of his heart. In his arms was where she most wanted to be. She thought, *I could so easily have missed this precious moment in my life. I could be back in England by now, sewing in the little shop in Bath, instead of living life to the full by being in this man's arms.*

Her lips sought his, and nothing came between their physical union. His strong male instincts demanded her surrender, but his love for her prevented him from taking more than she was ready to give him.

"Goodbye, darling Clementina," he whispered into her silky auburn curls. He kissed her ear. Then his hands gently cupped her head so that the pressure of his warm lips on hers made her melt towards him.

"Oh James!" She sighed with pleasure. "What shall we do? What shall I do?"

He chuckled. "Don't ask me that. I might be tempted to tell you."

She knew then that her love for him was too great to allow her to leave him. England she loved, too, but it seemed far away. She was now and always had been happy in America. It suited her. James suited her. But whether she was a special lady to him, she didn't know — because he didn't say. Perhaps he knew his future was uncertain and therefore didn't want to offer more than his loving friendship. If the rebellion continued, it was certain that more husbands, sons and lovers would die. James might be the target of a British soldier's bullet. She shuddered at this terrible thought and wished with all her heart the coming struggle could be avoided.

After they'd enjoyed their final kiss and he'd ridden smartly away, she gave a little pained sigh, as there was nothing she could do to bring him back safe and sound. Sadly, she was sure there was nothing she, as a dressmaker, could do to help anyone or anything during the coming revolution.

But she was wrong.

■ ■ ■ ■

As the summer of 1775 ended and winter came, there was a need for women as strong as Clementina. Many ladies were less able to cope with the trauma of war and needed · someone to talk to who understood their heartaches.

The Willoby dressmaking establishment soon became known as a place where ladies could go and express their grievances and their worries, no matter which side their menfolk chose to support. The Tory ladies had most to lose in the struggle, and those who had not left Philadelphia needed a calm, understanding person like Clementina to whom to pour out their fears and discuss the stupidity of men who preferred fighting to reasoned chitchat, as sensible women did.

The support the women gave each other by standing together helped Clementina too. She got to know many Tory ladies she admired, as well as many Patriot ladies. Some shared her love of Britain, while others openly despised the British. But as women with families to care for, their husbands and children were their chief concern. The causes of the conflict took second place.

Clementina's strength was tested one afternoon when James appeared unexpectedly. She was sitting sewing in the Redmarshes' parlor, because the stormy day with a heavy snowfall had made her daily trip to the shop inadvisable. So she'd stayed at home to sew by the fireside. When she heard his voice, she dropped her work and rushed to the door as the maid let him in.

He'd been riding hard in the stormy weather. And, although he held his hat in his hands, he'd not removed his greatcoat or his riding boots, which surprised her.

"James?" she cried, not sure whether to continue smiling at his grave face.

"I regret I have come to tell you some bad news," he said, dismounting.

"Oh dear, what is it?"

"Richard Wakefield has been killed at Dorchester Heights outside Boston. I was not there, but was told he was amongst those making a stronghold."

Clementina stared at him, horrified. It was monstrous news. That young, precious life gone forever.

James, whose face had become more lined of late with the hardship of a soldier's camp life and seeing men killed, looked at her strained face and said in quiet sorrow, "I shouldn't have let him become a soldier. I should have left him chasing about in his gilded chariot. He is dead now, Clementina, and I am to blame."

"No, James, you mustn't feel guilty! Richard told me being in the army gave him a purpose in life. You gave him pride. He wanted to fight against what he thought was unjust. You didn't kill him."

She was aware he was coming close to her. His bodily strength didn't protect him from the pain of losing his young friend. He had struggled through the bad weather to tell her the news, and now she could tell he wanted to shed his self-control and sob. He'd come to her for consolation. "I feel dreadful about it," he said, hanging his head.

Clementina's heart went out to him. Before, their love had been selfish, each enjoying the passion of it. But now she was sharing his pain. She loved him because he was suffering, and she felt his tears blending with hers as they clung together. It didn't occur to her to tell him that his war games with the British had resulted in this tragedy, because she no longer felt that she was on one side and he was on the other.

She let him cry and rid himself of his anger about the loss. And she felt unembarrassed to cry with him.

Eventually he got hold of himself and said

thickly, "I must return."

"Let me get you a hot drink, James."

He shook his head as he wiped his eyes savagely with his handkerchief and blew his nose.

"At least come up to the fire and warm yourself before you go."

This he did, putting his large hands out to the blazing heat.

He said after a minute, "I came to you partly as I was hoping you would tell Richard's parents."

Clementina closed her eyes. What a dreadful message had to be conveyed. She reeled at the thought of it. But James was already stamping about, fiddling with his hat, needing to be off. She knew she should accept the awful burden. He'd come to her, knowing she had the sympathy to tell Richard's parents and would be able to stay and comfort them, and he couldn't wait around. Since he'd always talked to her honestly about the revolution, she'd acquired an understanding of the beliefs both sides held dear. She'd developed a generosity of spirit that enabled her to sympathize with ladies on both sides of the divide. A woman weeping for her dead son, whether he was a British army lad or a rebel boy, was only a tragedy to Clementina.

"I'll go and tell them," she said, not mentioning the difficulty she would have getting there in the appalling weather.

"Clementina, my darling, I thank you." His voice was husky. That he was suffering endeared him to her. He could say no more, she could tell. But his eyes looked at her with a kindness she was never to forget.

Next minute, he had given her a brief kiss and was gone like a gust of wind.

So Clementina, numb with grief, struggled with Hawkes through deep snow to the Wakefield residence on Walnut Street, not to call on his mother for a pleasant visit, as Richard had wanted her to, but to give his parents the saddest message they could receive.

Eleanor Redmarsh and Nancy needed her support too.

By the time the spring approached, Eleanor told Clementina one day as they sat nibbling their sugar lumps with their after-dinner coffee, "I fear the British army might come here. Did you know the Quartering Act means that soldiers can come and live in your house without so much as asking your permission?"

Clementina was alarmed but was determined to hide it. "No, I did not. And I can't pretend I, as an Englishwoman, would like it if they did. But Eleanor, dear, we must not suffer it before it happens. I can't see why the British army would need to come to Philadelphia. They'll be quite content in New York."

In truth, Clementina didn't know any such thing. On the odd occasions James had paid them a quick visit, he hadn't said he thought it was a possibility. But it was sensible to keep her friend from suffering the vapors unnecessarily by saying something to quell her fears.

Clementina thought it best to change the subject. Nancy was expecting her first child. "We must prepare for your grandchild, Eleanor. Shall I help you to make some clothing for the babe, or a patchwork coverlet for the cradle? The mother and child would treasure anything you, the grandmother, made."

"Oh my, do you think I could?"

"With my help, Eleanor, that grandchild of yours will be the envy of all nurseries in Philadelphia!"

Eleanor pressed her hands together in delight.

Nancy's coming confinement was an excitement, and Clementina did everything she could to prevent Eleanor from thinking of her own sad childbed death memories by making her concentrate on the positive and enjoyable side of having a new baby in the family.

Nancy and Henry were thrilled at the prospect of being parents. Clementina was able to obtain the promise of Mrs. Cod's midwife services. Mrs. Cod quickly endeared herself to the nervous young Mrs. Fisher.

The child could not be coming at a worse time. But Clementina was determined that for Nancy and her mother the birth would be an occasion of joy.

Ralph Redmarsh never mentioned Clementina's passage back to England again. Neither did she. It was the wrong time to be thinking of leaving. Ralph was clearly pleased to have her living in the house to calm his anxious wife during the turbulent times.

And times quickly became more turbulent.

News came that the British had left Boston after the rebels brought cannon from a fort from up north and stationed the artillery on a hill overlooking the town, penning them in. So on 27th March 1776, British troops loaded onto their man-of-war ships and sailed away to Halifax.

When Mr. Redmarsh heard the news, he

commented dryly that the British were far from being beaten and might return, so they had better not rejoice too soon.

CHAPTER
TWENTY-ONE

The City of Brotherly Love, as Philadelphia was called, became a city of intrigue. While people of good will tried to come to terms with the revolution in America, there were those who did not want change.

Brotherly love, Ralph Redmarsh declared, was under strain.

Clementina strove to continue to do her work using the best of her professional skill, and to please her customers. It was just as well she was a practiced dressmaker and could make up a gown almost with her eyes closed, as her mind — like those of a good many others in the colonies — could not concentrate well, contemplating what fate held in store for them. Although James had told her he was convinced the Patriots would win in the end, skirmishes and battles suggested otherwise.

Nancy, whose child was due in late June, became upset because some of her former friends had become fractious under the strain of living in fear of conflict. The Timpson sisters, Nancy told Clementina, had been spiteful to her, which had made her tearful.

"I don't understand it." Nancy looked at Clementina who'd come on a visit, with eyes red with weeping.

"Oh, dear me," said Clementina, looking at her pregnant friend. Nancy had told her how the girls had worried her with old wives' tales about childbirth. She tried to think of a way to comfort her friend. "Personally, I think the Timpson girls are jealous of you being married and having a child."

"They are?"

"Indeed. Especially in the present climate of wartime. There are few social occasions for them to enjoy and few opportunities for them to seek husbands. Young men may feel unwilling to offer at this time. It is bound to worry the Timpson girls, Nancy."

Still, it didn't give the Timpsons an excuse to torment Nancy. Yet Clementina was only too aware of their worry, as two birthdays had rolled by since she left England and she was now a twenty-eight-year-old spinster. Nancy dried her eyes. "Henry says I should forget what they said and not invite them to my home again."

"Henry is quite right. All you need to do is listen to what Mrs. Cod says. She knows all about childbirth — and those silly girls know nothing. They are playing on your natural apprehension. It's very unkind of them."

"Oh Clementina, you're so sensible."

Clementina smiled. "And so is Mrs. Cod. You do like her, don't you, Nancy? You trust her to deliver your child when the time comes, don't you?"

"Indeed I do. I like her."

"So all you have to do is to do as she says and look forward to your little one. Now, dear, your mama and I have made you these small garments." Clementina took some tiny clothes out of her carpetbag and laid them out for Nancy to see.

"Oh Clementina, they are adorable!" Nancy's dimpled smile showed how much she appreciated the gifts. Her worries seemed forgotten. Clementina was delighted.

Clementina didn't mention to anyone about the tittle-tattle she'd heard from Nancy. She decided to pay a visit to the Misses Timpson herself.

Arabella Timpson and her sister Harriet possessed big mouths, which they used like cannons, shooting forth their loud opinions at whomever they pleased. Clementina was determined they should not upset the mother-to-be, believing there was enough fear and wild rumours about without the sisters adding to it.

Asking a maid to accompany her, she walked down to Second Street, as it was a pleasantly sunny day. She wore a fashionable, beautifully made *polonaise* gown, with fine embroidery on the bodice and skirt, to impress the young ladies. Upon arrival she was shown into the parlor.

Clementina came straight to the point, as was her way. "Young ladies, you should understand that Nancy Fisher, whose child is expected very soon, is under the care of Mrs. Cod, who has brought many children into the world without mishap. Therefore, neither Nancy nor Mrs. Cod need *your* advice on childbirth."

The two young ladies gaped, affronted. They might have turned her out of their house, but Clementina had the air of a mature lady that made them seem like schoolgirls again. They also admired her gown very much and hoped she might make one for each of them. Besides, Miss Willoby had gained a reputation as a straight-talking, no-nonsense, Philadelphian business lady. The dressmaker hadn't taken sides, as far as they knew, in the dispute with Britain, although she had an English accent — one that fascinated them. They couldn't fault her for being on the side of the British, if she was.

The girls looked at one another, embarrassed. They knew very little other than the basic facts about birth. When they married, their mother might enlighten them, but in the meantime they were receptacles for any old wives' tales about childbirth they heard. They were now a little ashamed of taunting Nancy with the most outlandish of these tales.

"Miss Willoby, we didn't mean to upset Nancy with our remarks," said Arabella, the older and worse offender.

"No, indeed we did not," the youngest lied.

Those statements indicated to Clementina that their consciences were indeed troubling them. She looked at them sternly. "Now," she said, watching them blush. "Perhaps you would tell me what you told Mrs. Fisher, so that I can correct any misunderstandings?"

Seeing them unwilling to repeat the tales, and glad they did not, as Clementina feared she might laugh, she went on, "If you wish to keep her friendship, and mine, then I expect you will want to shower her with little kindnesses at this time of her coming confinement. As you would want to receive when your time comes."

Arabella glanced at her sister and tittered at the suggestion that they would marry and have children of their own. They had come to wonder why young men were avoiding them. They were amazed to find the subject of childbirth, instead of being avoided as a subject unsuitable for young ladies to discuss, was accepted by Miss Willoby as the most natural subject for ladies to talk about. She reminded them that they, too, could well have swollen bellies in years to come and might want reassurance from their friends. By the time she had finished, Miss Willoby had given both girls more than sufficient to think about.

Before Clementina left, she was careful to promise the young ladies that, as they were friends of Nancy Fisher, she would be delighted to make them a new gown each. They knew this was a favor, as most ladies in Philadelphia were in line, hoping for her to make gowns for them.

As she went down Second Street, Clementina smiled to herself, thinking they wouldn't say anything unkind to Nancy again. But as she left the Timpsons' house, she sensed she was being followed, which bothered her. She was convinced someone was behind her as she went home.

It had been some months since she'd had that strange feeling.

The maid accompanying her said she wasn't aware of anyone behind them.

James came on furtive visits to the Redmarsh residence. He had to be careful because British spies were everywhere. He didn't want the authorities to think the house was a Patriot stronghold. He appeared sometimes in the evening for dinner, which, he said with a wry grin, was a deal better than the food he got in the army.

After the meal, Mrs. Redmarsh always said, "Now you two go into the back parlor for a little time together away from us old 'uns." She made sure a fire was made up in the grate and that Mr. Redmarsh didn't commandeer James to talk politics, or war, or whatever. "This time is for the lovebirds to be together," she whispered to her husband.

Having cried together in grief about Richard's death, there was little stiffness between Clementina and James now. They knew each other well enough not to be embarrassed to kiss and stay locked in close together, longing to satisfy their love, but unable to. For James's visits were always short. He had a long ride back to camp that was sometimes difficult, as he had to avoid any redcoats.

Clinging to his firm body, Clementina drank in his scent of soap and leather. Her hands combed through his untidy hair. She put her finger over his lips so that he gave her one of his devastating smiles that made them kiss again.

She always made him a little gift: a handkerchief she'd sewn, or a button she put his initials on for his vest. She put a lock of her reddish hair in a small pouch for him to wear around his neck on a thong.

"I love you and love your little gifts," he would say, kissing the end of her little nose. "And I love your soft curls and neat figure," and he would stroke her shoulders, her breasts, neck and ears. He made Clementina tingle and long for him to continue to please her as she felt the hard muscles of his fine male body. She knew he wanted to make love to her. But he never mentioned their future together. Would he ask her to marry him when the war was over? she wondered.

He never mentioned either the hardships that the soldiers' endured or their latest skirmishes or their preparations for battle. When he was with her, he wanted to forget his soldier's life and enjoy a lovers' tryst.

The time between his visits seemed like an eternity for Clementina. But what hope had their love in wartime, when they were apart? Stable relationships like marriage were the last thing on soldiers' minds when they were in the throes of war. Was that not so? The Patriots had managed to frighten the British army away from Boston, but General Washington, and James Hunter, now an officer in the Pennsylvania Rifles, were aware that the soldiers had gone to Halifax in Canada and would probably attack the rebel colonists again when their reinforcements from England arrived. New York, centrally placed on the eastern seaboard, seemed to be their likely objective. There were many loyal Tories living there. By June, British frigates had been spotted probing the defenses at the harbor entrance.

The Americans, realizing a peaceful settlement to the dispute was not forthcoming, began to prepare for the assault.

James Hunter, reorganizing and training his Pennsylvanian riflemen to be part of the 1st Continental Regiment, was dismayed when a miscreant by the name of Saul Smith came up before him for discipline. Smith had joined the rifles when General Washington was desperate enough to take any man to help build up the size of his fighting force. James didn't recognize his old bos'n of the *Heron,* Saul Hugill, because he'd never paid enough attention to the ship's crew in the past.

But Hugill knew who he was.

James disliked the man on sight. His crafty expression and mean mouth told him the man should never have been let in the militia, let alone given a rifle! "Give your firearm back," James ordered. Hugill reluctantly handed over his weapon, or one of them — he still had Mr. Redmarsh's pistol hidden on his person.

"Caught stealing, he was, sir," roared his sergeant. "From a young farmer's widow with young children. He'd bashed in their cottage door and was helping himself to their small food supply when I caught 'im . . ."

Despicable fellow, thought James. "Does Smith get the same victuals as the other men?"

"That he does, sir." The sergeant bellowed on, "He was taking no notice of the woman's pleas not to take her eggs — when they were all she had left to feed her children. He'd kicked their dog that lay whimpering. We don't want heartless men like 'im serving with us, do we, sir?"

"No, we don't, sergeant. Get rid of him."
James glowered at the hatchet-faced man
and got an insolent and vengeful glare in
return. What hope was there for the independent America he was fighting for when
evil men like Smith were around? Good
men like Richard Wakefield had died, and
others were dying now, and many were suffering for the cause of liberty from injus-
tices. This wretched man's behaviour made
a mockery of their sacrifice. James looked at
Smith and shuddered. He wished he had an
excuse to shoot the man. But stealing was
not a capital offence in the militia. If they
were in the British army, then he could have
ordered Smith to be flogged. But they were
not.

He didn't like to let Smith loose, either.
He was a good shot, having been trained as
a sharpshooter, and he might be a danger
to citizens. But there was nothing James
could do but to send the thief away and
hope the disgrace of being dismissed from
the army would make him mend his ways.

After Saul Hugill was turned out of the
army, he returned to Philadelphia. He'd a
little of the money he'd stolen from Hawkes
left, but no prospects. When he'd returned

to Philadelphia before, he'd found the *Heron* had sailed without him. He heard Spear and the ship's captain had been caught and ended up in prison, and thought it served them right for leaving him behind. As it turned out, it was just as well he hadn't been on the ship.

Now he'd no job and nowhere to live. But his days in the army had taught him to survive on very little and how to avoid being seen so that he could thieve.

Saul Hugill, with no purposeful aim in life, nursed revenge. He decided he would like nothing better than to get his own back on James Hunter and that interfering little whore of his, Miss Willoby. Oh, yes, she pretended to be as white as snow, but he knew she'd spent an evening alone with Hunter in that log cabin in the backwoods of Lancaster, didn't he?

That brick he'd thrown through her shop window before he'd joined the army, might have worried her. But Hunter had put a watch on the place, which made it difficult for him to do anything else to harm the little madam. And that Indian servant: he should have killed him instead of binding him up. Now he accompanied her when she was not with a member of the Redmarsh family. Consequently, Hugill lay low for a while, waiting a chance to strike again. His devious mind soon thought of a way.

Several days later, he was concealed behind an elm tree on the sidewalk while he was reconnoitering the large Georgian red-brick house that was surrounded by trees and shrubs, on Society Hill. He'd found out this grand house was where Miss Willoby lived with the Redmarsh family. On occasions, he'd seen Hunter visit — and, come to think of it, the redcoats might be interested in learning about that! He waited for the daylight to fade. This outskirt of the town had no street lighting.

Spitting out the wad of tobacco he'd been chewing, he patted the small box he had in his pocket to make sure it was there. In it he had put a candle and a flint, some gunpowder and fine-ground charcoal he had left over from his army days. It was an incendiary device similar to the one he'd used on the sawmill at Lancaster. Now he had only to get in the house. He'd already thought of a strategy. His features twisted into a smirk as he hummed his own version of an old nursery rhyme:

There once was a peddler whose name
   was Saul,
Fol, lol, did-dle, did-dle dawl,

He went to a house, a fire to start,
Fol de rol, de lol lol lol.

Hugill believed he had a right to sing about his clever plan. And he would sing again, when the fire took hold of the house. Life had been tough for him. He'd virtually done that drunken captain's job of sailing the *Heron,* only to have no one give him any credit. Even that swindling agent, Spear, had left him high and dry.

All his hopes of a comfortable life in his old age had vanished with the *Heron.* And it had all been the fault of that Willoby woman, who'd poked her nose in and found the indentured servants being shipped in the hold, then run off to Lancaster with tales of mismanagement to Hunter. She'd been the cause of his downfall. But Hugill would get even with her.

He was clever, wasn't he? He'd burned Hunter's sawmill to ashes. And he survived, unlike like that loony sailor, Big Jack. He remembered Big Jack's raucous laughter when the gunpowder had exploded in the forest sawmill, sending a shaft of fire way up into the night sky. Big Jack, like a besotted child, wanted to stand and watch the spectacle as if it was a celebration with colored fireworks.

"Come away," Hugill had warned him. "We must get going before someone sees us."

"Nope," said Jack stubbornly, tugging away from Hugill's grasp on his jacket. "I want to watch." The big seaman's eyes were alive with the flames reflected in them. "Look at it, 'ugill."

"By Jasus! Ain't you ever seen a fire before?" Hugill shouted, aware that some of the timber men waking from their slumbers were staggering out of their log cabins and howling when they saw their hard work going up in smoke.

"Come with me, or I'll leave you, so I will," Hugill had threatened.

Big Jack ignored him. With feet spread wide, he put his enormous hands on his hips and stood goggling at the spectacle of sparks and licking flames as the gunpowder they'd laid exploded and iridescent firebrands leapt out of the fiercely burning sawmill.

Hugill had no means of dragging the huge man away with him. He worried that Big Jack might get caught and would be stupid enough to tell the lumbermen that it was his, Hugill's, idea to set fire to the sawmill. And arson was a hanging offence. So Hugill walked smartly up behind the dancing giant, and pushed him into the fire.

Then Hugill saw Mr. Hunter come running up to the blaze and saw him drag a burning man away, rolling him to put out the flames. Hugill stayed long enough to hear Big Jack's screams die out. Knowing the seaman was dead, he sped off. It had taken him some time to get back to Philadelphia since he had to avoid that crafty Indian. The only satisfaction he got when he realized he'd missed his ship was knowing that James Hunter had missed it too.

Now, as the evening darkened, it began raining. Hugill trod stealthily over the road towards the house. His eyes glistened as he rubbed his hand over his wet, pinched face. Fingering Hawkes's flintlock pistol, Hugill pushed it down firmly into the leather belt of the breeches he wore, hiding the butt by covering it with his grimy jacket. Then, holding the peddler's tray he'd managed to steal, he found his way round to the back of the big house to the tradesman's door and knocked on it.

CHAPTER
TWENTY-TWO

The Redmarsh maid, Martha, was busy serving dinner when she heard the rap on the kitchen door. "Oh, bother!" she exclaimed, putting down a pile of unwashed plates. She wiped her hands on her apron and went to answer the door, hoping it might be her sweetheart, although he didn't normally call at this early hour. But as it had become a rainy evening, maybe he was keen to come and sit in her warm kitchen until she finished her work.

Martha took one look at the disreputable-looking peddler and said, "Whatever you're selling, we don't want it, thank you." She grumbled, "Fancy coming at this time of night when I'm getting the family meal. I ask you!" She was about to close the door on him when she found Hugill's foot preventing it. "Get your foot out of the door, you dolt!"

"I want to have a word with your Indian

servant."

"Hawkes?" Martha said, unwittingly giving Hugill his name.

"That's 'im. Hawkes. He's a friend of mine."

Martha hesitated. Hawkes had some friends, but none she'd ever seen looked as rascally as this one. She knew she had no right to judge him, however, or to refuse this man's request to speak to Hawkes.

"Come back later," she said. "The family is at table and have just this minute rung for me to serve the dessert."

His shifty look made her feel uneasy. Hawkes's friends usually had more presence than this fellow. Perhaps he was down on his luck and had been told by Hawkes that he would get some food at the Redmarsh house. So she explained, "There may be some leftovers for you in a little while," thinking he looked half starved, with those staring, hollow eyes.

Hugill's quivering nose sniffed the delicious aroma of food coming from the kitchen. His mouth watered as he spied the half-empty dishes of delectable meats, laid out on the kitchen table, that had been returned from the dining room. He had in mind to grab some of that food after he'd set the building alight.

He licked his lips and said, "Look, missy, I ain't got the time to hang around here in the rain, whilst the gentry finish eating. I'm a relative of Hawkes. Yes, you tell him that, my girl."

My girl, indeed! No way was she his girl, and she never wanted to be. She could smell his unwashed clothes and foul breath. Martha was suspicious. She felt sure there was not a drop of Indian blood in him. But you never knew. She shrugged. "Wait here, then, and I'll get him."

Holding her aproned skirts high, she quickly crossed the big kitchen, and opening the servants' narrow stairway door, she called up the stairs, "Hawkes, there's someone down here wanting to see you."

She waited a moment to make sure he'd heard, then rushed back to put the syllabub dishes on a tray, ready to carry into the dining room. She happened to glance at the kitchen door and found it wide open. The peddler had gone.

Hawkes had run downstairs and joined her at the door.

"Funny," said Martha over her shoulder as she carried the loaded tray towards the dining room. "A peddler called to see you, but he's gone. He said he was a relative of yours."

"A relative?"

Martha stopped walking and turned to face him. "That's what he said."

"But I haven't any."

Martha, anxious to take the heavy tray into the dining room, said, "I must say I didn't think he was."

When she'd left the kitchen, Hawkes went out of the house and looked down the road both ways to see if he could spot the peddler. It was dark and drizzly. He couldn't see much, and he went to search farther down the road, first away from the town and then towards it.

Hugill had listened to the exchange from behind the cellar door, where he'd hidden after slipping into the house while Martha was calling Hawkes to come down from his room. He knew he had just enough time, while that Indian searched for him outside, to start a fire and then hop it.

His skinny mouth widened into an odious smirk at the thought of the blast that would wreck the house. He carefully picked his way down the dark cellar steps after taking a light from one of the house candles.

Mr. Redmarsh possessed a vast wine cellar to house his good stock of fine wines. Entering the dank underground, Hugill looked about and found a place to put some dry tinder he'd brought hidden in the peddler's tray to burn.

In the meantime, Hawkes was running swiftly towards the town in the rain, his keen eyes searching the lamp-lit grid of streets for the peddler. He came across a rain-drenched pie seller trundling home, whose empty cart showed he'd sold the last of his wares. Hawkes gave a description of the man he was seeking.

The pieman scratched his forehead. "Yep, I remember seeing a man with a peddler's tray some time ago. I thought to myself, this cove don't look like a peddler. I know most of the street sellers round here — and he ain't one of them."

Hawkes's eyes glittered.

The pieman continued, "Now I remember. I heard from a mate of mine that a peddler had lost his tray a day ago —"

"What did he look like?"

"You mean the peddler that wasn't a peddler? Let me think . . . sharp as a ferret. I could have sworn he was a sailor. He had a sailor's walk, like my brother. My brother's a sailor."

Hawkes's hackles rose.

The pieman went on, "He was a sailor out of work — perhaps injured, so no captain would employ him, so he's taken to peddling. A lot of men are out of work since the troubles with the British began." As the pieman chatted on about the difficulties the revolution was bringing to everyone, including his family, suspicion about this false peddler struck Hawkes, urging him back to the house.

"Thanks mate," Hawkes cut into the pieman's continuing diatribe. "I must go."

Trotting briskly back towards the house, Hawkes suddenly realized the description of the so-called peddler fitted the mean-faced seaman who'd attacked him on the road to Lancaster — the seaman who'd set fire to the sawmill . . . He broke into a run back to the Redmarshes' house on Society Hill. Hawkes almost sent poor Martha flying as he bolted into the kitchen.

"Watch it!" yelled Martha. She tottered back, holding the big kettle, which splashed some water onto the kitchen floor.

"That peddler, Martha," Hawkes panted, rain running down his face. "Where did he go?"

Martha waddled over to put the kettle on the stove, saying, "I told you, he went ages ago."

Then, turning round and seeing the look of fright on Hawkes's face, she asked,

"What's the matter?"

"I think he's a villain. He might try and burn this house down."

"Mercy on us!" Martha grasped the corner of her apron and stuffed it up into her mouth to stifle a scream. She glanced this way and that, as if she expected the peddler to pop out of the bread crock or the oven.

Hawkes's eyes were also moving, looking for signs. "Are you sure he went away?"

Martha shook her head so violently, her frilled cap slipped to the side of her head. "I dunno."

"So he might be in the house?"

Martha screamed.

Hawkes crept into the pantry and looked around. He then slipped into the scullery where the scullery maid was washing the dishes, and asked her if she'd seen a stranger in the house. But she said she hadn't. Then he tried the stables, the woodshed, and the chicken run before coming back into the kitchen again. There he saw a rain-soaked visitor: Captain James Hunter, Miss Willoby's beau, who'd come late for dinner.

"I heard a scream." James questioned Hawkes: "Martha seems too upset to explain properly. Do I understand there is a strange man loose in the house?"

"Yessir, I think there might be. A peddler,

Martha said he was, but I don't know that he was."

James's experience told him that the Indian suspected something amiss. And, as the Indians he'd known used their sixth sense to a fine degree, he figured Hawkes was probably right.

James was always on the alert for a raid by the British authorities and regretted he'd left his rifle in the stables with his horse. He never liked to frighten the ladies by bringing it indoors.

"Where have you looked?" he asked Hawkes calmly.

"Outside, sir, but he may be in the house."

Seeing James's tall figure in the kitchen, Martha gave another muffled wail and took refuge behind a fan-back Windsor chair.

"Martha, stay where you are," James instructed her. His lips lifted at the corners to give her a weak smile of reassurance.

"Yes, sir," she replied, and obediently sat on the floor, less worried. Mr. Hunter was a man she trusted. She considered he knew what he was about and would soon chase the peddler off, and then she could make the after-dinner coffee as she usually did.

James and Hawkes looked at each other. They understood without discussing it that they needed to make a search of the house, using all their hunting skills. Hawkes had been taught from childhood to stalk prey. James had learned the art of searching for enemies in various terrains from his training as a soldier.

"You go upstairs," he said in a hushed voice. "If you find him there, chase him downstairs, and I'll deal with him."

Hawkes nodded and tiptoed cautiously out of the kitchen.

James had in mind to take the downstairs. He was sure that if the intruder were in the house, he would probably have in mind to steal some silver from the drawing room. As James passed the cellar door, he also thought some of Mr. Redmarsh's fine wines might well go missing.

With a fast, light tread, and keeping alert, James made a quick visit to the drawing room and then the back parlor, which held so many pleasant memories for him and Clementina. He found no one lurking there. Hearing Clementina's light laughter, he decided not to disturb the dinner party in the dining room, but went straight to Ralph's study to make sure there was no one in it before returning to the hall. Then he decided to check the cellar and walked towards it. Strange. He didn't remember the door being ajar when he'd passed it a moment or two before. With great care James opened the door wider and listened.

No sound came from below. But that didn't mean no one was there. Stepping cautiously down the stone steps, alert, he could hear nothing, but really needed a light in order to see. Going back up the stairs, he paused to listen again, in case Hawkes had found the man upstairs. But Hawkes was not calling him, so James darted into the kitchen, grabbing not only a candlestick, but also a rolling pin to arm himself.

Returning to the cellar, he went down the stairs, shining the light from the candlestick to see if anyone was hidden down there. The slam of the cellar door behind him made him jump. Damn! But as he had a lighted candle, James decided while he was there he might as well search the cellar.

His search didn't take long. Smoke and a crackle told him a fire had just been lit. He rushed to find it and stamp out the blaze with his damp boots.

When he noticed a trail of gunpowder, he gasped and he kicked the gunpowder to scatter it.

James realized in a flash that this was the work of an arsonist, and a deadly danger to everyone in the house. The fire raiser had planned to allow himself time to escape before the explosion.

Fury for the man who had started this fire enveloped James. He sweated as he vowed he would catch and punish the rogue. He ran up the cellar steps only to find the heavy wooden cellar door locked.

"Huzzah, Hawkes!" he yelled at the top of his voice, bashing his fist on the door. After a moment or two, he yelled, "The door is locked! Let me out!"

He heard a scuffle on the other side of the door.

"I can't find the key, sir," yelled back Hawkes.

"Break the lock then, man! There's an arsonist in the house."

Hawkes fled back into the kitchen, took the steps of the servants' back staircase two at a time, and tumbled into his room. Under his bed, he took out his tomahawk and raced downstairs with it. Smashing the cellar door with his tomahawk near the lock, Hawkes released the mechanism and let James out of the cellar.

The two men realized they'd been tricked. Their eyes met, foiled hunters determined to do better next time.

"I put out the fire," panted James, "but God knows where the scoundrel is now. We've got to get him. He's a killer, Hawkes."

A cry from the dining room alerted them.

"My God! He's in there!" James cried, aghast, pointing to the dining room. The Redmarsh family was at table. With his darling Clementina.

He thought quickly, then said, "I'll go into the room and try and reason with the fellow, while you nip outside and look in the window. Try to distract him so I can overpower him."

Hawkes gave a quick nod and was off.

James took a deep breath, worried about what he might find in the dining room. As he was opening the door many thoughts raced through his mind. Was this peddler the same man who'd burnt down his sawmill? One of the crew of the *Heron*? And had he escaped? Or was he a crazed Loyalist, who was after James's blood?

In this time of war, it was difficult to tell who his enemy was. Was an enemy waiting for him behind the dining room door? Or were there several men after him? Perhaps the British authorities had at last caught up with him, and he would be overpowered and sent to one of the dreadful British prison hulks floating off the coast.

All at once, James felt as if his death might be near. He was a soldier, and he knew death might strike him at any time. But surely not in the safe Redmarsh house! He had many regrets. For one, he wouldn't see the liberty he'd prepared to die for in his country.

But most of all, James thought of his love, Clementina. If he died, what pain she would go through. For he was convinced she loved him and was expecting to marry him. He'd never got around to asking for her hand. And now he might never have the chance.

CHAPTER
TWENTY-THREE

James Hunter, feeling like a man about to be executed, slowly opened the polished dining room door that, bizarrely, reminded him of a coffin lid. There in the elegant dining room he saw Mr. Redmarsh, standing and supporting his sobbing wife, while Clementina stood erect and ashen. An unshaven, ragged man pointed a pistol at her head. The villain turned to look at him as he came in.

"Smith!"

"The very same." The man sneered.

Smith, the rotten soldier he'd dismissed, had become as dangerous as wayward cannon shot. James could see by his wild eyes that the man was down on his luck and desperate.

Clementina said in a brave voice, "This man is not Smith. He is Hugill."

Hugill! His enemy who had burned his sawmill. And now Hugill threatened his most precious lady. Furious, James Hunter knew he couldn't spring at the man and fight him as a boy might. He had to act like a cool officer to overcome the crazed man. "Your fire is out," he told Hugill as evenly as he could, hoping Hugill would realize his plot had not worked and he would give himself up.

When Hugill realized his plan to set fire to the house had failed, disappointment made him livid. He cursed in a manner that would have shocked Eleanor Redmarsh had she been able to hear it, but her sobs drowned the vile words he uttered.

Clementina, with the gunman threatening her, looked too frightened for anything to register.

"That's enough!" barked James, bravely walking over to Hugill, with his hand out to take the gun. "Give me the gun. Your game is over."

Hugill's snigger was sinister.

James could tell the bluff didn't work when Hugill aimed the pistol at him.

"There now, Captain high-and-mighty Hunter. How would you like your head blown off?"

James didn't look at the madman's eyes; he looked at Clementina. She didn't scream or faint. Her self-control in this dire situation was inspiring. James longed to hold her in his arms for the last time. To tenderly kiss her goodbye . . .

A crash behind them startled everyone.

Hawkes had lifted the window sash with such force it shattered a couple of panes of glass.

Instinctively, Hugill turned to look, losing concentration.

In that instant, Clementina sprang forward. She took hold of Hugill's arm, which was pointing the gun at James, and dragged it down.

But Hugill was quick. He pressed the trigger. The gun fired, shattering the night.

James cried out and fell, as the bullet pierced his body. A gleam of metal flashed from Hugill's sailor's knife as Hugill made to leap on the stricken man, intending to stab James.

Eleanor screamed as a tomahawk whistled through the air. The weapon landed squarely between Hugill's shoulder blades. Hugill tottered and fell. His lean body jerked, then crumpled. His knife skidded across the wooden floor, and crashed against the skirting board as he died.

Hawkes climbed through the window and retrieved his tomahawk from the villain's body.

Clementina gazed in horror at the fallen men for a moment until her wits returned. She saw Hawkes appear and remove his axe from Hugill's body, and shuddered. But her attention was on the prone body of James, who lay writhing and moaning in agony on the floor.

Hawkes and Ralph immediately ran to his aid, covering him from her view as she stood swaying, stunned by the events of the last few minutes. Suddenly becoming aware of Eleanor's loud sobs, Clementina came to her senses. "Is James . . . alive?" she asked in a shaky voice.

"He is," Ralph replied grimly.

Seeing the two men attending to James, and knowing she could do nothing to help, Clementina rushed to assist Eleanor, who had fainted. Numb with shock as she knelt by Eleanor, Clementina lifted her shoulders, so that the older woman's pale face rested on her bosom, hiding her from the growing bloodstain on the carpet.

"We must get James upstairs, Hawkes, and put him on a bed," she heard Ralph say. "Prop the door open with a chair, that's it. Now you take his legs."

A cry of pain from James made Clementina's heart stop. But at least it proved he was alive.

Ralph said, "When we get him upstairs, Hawkes, I want you to run for Doctor Woodberry."

Still cradling Eleanor, Clementina was aware of Ralph and Hawkes carrying James out of the room and up the stairs with much heaving and panting. How she longed to go to James. But she knew she could do no more than the men were already doing to assist him. And Eleanor needed her.

The noise and scurrying brought Martha out of her hiding place to the dining room door. Visibly shaken, she asked, "What's happened, Miss Willoby?"

"Fetch the hartshorn for your mistress, if you please, Martha," called Clementina briskly, anxious that the girl do something useful before she screamed or fainted, when she saw the bloodied remains of Hugill. When Martha had scampered off, Clementina left Eleanor and hastily threw the rug that covered the dining room table when it was not in use over Hugill's body. Satisfied Martha would not see the corpse when she returned, she then returned to Eleanor and found her recovering.

"Where am I?" asked Eleanor, as the pink-ness returned to her cheeks.

"You had a little fall, my dear, but you'll be fine in a minute or two," fibbed Clementina, thinking it was better that Eleanor know nothing of the tragedy.

Martha came rushing in with the smelling salts and waved them under her mistress's nose until Eleanor protested, "That's quite enough of that, thank you, Martha."

Clementina said, "Now you are better, shall I take you to the parlor, Eleanor?"

"Where is Ralph? And James?"

Clementina's dry throat made it difficult for her to answer. Eleanor and Martha would learn that James had been injured sooner or later, but for the present she considered it was better they didn't know. So Clementina said as nonchalantly as she could, "They've had to go upstairs."

"Oh." Eleanor looked around at the uncleared dining table. "Have I had my dessert?"

Martha, seeming to understand Clementina was trying to keep her mistress calm, said, "No, ma'am. Shall I bring it to the parlor for you?"

Mrs. Redmarsh seemed happy with that suggestion, so Clementina and Martha assisted the lady out of the dining room and into the parlor. Once in the parlor and settled, Eleanor relished the syllabub Martha brought for her. "Didn't you want any?" she asked Clementina.

Clementina shook her head.

Eleanor chatted for a while, and then dozed on the settle, while Clementina paced the parlor softly, longing to rush upstairs and see James, but believing she should stay in the parlor and keep an eye on Eleanor.

A little later, she heard the doorbell and the doctor being greeted and taken upstairs.

She wept silent tears.

She must have sat with Eleanor and dozed. She awoke when she heard a tap on the door before Ralph and Martha came in.

Eleanor roused herself. "What time is it?"

"The hour is late, my dear," answered Ralph calmly. "You should go to your bed."

Martha, who looked forward to being in hers, went to assist her mistress.

Clementina was leaving the room, too, when Ralph put his hand on her arm and whispered, "I would like a word with you."

Seeing Eleanor being helped upstairs by Martha, Clementina and Ralph went back into the parlor.

"How is he?" asked Clementina, her mouth dry.

"The doctor says it is a nasty shoulder

wound, but with careful nursing he should recover."

Clementina breathed more easily.

Ralph asked, "Does my wife know what happened?"

"I can't be sure what she saw or remembers. But I don't think she is aware of all that happened. I don't think she would have enjoyed her syllabub if she'd known a man had just been killed in her dining room!"

Ralph gave a slight smile. "That's just as well, or her chattering would spread her account of it all around Philadelphia in the morning!"

Clementina smiled desolately back at him.

"Harrumph!" He now looked down at her with a serious expression. "Clementina, I'm sure you are aware we have a few difficulties to overcome."

"Yes, sir. We have James to protect until he is well enough to leave Philadelphia. And the body?"

Ralph nodded, indicating she had summarized the problems. Then he turned and walked up and down the room, as if deep in thought. He suddenly swung round. "I've been law-abiding all my life, and don't like to break the law. I should report the death. But the royal authorities here seem to have melted away. Philadelphia is not . . . how shall I say . . . normal, at the moment."

Clementina knew nothing about local government, and could only take his word for it. "Indeed," she murmured.

Ralph continued, "I believe too many inquiries about Hugill's death could raise awkward questions. If the British authorities got to know about the incident, we might be in trouble."

Clementina sensed that the British administration, although in disarray, could still punish wrongdoers. "Yes, it could," she agreed again. She could also have said that she'd always been law-abiding too. But was that so? When she thought about it, she could hardly believe how her sins had mounted since she'd left England. She'd stolen, told lies, assisted in the death of a man — and now she wanted to cover up that death.

It was humbling to realize she was so humanly frail. She was prepared to break the law and to be disloyal to her country, and all for the love of a man. Her beau. She knew Ralph had it in mind to protect James. James, as a Patriot — a rebel in the eyes of the British — had to be kept hidden from the British authorities. She didn't suffer any pangs of conscience about Hugill's death. She considered he'd brought it on himself.

He was an evil man. He would have killed her, as he'd tried to kill James. Clementina accepted Ralph's suggestion that he and Hawkes dispose of the body. In this time of strife, the authorities did not raise an eyebrow if someone reported yet another body found floating in the Delaware River.

Ralph explained, "The Indians have different laws from us. Hawkes killed Hugill, and has no remorse whatsoever for doing it, because he reckons he was protecting his tepee —"

"His what?"

"His tepee. His tent, his home. And he was protecting members of his own family, or tribe, from a man who would have killed them."

Clementina bit her lip thoughtfully and said, "Yes, I can understand his reasoning. It's not so different from ours."

"It is only different in that once the deed is done, he is not obliged to tell the authorities about it. He tells me he will take the body in a cart tonight to a secluded part of the countryside where he hides his canoe, and paddle upriver and bury Hugill himself."

In the silence that followed, Clementina closed her eyes. She was tired. It was difficult after the shock of Hugill's death, and

James's near death, to bring herself to listen to what Ralph was saying.

"We have another problem," Ralph went on as Clementina was still reeling from the first. "Who is to nurse James? He can't go to the hospital with a gunshot wound. The authorities might —"

"Question how he came to be shot," Clementina finished his sentence.

"Exactly so. So who shall tend the wounded man?"

"I can, and I will," Clementina said firmly. Then she asked, "Will he be safe here?"

Ralph shook his head. "It wouldn't be wise for him to stay here. But he has a house of his own on the lower end of Walnut Street."

"He has?" That was news for Clementina.

Ralph nodded. "He mentioned it to me some time back. A refuge, he called it. He has a housekeeper looking after it, I believe. That would be the safest place for us to hide him."

"Yes, I suppose it would." From everyone's point of view, it would be better to move him from the Redmarsh residence. Except her own. They both knew she would be compromising herself if she moved in with him. But she told herself in wartime one had to make sacrifices. She knew people might ask questions if he stayed with the Redmarshes. And Eleanor, not fully understanding the need for secrecy, might well gossip too much.

James had to have someone they could trust to nurse him, and who was more trustworthy than herself? The hour now was late. If lights were seen from outside the Redmarsh house, they would draw attention, and they did not want that to happen. Clementina had to make an instant decision. "We should douse the candles and retire for the night," Clementina said. "Tomorrow we can discuss the details of James and me moving to Walnut Street without anyone knowing. And Hawkes will be back to help us."

"You are a good, brave lady, Miss Willoby."

Clementina gave a little laugh. "A foolish one, don't you think?"

"No, Clementina, you're not foolish. You're prepared to risk your reputation and your life to save an American Patriot. You deserve praise."

"I would do the same for an Englishman." She did not add she would do the same for an Englishman if he were a good man and she loved him, but she presumed Ralph understood that. Clementina said no more but went to snuff out the parlor candles, noticing as she did so that her hand shook.

No, she didn't want praise, a medal, or a trophy, or anything like that. She just wanted James to get well.

As she lay down to sleep that night, she heard the groans of pain coming from James's room, and remembered what Mrs. Cod had frequently told her. She prayed, and trusted that God would help him recover.

The Second Continental Congress had been in session in Philadelphia since May. The journals, which recorded the meetings, were available for anyone to see — but they did not include some secret sections, in which plans were being laid for the thirteen colonies to become the United States of America.

Some countries were keen to see Britain lose their American colonies, and France was one. During the summer of 1776, a Frenchman arrived in Philadelphia from the French court to fan the flames of revolt and provide aid in the form of a loan of three million *livres* to the insurgents. His name was Paul Leblanc. He found lodgings in Walnut Street, almost opposite the house James owned. Monsieur Leblanc had a mission, but plenty of time on his hands, as the American delegates of the Continental Congress were secretly drafting the Declaration of Independence. He also had an eye for the ladies. And it was not long before he noticed a very nicely dressed little woman coming and going from the house opposite his lodgings. Someone told him she was a mantua-maker.

CHAPTER
TWENTY-FOUR

Clementina was surprised when she went to James's fine house on Walnut Street. In the back of her mind she'd stored the information that James was a wealthy man. But seeing him mainly in the backwoods in workingman's clothes, and then as a soldier in uniform, and now, as an invalid in bed, she'd forgotten what an important Philadelphian citizen he was. His house reflected his wealthy status without being ostentatious. It was well situated in a tree-lined, lamp-lit street near the Pennsylvania State House where the Congressional delegates met. And the Wakefield family was nearby, which prevented her from feeling isolated from everyone she knew.

His four-story brick home had plenty of room for her to live in a spinster's apartment within the house. The whole house had a comfortable air about it, with well-polished wood, and it showed James to be a practical, rather than an elegant, owner.

The housekeeper, she was pleased to discover, was a pleasant and efficient person. A Quaker widow of advanced age, Mrs. Norris kept the house in immaculate condition. This meant Clementina had no housework to do.

"I'll cook meals for thee if thee wishes, as well as for Mr. Hunter," offered Mrs. Norris.

"Thank you, Mrs. Norris," said Clementina, only too pleased to be relieved of the shopping, washing and cooking tasks, so that she could concentrate on nursing James and her dressmaking work.

Mrs. Norris was no gossip, either. Her employer had instructed her, when the troubles began, not to discuss him or what he did or tell her friends his whereabouts.

Clementina felt sure she was a tight-lipped woman who would not trot down to the market and mention that her master was back in his house, injured, watching their eyes grow wide as she whispered behind her hand that there was a young lady come to live in the house to nurse him.

James lay in a poor state for days. He was in pain from his injury and tossed about so much, Clementina had to keep checking to make sure his bandages remained in place.

She had to change them daily to keep the wound clean, and she hoped and prayed she would find no sign of infection.

As she washed and tended him, he sometimes murmured. But his replies to her questions were confused. He opened his eyes to the sound of her voice, but closed them again as if he couldn't see her. "Drink, please drink," she would beg him, offering him water in a cup. Sometimes he did take a little water, although the effort quickly exhausted him, just as the effort exhausted her. Ominous signs that he might be slipping away made her call frantically to get him to respond, but if he did flicker his eyelashes, it was only briefly before he'd slip back into a coma again. She liked to think his strong, healthy body was taking time to get over the harm that had been done to it. She remembered the doctor's assurance that he would get well and knelt by his bed holding his limp hand, praying he would.

Then one day her prayers were answered.

He stirred. "Clementina," he said, his blue eyes looking straight at her. "What are you doing in my chamber?"

She almost smiled, but said, "Do you not recall you were injured? I've been nursing you."

He seemed affronted. "But you can't!

Young ladies don't nurse men."

"This one does. Have a sip of water. Now lie quietly. I'll ask Mrs. Norris to bring you some broth."

He lay looking at the plasterwork decoration on his ceiling as if it was a puzzle, then said, "I don't like broth."

Clementina was about to leave the room, but stayed by the door, holding it open. "The chicken broth she makes is very good. I'm sure you'll like it."

His head turned towards her. "How do you know?"

"Because she makes some for me, too."

She left him and trotted downstairs in the lightest mood she had enjoyed for days. She told Mrs. Norris her master was recovering and would like some of her excellent chicken broth.

The housekeeper said, "He don't like broth, Miss Willoby."

"He will take it nevertheless, Mrs. Norris," she replied with spirit. "So please get it out of the larder and put it on to boil."

Leaving the kitchen, she heard Mrs. Norris chuckle. "Thee are right for him, I can tell," she said to Clementina's departing back.

When she got upstairs, she found James had eased himself into a sitting position. He

405

said as soon as she got in the door, "I would like to know —"

"You won't hear anything from me until you have taken your nourishment."

Weakly he gave her the tiniest smile. When he'd been fed and drunk some water, he fell asleep. Clementina noted his breathing was easier and rejoiced. She had a message sent to Ralph to say that, at last, James was on the mend.

The invalid made rapid progress.

His questions came fast, and Clementina answered them reassuringly. Yes, Hugill was dead and buried. No, Mr. Redmarsh did not report the death, as Hawkes took the body and disposed of it as an Indian would dispose of his enemy. No one had inquired after, or indeed missed, Hugill.

James was glad to be back in his own home, although he also seemed anxious to recover his strength as, he hinted several times, he had work to do.

The doctor called and was closeted with James for some time. "You have nursed him well," the doctor remarked as he left the house.

"When will he be able to use his arm again?"

The doctor shook his head, "I fear he will be disabled."

Shocked to hear this grave news, Clementina saw the doctor away and went immediately to see James. He was sitting in a chair near the window as if in a trance.

"James, I —"

"Know what the doctor told me. I'm not able to be a soldier, or a timber man, again."

"Yes, that is so," she said simply. What use was there in pretending she didn't know the effect his frozen shoulder would have on his life? He would no longer be able to fell trees, or use a rifle. He looked momentarily like an older man, strained with the knowledge he had to bear the burden of coping with the result of Hugill's wound all his life.

"You could have been shot in battle," she said, trying not to let her voice quaver.

"So I could, Clementina." He was searching her eyes. Was he looking for strength or pity?

"But you saved my life. And you are recovering well, the doctor tells me. You will be up and about in no time and learning to ride again. You can use a pistol with your left hand if you practice."

He chuckled. Perhaps it was with bitterness as he assessed his predicament, or perhaps it was because the positive suggestions Clementina was making helped him see a way forward. Then he calmed down and she saw him use his handkerchief to wipe away the tears that had rolled down his face.

"Come here," he said softly.

She came and knelt by him, brushing his curls from his forehead. "It won't be too bad for you," she said. "It's surprising how well people cope with physical disadvantages when they get used to them."

"I'm in no worse case than many a battle-worn hero. Except if people think I was wounded in battle, I will know — and you will know — I am a fraud."

"No!" she said, shocked. "I have seen you perform many a brave act. You are a hero."

He smiled wryly at her. "I think one could say my injury is my punishment for neglecting my duties. Hugill should never have been hired as bos'n on the *Heron.* You saw how he inflicted suffering on the indentured servants. I should have known what kind of a man he was. Then I should have recognized him when he joined my rifle company."

She leant forward to kiss him. "Perhaps you should, but that mistake was made a long time ago," she murmured, and kissed him again. "Now you must look forward to your future."

"It is not very promising," he said sorrowfully, looking at his injured arm.

"Indeed it is," she rejoined.

"What do you suggest? I don't suppose General George Washington will find me useful now."

Clementina had no answer for that. All she wanted to do was to comfort him. Her hands slid around his body, and she laid her head on his chest.

Stroking her hair with his good arm, he said, "I have a lot to thank you for."

She didn't answer because tears had come into her own eyes. They were tears of bitterness, although a different bitterness from his, because hers were from knowing she loved him more than anything in the world, and yet her future was as uncertain as his. He might have thought she was crying for him, because he made no comment. Life had to go on, and she had to get up and get on with her daily tasks. She also believed that James had to be left alone to come to terms with his disability, to decide on his future.

But in a physically limited way they could make love when they were alone. She felt no embarrassment when their kisses became longer and deeper. His hands strayed to touch her neck and breasts and brought pleasure to her, although she had an acute longing to have him all to herself. She did wonder if he intended to ask her to marry him. He had plenty of opportunity to ask. But James was, she thought, still more concerned with his country's troubles and his future than with her.

Or perhaps he realized the conflict with Britain had only just begun. General Washington refused to negotiate terms of peace, and the British wouldn't recognize his status. They kept referring to him as Mr. Washington, as if he were nothing but a rebel instead of the leader of the revolutionary army. Therefore, James didn't want to get her, an Englishwoman, involved with a rebel, as he was classified.

So she didn't bombard him with questions. She sensed James would make up his own mind in good time. In the meantime, their relationship was tender and loving, and they suffered as all lovers did who had to delay the consummation of their love.

But she had plenty to do. His recovery meant Clementina had the opportunity to slip along to her mantua shop more often, which, fortunately, was only a short distance away. She could make sure all was in order. And it was, of course, because she'd trained her girls well — so well, in fact, the town's ladies continued to push in front of each other to order new gowns, despite the colonies' troubles with their British overlords.

Clementina was in her element, designing the simpler styled gowns of wartime and making do with any materials that became available to make them up. This included unpicking old gowns and salvaging their materials to make new ones.

It was a lovely summer evening when she was walking back from the shop, anxious to be with James, when she met Monsieur Leblanc.

"Oh, la la!" he exclaimed as if he hadn't deliberately collided with her.

At first Clementina thought she'd been in such a hurry she'd accidentally brushed up against this elegant gentleman. "Excuse me," she said, stepping sideways to walk past him. But he also stepped in the same direction, blocking her way.

It was possible for two people trying to pass one another to find themselves moving in the same direction and still find they are blocking each other's way. For a moment, Clementina thought that was what had happened.

"Madam." The Frenchman gave an elaborate bow. "I see you are determined to waylay me."

"Indeed no, sir!" she said quickly. Then she gave him a polite smile. "I regret I was in a hurry to get home."

"Home?" he questioned. He sported a little moustache, which he smoothed with his finger.

"I mean where I am staying . . . I mean my lodgings."

"Ah, your lodging house. The house of Monsieur Hunter, I believe?"

Clementina was cross; she was almost at James's front door, and to be accosted by this stranger and questioned was intolerable. It was unfair to have been captured like this when all she wanted was to get in the house. How did he know where James lived, she wondered. He couldn't be a British spy because he was obviously a Frenchman and she knew the French were hostile to the British and supported the Americans, even though they pretended they didn't.

"You have such wonderful eyes, madam," he said. "A graceful figure I always admire. And a face that would fit on a statue of Venus."

Clementina gasped. What forwardness! And what downright stupid things he said. If this was the way Frenchwomen liked to hear their men flirt with them, so be it. But she found it ridiculous. Besides, the sentiment was untrue. She possessed no more than tolerable features, and believed her eyes to be a rather ordinary light brown color.

"Monsieur," she said crisply. "Pray let me pass."

His true nature came out when he smirked at her and suggested, "Madam, shall we take a glass of wine together, eh?"

Clementina wanted to escape from him. She tried to dodge by him, but he was too quick and held on to her. "Unhand me, sir, at once!" She raised her voice so that a group of men walking along the sidewalk opposite turned to look at her.

"Madam," her tormentor hissed, "there is no need to raise your voice. I know you are the mistress of Monsieur Hunter. I have seen you come and go from his house. And every night you stay there."

Clementina's temper bubbled over. "I beg your pardon, monsieur," she cried. "You have enormous audacity to accuse me thus, when you know nothing about me."

Because she made such a loud protest, the gentlemen across the street stopped and came over. "May we be of any assistance to you, ma'am?" a short, portly gentleman enquired, looking over the top of his glasses at her.

Clementina did not have to say yes, because the Frenchman, taking a look at the party of gentlemen, had rushed away. Crimson-faced, Clementina was at a loss before the gentlemen offering her help.

"May I escort you home, ma'am?"

The courteous Americans appeared genuinely concerned. Clementina knew she was shaking. Her knees were threatening to give way. "Thank you, kind sirs," she answered in a thin, quivering voice that didn't sound like her own at all. "I'm almost home. I live in the next house." She pointed to it.

"Why, that is James Hunter's house, is it not?"

Fear crept over her. Not only had that flirtatious Frenchman accused her of living with James, but now these professional gentlemen might scorn her too. She didn't answer.

"Are you his wife?" asked an erect gentleman.

She couldn't help blushing. "N-no," she stammered. "I've been nursing him."

"Has he been injured, ma'am?"

She looked at each gentleman in turn. They seemed genuinely interested to know the answer. But how did she know if they were Tories who might betray James? They might even have him cast into prison!

CHAPTER
TWENTY-FIVE

Already reeling from her encounter with the lecherous Frenchman, Clementina strove to think how she could get over the hurdle of being questioned about James by these inquisitive gentlemen — and without allowing her concern about him to show. A threatening headache made her put her hand to her forehead as Clementina found herself clenching her teeth.

"Yes, Mr. Hunter has been ill," she said cautiously, with as even a voice as she could manage, hoping she would not have to say more about him. "But he is now almost recovered."

The gentlemen murmured their sympathies.

"Thank you, gentlemen," she said with a polite smile. And after giving them a little curtsy, she turned to walk towards James Hunter's house.

"Wait!" the portly man cried, coming up

to her with a lively step. "Is he at home right now?"

Having extricated herself from the mire, Clementina now felt herself in it again. What should she say? Her head throbbed.

"Well, I don't know if he would want to meet you," she replied in her prim manner, sidestepping the question.

For some reason, the gentlemen found this exceedingly amusing and roared with laughter.

She gave them a thin smile and turned again to enter the house.

"Tell him," said the round-faced, long-haired gentleman, "that Dr. Franklin would like a word with him."

"Dr. Franklin?"

"And Mr. Jefferson and Mr. Lee, who are members of Congress."

"Oh!" Clementina's mind whirled. They were congressmen. They must be men who supported the rebels. She didn't have any fear about letting them enter the house, if they were telling the truth — and giving them a critical stare, she decided they were. Indeed, there were no fancy clothes or haughty manners to be observed about these gentlemen who stood bravely against British domination of their colonies.

One of the gentlemen came nearer her

and said confidentially, "We know Mr. Hunter, my dear, and would like to discuss an urgent matter with him."

Clementina decided to show them into the house. Then she would go upstairs and ask James if he wanted to meet them. "May I suggest, gentlemen, that you step into the parlor? Then I shall ask Mr. Hunter if he is well enough to meet you."

The gentlemen seemed to be amused by that statement, too, but trooped into the house after her, and seated themselves around the oval table, where they began talking earnestly with each other.

"Excuse me, sirs. Would you care for a drink?" she asked.

The gentlemen turned to her. "Why that is most civil of you, my dear," Dr. Franklin said. "I am partial to a glass of Redmarsh's Madeira wine."

Clementina smiled. "And a slice of cake?"

"Yes, indeed. Wine and cake would not come amiss."

As Clementina rushed into the kitchen and asked the housekeeper to provide some refreshments in the parlor as soon as she could, she thought James might be glad to have some visitors as he had become bored of late. He'd been wandering around the house during the last few days, not knowing quite what to do with himself. The healthier he got, the more unsettled and tetchy he seemed to become. She found him upstairs in his study, reading. "James," she said cautiously, "there is a Dr. Franklin in the parlor, who would like to speak with you."

He leapt to his feet. "Who did you say?"

She swallowed, wondering if she'd done the right thing to let the gentlemen in. "I said Dr. Franklin is waiting in the parlor to speak with you."

"My God. Not *the* Dr. Franklin?"

She shrugged. "I don't know what you mean. He came with a Mr. Jefferson, I think he said he was. And another congressman . . ." She stood with her mouth open in amazement as James gave a whoop of delight and rushed to the door, saying, "Benjamin Franklin and Thomas Jefferson, I think you mean."

As she watched his enthusiasm, she smiled, her headache easing. "Well, I'm pleased you didn't mind me asking them in. I wasn't sure . . ." Her voice faded into silence because James was already halfway down the stairs. Clementina rested her arms and head on the banister, relieved to see James moving so rapidly. He had overcome his illness, and was well at last. She knew his shoulder would always be stiff, but that was only a slight disablement. It wouldn't prevent him from doing most things.

It wouldn't prevent him from making love with a woman, for instance. But she didn't know if she was the woman he wanted now that he was better. He'd recovered and was his handsome self again so she knew he could attract many other ladies.

She had now almost reached the old age of twenty-nine. Wouldn't James want to marry a younger woman? Unfortunately, she thought he might. She'd been useful to him and he'd been kind to her, giving her the shop in Bath. But now it was all over. She had no reason to stay here, had she?

She had a thriving business in England to return to. Ladies always wanted new clothes. And an attractive, orderly shop with skilled seamstresses, would always be in demand in England, as well as in the growing colonies. She was lucky, she supposed, to have her dressmaking skills to fall back on.

She had to admit though that, deep in her heart, she wanted, above all, a man to love. A true love. A man she respected. He wouldn't have to be perfect in looks or body, or be free of any slight defects of character. After all, she wasn't free from imperfections, was she? And as she weighed everything in her mind, she kept thinking

419

James was perfect for her. It was just a shame it couldn't be. She would just have to be content with her professional success.

Remembering that it was necessary for her to help Mrs. Norris with the refreshments, Clementina immediately cast aside her own concerns and trotted downstairs to help.

When the trays were ready to be carried into the parlor, Clementina knocked on the door, and in the ladies went.

It was obvious to Clementina that the gentlemen had been discussing some secret business. The conversation halted and papers were hurriedly put away, as the men rose to greet the ladies with polite comments.

James, Clementina noted, seemed easy with his visitors. After Clementina had put down the tray and poured out some coffee, Mrs. Norris offered coffee or Madeira wine to the visitors. She then handed round the plate of cakes.

James was talking to Dr. Franklin when she came up to them, smiling. "Clementina, I would like you to meet a most distinguished American gentleman."

James went on to tell Clementina that the portly gentleman was not only a statesman, but also a scientist. He'd traveled widely and was very learned. He'd designed the

Franklin stove.

After listing some of his achievements, James then went off to talk to another gentleman. So Clementina gave Dr. Franklin a low, respectful curtsy, as she used to curtsy to Princess Amelia.

"Oh, you must not bow to me, ma'am. I'm an American. And all Americans are equal."

"But I am English," she said, lifting her chin to show she was not ashamed to admit being a citizen of Great Britain.

"So James told me. You are his intended, I believe?"

Clementina went scarlet. She thought quickly that perhaps James had said that to explain her presence in his house. She didn't deny it. She kept her head up and retained her composure as he looked at her over the rims of his glasses. She said, "I am a mantua-maker by trade, sir. From Bath, in the county of Somersetshire."

"And my family came from Northamptonshire," he announced promptly, "and I am a printer by trade."

Clementina warmed to him. His soulful eyes reminded her of a spaniel. But there was an active, intelligent brain in his head.

So when he asked her directly, "What have you to say about colonial liberty and freedom from imperial authority, ma'am?" she almost died of fright.

Her natural honesty came to the fore. "I believe, sir, we should endeavor to be tolerant and work together."

"Ah, yes, ma'am. So do I. But when good will turns sour and conflict comes, what then?"

He was making her decide about her position in the revolution. She frowned as she thought hard. Then she said, "I think when a child grows to be an adult, it is right for that child to be independent, however much the parents wish it to be a child forever. Some family battles may take place. But in the end, the parents will be pleased to see their child become independent. A new relationship will be forged between the older parents and their maturing young. Tolerance on both sides will always be needed."

She then realized James had returned and was standing by her side, listening to what she said, so she went on to make it clear to James what she thought. "England and America will, I believe, always be friends, no matter what quarrels they may have at present. My heart is with England, but I have grown to love America, too. I accept that the colonies are too big to be governed by England and want to determine their own future."

Dr. Franklin turned to him and said, "There now, Mr. Hunter, you couldn't want a more intelligent and reasonable lady."

Happiness spread through Clementina as she saw the wide smile James gave her.

The congressmen said they had to leave then and courteously made their exit.

Watching them walk away James remarked, "They have asked me to assist them as a confidential clerk."

"Oh, and are you able to do that?"

James smiled. "I was once an Oxford scholar. I haven't forgotten how to write."

She smiled back at him. "Of course you were." He was once a successful sawmill designer and a successful soldier, so why couldn't he become a successful scribe as well? She was so pleased he'd been given a job to do. And it was an important job, too, she deduced from the company who'd just left. "I have often wondered why you were sent down from Oxford University?" she asked.

"I was accused of stealing."

"And you did not?"

"I did not. I made the mistake of trusting a student who was a thief, and who craftily managed to put the blame on me."

"And your father didn't believe you were

innocent?"

James sighed. "My father sent me away to school at an early age. We were never close. He chose to believe the authorities rather than my own account of the event."

Clementina bowed her head. "That must have been hard for you to bear."

"It was. But I had not yet learned to be careful whom I trusted. As you know, Nathaniel Spear was able to abuse my trust. And that led to many people suffering."

Clementina inhaled deeply. She couldn't deny that was true. "Nathaniel Spear has been caught and punished. You are free to start again. And just take care whom you trust in future."

"I will," he said. He took her in his arms and held her close.

He would have kissed her then, she felt sure, but Mrs. Norris came bustling in to clear the plates, cups and glasses away.

Nancy's baby was due and Clementina, free from her nursing duties, was able to visit her friend. Nancy had long forgotten the old wives' tales Arabella and Harriet Timpson had told her. Prompted by Clementina, both girls had visited Nancy, bringing gifts for the coming baby. They'd all became friends again.

Mrs. Cod told Nancy she was ready to act as midwife the moment she was needed.

When Clementina visited Eleanor and Ralph Redmarsh, they were pleased to see her. Sitting in their elegant drawing room, Eleanor asked her the question she most dreaded to hear. "So what are your plans for the future now, my dear?"

"I can't think what to do," she said sadly and with perfect honesty.

"Your dressmaking business is going well, I trust?"

"Oh yes, indeed it is, thank you."

"So it is James Hunter that makes you sad?"

The color rose in Clementina's cheeks. She was aware that Eleanor was a chatterbox and would pass on anything she told her, so she replied, "Oh no. He is quite well now." She lowered her voice. "He's working for some congressmen. It is most gratifying to see him looking so well now, and so happily occupied."

Clementina was aware it was she, rather than James, Eleanor was enquiring about. But she was anxious not to allow Eleanor to pursue the subject of her relationship with James until she'd had time to sort it out in her own mind. "I must leave now," she said, getting up, "if you will excuse me. I've just remembered I promised to visit a customer about a gown she says has been made too long for her. I need to see it on her, as I offered to alter it." It was a lie. But Clementina had to think of something to leave quickly. On the way back to Walnut Street, she felt tears threatening. She hoped she would not meet that dreadful Frenchman again.

Should she, perhaps, start calling herself by the courtesy title Missus, as Mrs. Hunter had done in Bath, and begin to wear matronly clothes? That would be a shame, as she enjoyed dressing in the pretty, fashionable gowns she'd made for herself to inspire the Philadelphian ladies.

She developed a throbbing head again, thinking about what it was she should do.

Then she smiled when she remembered kindly Mrs. Cod, who would tell her to let God sort the matter out. Consequently, she went back to Walnut Street in a serene mood.

At dinner James announced that tomorrow would be a significant day.

She smiled at him. "Indeed? Why?"

His endearing smile made her catch her breath. She wanted to cry. She loved him so much. Too much to stay in the same house with him any longer, she decided. Could she have an apartment for herself over her shop, as Mrs. Hunter had over her shop in Bath?

"The delegates from the thirteen colonies are going to vote," he said, and continued eating his roast duck.

He was only interested in the Continental Congress now, thought Clementina. Piqued, she said, "James, I'll have to think about moving out. I need to make a home of my own."

That made him put down his fork with a clatter.

"Yes," she continued, "I can't continue to stay here now that you are well. I've stayed too long as it is. I wondered if I should —"

"Hold on!" he cried. "I mean, give it another day before you make any decisions, eh? I've just told you, tomorrow you may change your mind."

Amazed and intrigued, Clementina nodded. "Very well."

CHAPTER
TWENTY-SIX

On a sunny morning in July, when Clementina awoke, she remembered James had told her it was to be a very special day. The thought fascinated her and she pondered the possibilities.

She was worried though, because, although they'd enjoyed a companionable evening together, he'd not attempted to make love to her, and she desperately wanted him. She feared he was disappointed after she told him of her plan to move out, and he might want to break the amorous attachment they had begun.

She didn't want to leave his home, because if she went, she might break their tenuous tie forever. But she refused to be his mistress, or to linger while he formed an attachment to another lady.

Forlorn because she had no idea where to go if she left his house, she sighed. The kindly Redmarshes would most likely have her back, but was it wise to return to them? It would take time and a great many arrangements for her to make her home over the shop.

Disturbed by a strange feeling she was living in a kind of limbo, she found it difficult to make any firm decisions. She was not happy — but she wasn't exactly unhappy, either. Her mind seemed unable to cope with thoughts of her future.

But James had told her the day was going to be significant. So she took trouble with her toilet, brushing her auburn hair till it shone, and washing with lavender-scented soap, as well as dabbing a delicious-smelling French perfume onto her neck and wrists. Then she took her time selecting from her considerable array of fine gowns hanging in her wardrobe the one that would best suit this momentous day — if indeed it was, as James had said. She smiled as she looked through her gowns. She'd come a long way from the little orphan girl who'd owned one dress.

In the end she chose her favorite, well-worn mantua made from woven silk with a floral design, with a cap to match.

James Hunter's house on Walnut Street had been pleasant to live in. Clementina loved its warm, polished-wood interior. Beautifully grained wood patterns were sufficient decoration, without the addition of a great many pictures and ornaments. And yet the house's very simplicity seemed to be waiting for something more. Did it need a lady to bring a softer touch to the interior?

To her disappointment, James had gone out by the time she trotted down to breakfast. But he'd left a small posy of red rosebuds on her plate, with a note saying he'd something that had to be done, but he'd be back as soon as he could, and would she please stay in. She was touched to see the nosegay and wondered if he felt a trifle guilty because he intended to cast her off.

She gave a little shudder as the thought crossed her mind that perhaps he had another woman. But she would have to brace herself because she knew he surely would get married one day. *I'll wait and see why he wants me to stay here today. My dressmaking shop will run smoothly without me. I'm sure the girls will continue their work whether I'm there or not.* She relished the idea of having a holiday on this sunny morning. For her it was a treat to have time to do as she pleased. It was a luxury known to ladies, but not working girls. Mrs. Norris was such a wonderful housekeeper; it really wasn't necessary for Clementina to do a thing.

Clementina knew she was very fortunate. Or was she? The thorny question of her future still hung over her. She was arranging some flowers in the hall when the doorbell rang. "I'll go," she called to Mrs. Norris, who was working in the kitchen.

Opening the front door, she saw Hawkes outside with a broad grin on his face. He held out a note for Clementina, but she didn't have to open it to guess his good news.

"Is it a boy or a girl, Hawkes?" she asked, smiling at him.

"A fine boy, ma'am. Born this morning at four o'clock."

Clementina laughed and pressed her hands together in joy. "A male addition to the Redmarsh and Fisher families. What wonderful news!" she exclaimed. "Tell them how happy I am. And Mr. Hunter will be, too, when I tell him."

A visit to see Nancy and her new baby was something she would look forward to. But she would wait a day or so, because Nancy would need rest, and her family would be joyfully fussing around her and admiring the infant.

After that exciting news, Clementina felt

unsettled, waiting for James to return. She wandered into her room and sat on her bed, wondering what furniture she would be able to find if she had her own home. Perhaps one of her seamstresses knew of some she could buy secondhand.

She looked at her accumulated belongings. She had some pretty things now, as well as a good wardrobe of clothes. Little presents had been given to her. She smiled, thinking she certainly wouldn't be able to fit all her things in one small trunk as she had when she came to Philadelphia.

Looking through her drawers, she came across the drawing Thomas Gainsborough had made of James when he was young. What a fine picture it was. As she stood looking at it, there was a tap on the door.

"Come in," she called, thinking it would be Mrs. Norris.

"Are you sure?" James's face peeked round the door as he opened it.

Clementina, momentarily shocked he'd come to her bedchamber, didn't want to remark on it, so she said nothing.

"What have you got there?" he asked, strolling in and looking at the drawing in her hand.

She gave him the picture. "I took it from your aunt's drawer before I left England," she confessed, shamefaced, but he didn't mind.

He grinned. "Oh, I remember Mr. Thomas Gainsborough doing this drawing of me in Bath," he said. "It's a portrait of a gullible youth."

Clementina looked at the hardened man standing close to her, thinking he was no longer an untried boy. "I think it's a beautiful portrait of a fine young man by a master painter," she said. "I liked you as you were then," she said. "I don't think you were gullible. Only a little too trusting perhaps, before life dealt you some hard blows."

He put his arm around her slight shoulders. His closeness delighted her. His deep voice sounded in her ear. "Don't you like me now, Clementina?"

She flushed. She could smell his manly scent. She dared not trust herself to say how much she liked him.

He sighed. "I was hoping you would say you liked me," he said in a disappointed voice.

"I do," she said suddenly.

"And perhaps you harbor a feeling a little more than mere *liking* for me?"

She dared not look at him. She was annoyed that he was teasing her. "James, I cannot say what I am thinking."

"Why ever not?"

"Because . . . well, because you would not want to hear it."

He pressed his lips together. "I suppose you think I disgraced my family?"

"No, I do not. If you didn't steal that money years ago, James, there's no disgrace, and you should never have been exiled."

"Then you consider me a fool to have lost my sawmill?"

She shook her head. "You were unlucky. I've told you before: you can build it again."

"Then it must be that you think I am a traitor to England?"

Clementina cried, "No! You are following your conscience. I see no fault in that. Pennsylvania has given you a home, and you are doing your best for the people who live here."

His engaging smile seemed to melt the bones in her body, and she wanted to fall into his arms, but didn't dare.

"So," he said slowly, "was I mistaken in thinking that you love me?"

"Oh James!" Tears sprang to her eyes and she turned her head so that he could not see them.

"Oh James," he mimicked. Then he thundered, "You don't usually mince your words. Do you love me?"

Turning her head to look up into his eyes, she said fearlessly, "I have loved you since I first saw you as a little girl, and you looked just like this drawing."

His arms came tight around her, and Thomas Gainsborough's picture fluttered to the floor.

"My darling Clementina," he said, kissing her tenderly on the lips. And then he kissed her again, strongly. And again, as she was kissing him too.

Then he held her at arm's length. He lifted her firm little chin as he gazed into her brilliant amber eyes. "Do you love me enough to marry me?"

She wiped more tears from her eyes. They were tears of happiness.

"Well?" he asked anxiously.

She dabbed her face, crying and laughing, as he waited for her answer. "Yes," she managed to say. "Yes, yes, yes, James."

He laughed then. "I thought for one awful minute I might have to take the betrothal ring I brought you this morning back to the jewelers!"

He produced a small, scarlet leather box, containing the shining ring, and taking her left hand, he slipped it onto her finger. The gold ring glowed, looking as if it belonged there.

They hugged and kissed until they sat and then lay on Clementina's bed.

Time disappeared as Clementina allowed the last of her inhibitions to melt away. She was no longer feeling repressed in any way and was free to feel, hold and kiss the man she loved. And she did, with all her heart and body.

His gentle kisses and caresses gave her a sense of worth. She was a woman in love like any other, and as his hands stroked her body, she longed for his fingers to undo the buttons of her gown. But he seemed content to take their lovemaking slowly. She felt he was holding back his natural urges.

The strong, clear sound of the chiming bell startled them.

"What is it, James?"

"Can't you hear the bell?"

"Yes. But why is it ringing?"

He grasped Clementina's hand, saying excitedly, "Come on." And he pulled her off the bed and out of her chamber, down the stairs, and into the street.

"Where are we going?" she asked.

"My darling Clementina, the bell is sounding because it is summoning the citizens to hear the first public reading of our Declaration of Independence. This is the birth of our new nation."

MAURY COUNTY PUBLIC LIBRARY

She could feel his excitement and laughed with him.

"You can choose to be a liberated American with me. Will you, Clementina?"

Struck by his proposal, she gasped. Her mind was clear as she reasoned: she was an orphan and didn't know who her parents or ancestors were, but she could now choose to start her life afresh in this new nation. "I will be an American who will always have a fondness for England," she replied solemnly.

He looked at his radiant bride-to-be, gently pressed her hand, and said. "I will, too."

And there in the street they kissed to seal their agreement and betrothal, for all to see. The bell was still ringing. In the distance they could hear fireworks and people cheering. They looked into each other's eyes with love, realizing the significance of this historic occasion. They were wise enough to know the conflict with Britain was not yet over and that many battles and heartaches lay ahead.

But with their deep and lasting love for each other, Clementina sensed they would survive the troubles, and that one day would be able to tell their grandchildren about the 8th July 1776, when they heard the Liberty Bell ring out over Philadelphia.

ABOUT THE AUTHOR

As an English Speaking Union graduate student at the University of Wisconsin, Madison, **Anne Holman** became interested in American Colonial History. She now lives with her husband in beautiful Devon, England. Anne has written many historical novels and is one of the top authors whose books are borrowed from English libraries. Eleven of her books are available from Amazon.com.

The employees of Thorndike Press hope you have enjoyed this Large Print book. All our Thorndike and Wheeler Large Print titles are designed for easy reading, and all our books are made to last. Other Thorndike Press Large Print books are available at your library, through selected bookstores, or directly from us.

For information about titles, please call:
(800) 223-1244

or visit our Web site at:
www.gale.com/thorndike
www.gale.com/wheeler

To share your comments, please write:
Publisher
Thorndike Press
295 Kennedy Memorial Drive
Waterville, ME 04901